FRAM

FRAM

A NOVEL

STEVE HIMMER

PUBLISHING
BROOKLYN, NEW YORK

Printed in the United States of America
10 9 8 7 6 5 4 3 2 1

Ig Publishing
392 Clinton Avenue
Brooklyn, NY 11238
www.igpub.com

Library of Congress Cataloging-in-Publication Data

Himmer, Steve.
  Fram / Steve Himmer.
     pages ; cm
  ISBN 978-1-935439-98-1 (softcover)
  1. Spouses--Fiction. 2. Quests (Expeditions)--Fiction. I. Title.
  PS3608.I49F73 2015
  813'.6--dc23
                                        2014045365

To Sage

Everything is burning. What is burning?
                              —The Buddha

…everything happens but nothing goes on.
                              —Dominique Jullien

1

Rumor had it the lightbulb was already there when the Bureau of Ice Prognostication was founded at the height of the Cold War—the first one, the one that was actually cold, not the one with the bombs and Berlin Wall that came later. Oscar had held that line ready for years in case he was ever allowed to talk about what he did for a living.

That bulb had crackled and hissed through his years in BIP's office, hanging from the same few inches of cloth-wrapped cord it had in the early days long before Oscar's time. It persisted despite losing some luster, despite ancient filaments fraying and sizzling and threatening to snap. In winter it took longer to warm to a glow and on hot days in summer the bulb darkened so slowly it never quite dimmed overnight, their very own Arctic sun deep in the bureau's basement domain. Without any windows, that varying light was the only sign of seasons passing. But the bulb reported for work every morning and had outlasted decades of prognosticators and their supervising directors. Policy stated it could not be replaced until it actually failed and heaven help the traitor who tapped at the glass or jerked the lamp's chain or otherwise caused that noble, inspiring star to exhaust itself prematurely. Men above Oscar's pay grade had been fired for less, for cursing the bulb when its light was too weak to get on with their work.

"Efficiency," Director Lenz told Oscar and his partner Alexi in their weekly productivity lectures, first thing each Monday morning. "Efficiency and perseverance! That lightbulb can teach us all something about commitment and making do. You should spend a whole day—your own day, not ours, not for pay!—staring into that lightbulb to learn what it knows. Stare until you are blinded by its inspiration."

Director Lenz could make anything sound like a slogan.

In Oscar's first weeks at BIP, at his first productivity lectures, he'd nodded along vigorously. But after noticing the scant attention paid by Slotkin, his partner then, he realized how little it mattered to the director if his subordinates listened at all. So he aped Slotkin's slight motions, his minimal nods reminiscent of the bulb at sway on its cord and always in motion despite the absence of wind in the office. Stirred by warm air rising from humming computers and working bodies, perhaps, or the hot air of directors' lectures still circling the basement with no way out.

Sometimes supervisors from other departments brought their own charges down, to stand under the lightbulb and deliver their own inspirational talks. Such visits required careful concealments to make the Bureau of Ice Prognostication look more like the Bureau of Informational Policies it was known as to everyone not in the know. Files and paperwork had to be hidden and the big map of the Arctic turned around on the wall to instead show a colorful hierarchy of interdepartmental and interagency color code schemes—the work BIP was publicly responsible for.

Whenever it happened, the anxiety of being colonized even for a few minutes hung on Oscar for days, a lingering feeling of someone looking over his shoulder, even though one of the first things he'd done at BIP was to drag his desk—it had been Wend's desk until then, Slotkin's previous partner—away from the wall to sit facing the door. Slotkin had assured him no one would mind because not even Director Lenz made his way down the hall more than one or two times per year and they rarely heard from him at all between Monday lectures unless he leaned on his intercom's button by accident. Oscar had assured Alexi of the same thing, when his time came after Slotkin's was up.

Other than those rare visits, it was easy to forget the world existed apart from themselves and their work, apart from the Arctic they
explored daily from the privacy of a cinderblock cellar. The world
shrank to a pair of prognosticators, working in twos per tradition,
and the lightbulb above with that long history of its own. They were
a trio as cut off for a few hours each day as the men of Franklin's first
expedition had been while crossing the Canadian wild, though without yet resorting to eating their shoes or each other. Oscar brought
his lunch from home on most days and Alexi preferred to go out.
Director Lenz' eating habits were a mystery to them.

The bulb wasn't bright but its wan glow was faithful and always enough by which to stare at the minimal map of the Arctic
spread on their wall and to think about what should be there and
what, perhaps, already was. Enough to make notations and to
write reports and to file them for Director Lenz to inspect or not
bother at the end of each day. Any more light risked reminding
the prognosticators their basement room had no windows. Any
more and they might look past the important task at their hands:
the task of determining what had been found in the wild white
spaces of the far north and, more importantly, of filing the paperwork and electronic records to prove it.

"Paperwork is destiny," as Slotkin had been fond of saying.

Oscar thought often of the men who had worked in that
light before him, those men and the discoveries they'd made.
The same lightbulb shone on Sarno when he speculated about
mineral deposits deep under Kamchatka, and when Rudnik
proposed Greenland as the ideal location for airfields and
refueling stops. While an inspired Dimchas drew up plans for the
first shopping center north of the Circle, the lightbulb watched
over his shoulder and cast its fatherly glow on his pencil and
page. That proud history—and his own modest link in its chain—
spurred Oscar forward each morning onto the snowfields and
into the storms, toward that vast sheet of paper with pencil in
hand. The prognosticators who paved the way had been driven

by the dignity of a day's work well done no less than Peary or Nansen or Franklin had been, navigating the unknown by compass or computer and not giving up until they arrived, and Oscar endeavored to do those men proud.

"A glorious tearoom in the name of the people," Alexi offered as the day's first proposal, as he had every morning since his arrival in BIP. The elaborate phrase, the old-fashioned ornament of it, was already a signal between the two men, an indication the junior partner wouldn't be ready to work until his first cup. He hadn't looked at the map yet to see where Oscar was working and Oscar didn't need to look to know that. Slotkin had always been first on the ice, as he'd liked to put it, and tall enough to reach the top of the map without rising onto his toes. He'd carried two extra pencils in his shirt pocket in case one broke while he worked those several steps away from his desk—no time to waste on backtracking, he'd say, you bring what you need to the north.

"Here," Oscar said, drawing his finger along a jagged coastal outcrop north of Mould Bay on Prince Patrick Island, one of his favorite haunts. "There's a settlement where an expedition arrived decades ago but their paperwork was never filed. They've been living there ever since, cut off and forgotten, generations of birth and of death."

"But Oscar, last week we agreed that area was impenetrable wilderness. Are we changing our minds?" Alexi hardly peeked at the half-empty spaces, rummaging instead through a plastic bin on the table. His whole stringy body got into the search, hands and arms swimming through elastics and napkins and office detritus, legs dancing along. "But I'm sure there's a sugar factory in that region, producing packets of sweetener."

Alexi never stopped moving, keeping his body so lean you'd never imagine his prominent amateur standing as a competitive eater at the national level (a hobby Oscar, for his part, was happy enough to know little about). Alexi burned more calories in a couple of hours than most people do in a day, which had been common once in their line of work. Sedentary as prognosticators tended to be, in the old days Arctic explorers burned thousands of calories daily, honing their bodies into lean angles of muscle sharp as tiny slashes against the ice fields. Exploration had become a softer man's game.

But Alexi was right about the wilderness: they'd agreed upon it a few days before. Oscar tapped his pencil's nub of eraser against a faintly sketched line marking the boundaries of a dense forest full of wild beasts filling almost the entire upper region of the wall. It was a tall map and writing up high tired their arms quickly—he was no Slotkin, Oscar had to admit, and Alexi couldn't reach the top of the map unless he stood on a chair—so for the sake of their shoulders they had agreed on the forest, an unbroken, unchanging forest covering those inaccessible regions. Also to get more work done in a day; efficiency, after all. Efficiency and perseverance.

"We may have made up our minds," Oscar said, "but the world has remade itself around them. Last week was a long time ago and perhaps that wilderness has been cleared. At least enough for a small settlement. Or perhaps... yes, perhaps when we discovered the forest we weren't aware yet of the settlement being there because it has been so fully forgotten. It took time for us to find it, hacking our way through the forest." He swung his pencil like a machete, though a chainsaw might have been more effective as thick as they'd imagined those wilds.

"How's that?" Oscar continued. "Slotkin always said...," but Alexi's attention had wandered. Oscar reminded himself not to pressure his new partner to do things more like his old. He'd have to find his own course, his own manner of mushing, and constant comparisons weren't going to help.

He knew Alexi wouldn't be happy about venturing toward the top of the map and wouldn't appreciate the strain on his body, but Oscar had a feeling that morning, a spark he hadn't felt in some time—the promise of new land on the horizon. What the Inuit, or so Oscar had read, call *iktsuarpok*, the feeling that something is going to happen, that someone is about to arrive at your house and you're distracted by constantly checking for them.

"I'm thinking... yes, I've got it: this settlement was just stumbled onto by the settlers at Symmes' Hole, who made contact on a hunting trip over their mountains and it only now made it onto our maps. Symmes' Hole is so remote, they're in touch so rarely, it was their first chance to let someone know." He stood back for a moment, pencil poised at the angle of a rocket about to launch itself at the Arctic in its paper form. "Trust me on this one, Alexi. I'll work on it today to see where it goes."

"I don't know... it seems pretty far north for a forest. I think it said in my training binder...," Alexi broke off to push a pile of papers aside on his desk in search of the binder, lost in the year's worth of rubbish he'd somehow built up in two weeks on a desk Oscar was used to seeing kept clean. As he watched rubble spill to the floor Oscar's body tensed against the impulse to catch it, to return it to where it belonged. The urge rose to yell at Alexi or just to yell but he clenched his fists and curled his toes and pictured the clean, clear view of the icesheet he'd seen that morning when checking the North Pole web cam on his phone—an unremarkable device, like any other of today's gewgaws and gadgets, but to which he'd added a plastic case textured and printed to look like a shell of grained wood, to make it look like an object that mattered and was worthy of an Arctic explorer—and with deep breaths of that icy air Oscar came back to himself.

"You said that before," he told his still-rummaging partner, "but remember what we decided? The not quite dormant volcano, the geothermics... there's a warm microclimate at the top of the island where the settlements are. That's always been how Symmes' Hole succeeds, drawing power and heat from underground. Off the grid. And remember? The forests are different, practically boreal because of that underground heat."

"I guess it still seems a little unlikely."

"Oh it is, it is unlikely, Alexi. But even the unlikeliest things have to happen sometimes—that's the law of probability, right? Or is it the law of coincidence? Either way, a million monkeys and a million typewriters, that sort of thing."

"I wouldn't mind one monkey with a donut right now."

Oscar sighed and strained for the far northern tip of Prince Patrick Island, where he sketched in some building shapes and made a few notes.

The map on the wall, the pencil and paper, were little more than a nod to tradition by now. That's how they started each morning because prognosticators had always started that way, for as long as there had been a bureau, ever since the US government learned via some intercepted communication the better part of a century ago that the Soviets had a Bureau of Ice Prognostication to make the most of their Siberian exploits. What it did, exactly, no one could say, but rather than sit around waiting for answers they acted and created a BIP of their own, doing just what the words in the translated name of the department suggested and that's what they'd done ever since. They'd outlasted the era of real expeditions and they'd outlasted the Soviets, too, though Oscar liked to imagine there were still underground agencies like his own hard at work in modern day Russia, still charging across the tundra from their own basement offices toward their old Arctic. He took comfort in having those counterparts, in justifying his own work against theirs as prognosticators had always done. He'd read of a monastery secluded in Siberia, expanded over the centuries to make space for all the secrets and relics of the Tsarist then Soviet then post-Communist Arctic, a museum with no visitors, and what was a building full of important objects but a database made tangible, albeit it a bit less efficient than the lines of numbers and code in BIP's own digitized archive?

By Oscar and Alexi's time paper was only a means of brainstorming, of clearing their heads, and the real work happened once they sat down at their terminals and logged into BIP's database where they could populate the records to confirm a place they'd pinned on the map—that forest, the mountains between settlements, or whatever they'd found. There can be no place without records, no discoveries without files and forms, so someone had to draw up and fill out the paperwork to bring the Arctic into being and those someones were Alexi and Oscar, and Slotkin and Wend and Dimchas and the others who had come before.

None of them had been to the Arctic, of course, but who has? Who but the great men: the Pearys, the Franklins, even the Cooks, more or less. Greater men than worked in BIP's basement. But that, as Director Lenz often said, was their advantage, the edge that allowed generations of prognosticators to get on with it: a lack of actual knowledge made the job easier and their work more useful to their government and its people. The important thing was professionalism untainted by sentimental attachments to snowfields and icebergs and unvoting tribes who never pay taxes, as he reminded his underlings each Monday morning. He hadn't taken this promotion from the Office of Government Standards on Filing Systems downtown to have his new Bureau (it hadn't been "new" to Director Lenz for some years but he still said that as part of his speech, perhaps for its inspirational value) get bogged down in the truth. Prognosticators had focus unbroken by refracting light or the shifting appearance of ice and of sky so problematic in the Arctic itself: if blue turns to green and yellow to red, if a day or a night lasts for months, how can anyone know anything? How can you make sense of a place if it won't hold still to be counted and even its colors aren't fast? Their job was to imagine, never to know. The truth, as generations of directors had reminded their charges, would only get in the way.

But Oscar had always dreamed of the Pole, like all boys and all men who still have boy in them, men who can't quite get rid of that box of Arctic Greats trading cards at the back of a closet and who still have a carton of action figures—Amundsen and his real-fur collared jacket, Robert J. Flaherty and his tiny plastic movie camera—tucked away where their wives won't tease them about it. That's why he'd taken the job at BIP when it opened, despite the cut from his salary as a database developer in Weights and Measures, despite the loss of his windowed office upstairs with its view of the National Mall. Oscar had given up on the actual Arctic a long time ago, abandoned his childhood dreams of mushing across snowfields en route to the Pole and charging north into the wind on a mammoth icebreaker. He'd left those dreams behind like cairns stacked on the ice for fallen shipmates, but when the position downstairs in BIP appeared on the government jobs board it looked like a second chance at something he'd lost. A basement office with a map of the Arctic was closer than he ever expected to come by that point in his life and so much closer than most daydreaming boys ever got. All but those lucky few who somehow have what it takes, who have more than a John Franklin lunchbox and its plastic thermos with most of the *Erebus* faded away. Those lucky few who reach the blank spaces of which we all dream.

The lying had taken some getting used to. Not being able to tell his wife, Julia, where he really worked—especially when it was a lifelong dream fulfilled against all the odds—had been hard and still was. He'd had to practice, at first, testing funny stories about informational policies and color codes on Slotkin before bringing them home. But in time the lie grew familiar, part of his routine, and he found ways to talk about what he'd really been doing without talking about it at all. A code between husband and wife, even if only he knew.

Triumphant, Alexi raised a fistful of sugar packets out of the bin and said, "Yes, I can see the settlement now." But a concerned look crossed his face and he returned to rummaging. "And I propose a spoon works as part of that colony, providing much needed jobs and producing the finest utensils in all of the north."

It's hard to imagine Alexi dreamed of the Arctic when he was a boy. It's hard to imagine him wanting more than an easy day's work and swift subway ride home, to be greeted by a new issue of the magazines that awaited him in their subtle black wrappers and perhaps a coupon for free pizza from the parlor he favored—the one where he trained for competition, and had already invited his partner to watch him "work out," which was about as much of his outside life as he'd shared in the two weeks he and Oscar had worked together. With Alexi the map was the territory, for the most part. But maybe he, too, had once longed for a fast sledge and a strong team of dogs, or daydreamed of drifting over the Pole with Greely or Andrée and being the ace pilot who saved their doomed missions from failure and kept them on course.

Perhaps he shared Oscar's nostalgia, a nagging sense things were if not better in the cold war for the Pole that they were *clearer*, at least: black and white as the expanses of an incomplete map—what was known, what was not. North was north and south was south, either you reached the Pole or you didn't—never mind what those lying Cookies might say about Peary—and a journey from one place to another was an actual journey, not a phone call or a satellite broadcast or some entry double-confirmed in a database managed many rungs down the ladder of latitude and historical value. Explorers went somewhere and they came home or they didn't, they led real expeditions and never dreamed they would give that work over to bureaucrats digging through filing cabinets and databases of old ideas.

But one age cannot be another and you make due with what's available when you come along, as Oscar often reminded himself. He was lucky to be where he was, exploring the Arctic with a pension plus health insurance.

Before he could consider Alexi's proposal of a spoon works and before Alexi located a spoon, their desktop intercom buzzed so hard the whole cube of yellowed plastic—somehow discolored by sunlight despite never leaving the basement—rattled and shook as Director Lenz' voice crackled out of its tinny round speaker. "Oscar. Alexi. Into my office. Fast as a lightbulb in front of my desk!"

And with that command they were off.

A chemist fingered his black desktop polar bear statuette in a windowless laboratory, surrounded by beakers and burners and samples of the various weights and textures and durabilities of plastic he was paid to perfect. The blue glow of a stark white monitor—its casing molded from one of his own earlier formulas—gleamed on the glossy curves of the figurine as he rolled it around in his fingers like a real bear might roll the chemist's own corpse in its far-reaching paws if given a chance. A gold sticker affixed to one unvarnished pad read MADE IN CHINA and some gum, some glue residue, peeked from beneath where the chemist had once tried to remove it but given up for fear of leaving behind a bigger mess than the sticker itself.

Somewhere, he knew, was the original of that statuette. A real bear, or not a real bear but a real statue of a real bear, not re-carved by machine, not measured by lasers and cut into a template and mass-produced for souvenir seekers in art museums like the one he had visited on vacation the previous summer in Washington, DC, his eye caught by that palmable polar bear as he exited through the gift shop.

Who knows why? Who can say what he saw in that polar bear stripped of its translucent fur, its secret black skin rendered by whose hands first in stone then re-rendered in reconstituted stone substitute?

Somewhere that original was showing its age, more worn now by time than the infinite souvenir copies of its former self could ever become, its once accurate measurements preserved now as numbers in the memory of some fabrication machine. Perhaps that original had been scorched and shaved by the very laser that took its measure for preservation. Perhaps taking its measure destroyed the real bear altogether. But this bear, the chemist's, gleamed with a surface as shallow and dark as the computer display on his desk where green text flickered and blinked (because this was back in those days). Ageless as the computer's white plastic housing in that sunless lab where every morning he arrived a bit older, a bit grayer at the temples and sideburns and eyes, a day thinner up top and in his soul, too.

And it took years of experimentation, trial runs upon runs and failed batches and hours of secret off-the-books overtime but he found the solution, a formula for plastic that would wither and yellow in the glare of time's passage whether it ever saw sunlight or not. His legacy would be the secret to making machines as mortal as users, and the chemist snuck his new formula into the company-wide database from which it would be implemented by manufacturing plants in China and Korea and all over the world.

It was only a few months until complaints started coming and his employers connected the dots in a trail back to him, to his lab, but not all the way to the bear. The chemist had expected that. He'd expected to be fired but he was wrong. He was given a bonus and a new title and he got bumped upstairs because old-looking machines made their users feel old, made them anxious, made them purchase new keyboards and computer towers and, later, when the formula spread, new televisions and intercoms, too, as they staved off the creep of the bear without knowing that hot breath was his on the backs of their necks when they hunched over desks, assuming the shapes of busy people as if they'd been carved into the form—measured and fit for it—without knowing quite why.

And the chemist, wealthy now and too important to his company to do any more work, spent long afternoons at the zoo across town, where the real polar bears glinted green with algae if they caught the light, the green of those formula lines he'd once typed on a screen (though by now, on computers employing his plastics, typing spaces were as white as a bear was expected to be instead of as black as bears actually were). He watched them swim and he wondered why the bears didn't break out and head north, and he wondered that about himself, too.

And his intercoms and keyboards and monitor casings, replaced and cast off of desk after desk, piled up to outlive him in poisonous swamps where circuit boards float like squared lily pads in parts of the world that don't show up on paper, the places that fall between places on maps, the numbers between the numbers in GPS units imbued with the chemist's own alchemy.

2

"I hope," said Alexi, "there's breakfast or bagels or something." He stopped for a moment in the long hallway to sip from his steaming though still spoonless cup, and when he raised the rim to his lips Oscar glimpsed a large, black letter "A" markered onto the white enamel underside, obscuring the fainter curves of an old "S" underneath.

"Why would there be?"

"Your anniversary! You've been with the Bureau ten years today. If that isn't worth a few bagels, I don't know what is. And I've got the Eastern Seaboard Pancake Grand Stack coming up—bagels are better practice than nothing."

"How do you know that? You've only been here two weeks and I hadn't realized myself."

"Oh, you know…," Alexi said before tilting his cup so it hid his face.

Upstairs in Weights and Measures all had been precision and numbers. Oscar had started in filing then advanced to be a troubleshooter for databases, finding all the ways the data entry pool might make mistakes and fracture a table or form. His job was to make those mistakes first, to see how the database broke then ensure no one could make that same error again before moving on to new failures.

Upstairs, fields were never left empty at the end of the day. Everything had to be balanced and accounted for in double-entry—data was highlighted blue after it had been entered once, and turned red when entered again—and it took time for

Oscar to adjust to thinking of emptiness, of BIP's square miles of nothing veiled by a layer of electronic something, as a day's work. Time and the teaching of Slotkin, whose imagination had gone over the past several months until every day he invented the same beachfront resort, the same volleyball courts and bikinis, in whatever stretch of the North they were prognosticating on at the time. He hadn't made any discoveries in weeks when the two of them were finally called before the director.

"Who plays volleyball on Ellesmere Island?" Director Lenz had thundered. "It's below zero most of the year! How many courts could they possibly need?"

Neither man had an answer to offer. The fact that those volleyball courts were pure speculation, that none of them would ever be built, was irrelevant to the work they were doing, to the building material requisitions they had filled out and filed and to the construction agreements with contractors they'd created and stamped and signed featuring all the appropriate logos and seals made with the Bureau's own image editing software. That it was all prognostication didn't matter to the database or to the director.

"You have to at least make a damn effort," Director Lenz scolded his men. "Your discoveries have to make sense. A beach resort? That close to the Pole? Are you asking for us to be shut down? Do you know how hard is to hold onto our budget these days? Even the Post Office is at risk of closure. The *Post Office*, my God," and he paused perhaps in reverence of that most venerated of agencies before adding, "Do you two have any idea?"

They didn't, but the next day Director Lenz hosted a party in his office for just the three of them. An extra productivity meeting, really—on a Wednesday this time and with cake— at which Slotkin was given a shining brass compass engraved with his name and an unfilled outline of the whole Polar region etched on the round back of its casing as if his years of work at BIP had all been undone though it probably wasn't meant to be taken that way. But Slotkin hardly noticed, too busy shuffling into the corner of the director's office where he muttered under his shaggy mustache and sketched the dimensions and details of his Ellesmere Island beach resort on a gray paper towel. He was gone the next day and Oscar hadn't heard from him since. He wouldn't have known how to reach Slotkin if he'd wanted to, but he imagined his old partner whiling away his elderly years at a beach resort somewhere, playing volleyball high in the Arctic. Or maybe—who knew?—he was already dead. They would say the same about Oscar someday, and Alexi and Director Lenz, unless forms were filed to prove otherwise. It's an outcome as inevitable as the top of the world.

"Ten years?" Oscar asked. "Have I really been here that long?"

"You have," said Alexi. "You might be presented with a plaque to hang on the wall of our office, above the electric kettle. I can see it now."

The hallway hadn't changed since Slotkin's departure. The same faded green walls and the same buzzing fluorescent tubes overhead. The same director in the same office at the end of the hallway and the same number of echoing footsteps from their door to his. Nothing changed but the Arctic, reimagined in hundreds and thousands of configurations, and some of the prognostications Oscar had made with Alexi in those last two weeks were the same ones he'd made with his previous partner over the years, and no doubt those same discoveries had been made earlier, too, by men who came before all three of them and before even Wend, in the days of Rudnik and Dimchas and other names lost to the obsolescence of file formats that eventually corrupts us all. The excitement of a new discovery lasted only until the duplication was revealed in their files—which became so much easier, infinitely, after all the old records were scanned into a database and made searchable—and instead of filing originals they filed updates, filling in what had happened in those locations since the last time the files were addressed. Perhaps a school building had become outmoded and had been torn down or replaced. Perhaps a town's population had boomed—was a streak of silver discovered and a spoon factory built? Or perhaps a coal vein ran dry and the families of miners packed up and left it behind. Generations of prognosticators could return to the same parts of the Arctic and find something new, a clear space to continue what their predecessors established, as if they'd sailed to Martin Frobisher's abandoned colony at Meta Incognita to rebuild on the brick stumps of his long-crumbled walls. They were steadfast as Lady Franklin's search parties, setting out one after another without ever stopping to think how an accurate answer, a once and for all, could put them right out of work. They didn't worry because they were safe from the truth: an accurate answer might come and go—it might do so three times in a day—without any one of them realizing how close to danger they'd sailed.

Alexi slurped the dregs of his tea as they reached the door to their superior's office, already open a crack. From inside came the director's voice grumbling, "I don't know how the fuck it got out..." He paused, on the phone, then said, "No... It got out, that's all I know... The damn internet... well, fucking plumb it! I'm doing my end."

"Just in time," said Alexi, gazing into his cup, and Oscar knocked on the door with the one-two-(pause)-three knuckle raps Slotkin had taught him the director preferred.

"Come," Director Lenz yelled and Oscar pushed the door open and held it for Alexi before slipping into the office himself.

The director loomed behind a desk so small his round body peeked out on both sides. Everything about the director was round—his body, his face, his bald head laced by the few long white hairs he combed over—yet he was not, per se, a large man. And beneath those white hairs bright red skin on his face and what showed of his arms. He looked, always, like he'd just stepped from a bath drawn so hot it boiled him red as the lobsters he posed with in a photo on his desk from a *National Geographic* gala to celebrate the seventy-fifth anniversary of Richard Byrd's Polar flight—another great man nearly undone by hobgoblins of gossip, by petty desires for him to fail. Had Byrd only kept better records—had BIP been established a few years earlier—he might have fended off those attacks, those charges that sloppy erasures in his flight log were "proof" he had not reached the pole... As Slotkin had said more than once while he and Oscar discussed some expedition or another over their lunch (they hadn't been prone to chat while they worked), it's a wonder explorers ever come home at all when such unwelcoming welcomes await. The way they worked, the way BIP explored the far reaches without ever leaving their office, made it all so much smoother by controlling the whole story start to finish without leaving loose ends and left-open doors where doubt and distrust and after-the-fact changes of heart could creep in.

Behind Director Lenz in his office, where a window might have been if the Bureau weren't housed in a basement, hung a window-sized photograph of the mysterious centenarian lightbulb from Oscar and Alexi's own office, a photograph many times larger than life in which curled filaments shone more brightly behind the glass of the frame than behind the glass of the actual bulb. Though perhaps that brightness was a reflection, some trick of the light trapped between photo and glass and so magnified; that sort of thing happens all the time in the Arctic. Light makes you see land where there is none, land where you want it to be when you most desperately hope to find some, and many a man —good men and even great ones—has steered a wrong course toward those vanishing shores of Fata Morgana.

In short, all was as expected in the director's office. All was as it had been every Monday when the prognosticators stood on the threadbare gray carpet before him and as it had been for years before that, with the exceptions of being called to his desk on a Wednesday, and that Director Lenz wasn't alone. In ten years Oscar had never seen anyone else in that office, but on that morning two stiff men sat in stiff chairs to the director's left, one in a dark green army uniform festooned with ribbons and medals and a whole sky of stars on his shoulders amidst other decorations and badges no doubt impressive enough in their own right for reasons indecipherable to Oscar and his limited fluency in regalia. Close-cropped gray hair crept from under the rim of his cap and a thin, steel-colored mustache had been drawn across his face like a blade. The other wore a gray pinstriped suit that fit him so well even Oscar could tell it was nicely cut, and he knew as much about the way suits should hang as he knew about lunar travel. Neither Director Lenz nor his guests offered an introduction and it isn't a prognosticator's place to speak first, so the partners waited to be spoken to.

"Listen, both of you," said the director, leaning across his small desk, wide red hands wrapped around its plastic woodgrain veneered ends. "Sit down and listen." He always told them to sit though until that morning there had never been any chairs but his own in the room (who knows where the chairs for his guests had come from) so generations of underlings stood where they were despite the instruction, shoes slotted into old footprints left in the pile of the carpet not only by their own feet but by those that came first, varying a size up or down over the years so the impressions in the carpet were blurry.

The man in the uniform and the man in the suit sat glacier-still with a posture in common: backs straight against straight-backed chairs, knees together with hands flat upon them. Oscar thought of sleeping skuas hanging impassive on the edges of cliffs but had only seen skuas on the pages of *National Geographic* and they might move around more in those crowded Arctic colonies than he imagined them to. Real skuas might be nothing like those two rigid men but skuas were what he was used to—their still images, anyway—so thinking of them helped Oscar stay calm in the face of strangers appearing in BIP.

Director Lenz crabbed his fat fingers back and forth on a sheet of paper, crumpling until it lifted away from the surface of his desk enough to allow him a grip. Triumphant, he waved it around. Oscar spotted BIP's bright red stamp in one corner and some other stamps he didn't know: blue stamps and green stamps and brown. Out of the corner of his eye he saw Alexi's head look one way then the other, no doubt scanning the office for bagels.

"You two," Director Lenz said, and Alexi's face popped with surprise. He pointed back at his own chest as if the director might mean someone other than the underlings he'd called to his office. "This paper here just came down. It just came down from upstairs who said it came from downtown on the hill and it says the two of you have an assignment. A very important assignment. Are you listening?"

"Yes, sir," Oscar said and Alexi nodded while holding the empty teacup near his face where the director would be sure to see it, as transparent as those dark slipcovers fooling no one on his magazines when he pulled them out to read over lunch. Not that the director would care, on either account.

"A very important assignment and it's going to supersede your regular duties. You'll be on this assignment as long as it takes. But it shouldn't take long. It had better not take you two long. Only as long as it takes."

Oscar knew better than to ask, he knew Director Lenz would get there when he got there if he got there at all, but Alexi— perhaps because of his tea-deprived state or because he was new—couldn't hold out and asked, "What's the assignment?"

"Let me talk!" roared the director. "How can we maintain efficiency if you won't stop talking?"

"Sorry, sir," Alexi mumbled into his mug as the strangers in chairs shook their scowling heads.

"Where was I? Yes! You two are being sent north. You'll go, get the job done, then come right back. Take too long and it's your vacation days."

"North?" Oscar asked, body aquiver as a compass needle at high latitudes.

Director Lenz turned toward the Suit and the Stars in exasperation and all three of them raised their eyebrows at once. Then he turned back to his prognosticators with those big, bloodshot eyes. "North. Yes. The Arctic, you dolts. The fucking Arctic. You've heard of it, yes? That bastard map on your wall? Where else would you be going, the moon? The goddamn moon? Are we NASA now, for Christ?"

Oscar's face grew hot at the shameful suggestion and it was all he could do to hold his tongue and not defend himself against the vile charge. He was glad to see Director Lenz look away, underlings already dismissed from his mind. Focused now on some papers fanned over his desk, with more seals and stamps unknown to his subordinate's eyes, he said, "Now get back to work. You'll receive the details when it's time."

They turned toward the door, and Oscar was shocked at the slump in Alexi's cake-starved and tea-deprived shoulders. Hadn't he heard the director? Wasn't he listening? They'd be going north, for some reason, for whatever reason—and who cares what reason so long as it would deliver them to Arctic?

Then he realized what was obvious and only briefly obscured by the excitement of going north: it meant going somewhere, traveling, and probably meals in strange restaurants and sitting on planes and other things Oscar wasn't quite crazy about. But the Arctic! He'd be willing to sleep in a roomful of strangers for that, which was easy enough to tell himself while he was still comfortable in BIP's basement.

He knew it would be hard to stay focused on the day's prognostications with so much more to think about now but as senior employee it was his job to keep Alexi on task, to get him his tea then get him to work and to get a good morning's hypothetical mapping accomplished by lunch so they might get on with filing and copying the corresponding forms in the afternoon to prove what they'd invented was actually there, and not end up working through dinner again. Not that Alexi would work through dinner. He'd be off like a lost ski at 5:00, leaving Oscar to stay behind in the basement until the day's discoveries were made.

The Arctic won't imagine itself, after all.

3

Back in their own office, back down the hall, the prognosticators set to the day's agenda. Alexi proposed a lumberyard and sawmill and Oscar added a workers' café. They agreed on a technical college founded on the south shore of Cornwallis Island only to discover the tractor and plow factory built there by Dimchas years earlier, so relocated the college to the north end.

At lunchtime Alexi stepped out, saying he needed to make a phone call—which required a trip upstairs to street level to have any chance at a signal—but Oscar ate a sandwich at his desk and kept working. Director Lenz' announcement was enough disruption for one day to handle. When Alexi returned, Director Lenz buzzed the intercom and asked for him—and only him—to come to his office. Oscar had never been summoned alone to the director's office and in all his years at BIP he'd never seen Slotkin called alone to the office, either. Alexi wasn't gone long before he came whistling back to his desk and Oscar tried not to wonder what his new partner and Director Lenz might have talked about. Paperwork, probably. Tax forms.

He spent the afternoon filing building permits backdated a decade, creating receipts and invoices for the materials used in constructing the college, and entering that paperwork into the database that made it all real. Meanwhile, Alexi, with his knack for everyday appetites, compiled electronic records of ten years' worth of paperwork related to groceries and other necessities of daily living a technical college might have: the pencils and notebooks, the toilet paper, the aspirin and condoms and antacid tablets to stock the campus infirmary. Between the two of them they created a whole institution that existed only on paper, or not even on paper but only in electronic records of paper that never existed. Oscar made the blueprints by copying some standard BIP templates for education (designs that had been adapted, slightly, for hospitals and prisons over the years) and once they were ready he logged them into the records of Northern Branch, the satellite office responsible for administering all Arctic construction. In theory, at least: Slotkin hadn't known if Northern Branch really existed so neither did Oscar; it may have been another shell in the game of BIP records and perhaps there was even another office, some other department, responsible for inventing government offices when they were needed, a Bureau of Bureaucratic Prognostication. Whether Northern Branch was actually up there or not was irrelevant to Oscar's work so he'd never worried about it and didn't that day. Meanwhile, Alexi wrote rosters of past and present students, even those set to enroll for the fall term, and logged those records into the database, too.

The Cookies, those bitter losers, complained the BIP way was to rest on their laurels, to keep talking up the same old expeditions without taking fresh risks, not that they knew the half of how BIP actually worked. But BIP were government and the NGO Cookies assumed they had infinite funding, so they went on in their bulletins and listservs about the nobility of "real" exploration, of actual men going to actual places, always toward the goal of bumping off Peary as first to the Pole and restoring their own Frederick Cook to history's good graces. They'd been at it for years, spreading rumors and sparking arguments the wider world knew next to nothing about, verbal skirmishes in Arctic enthusiasts' magazine pages and later online, the occasional theft and counter-theft of some artifact or some piece of supposedly "last word" evidence, since April 1909 when the fight over who'd reached the Pole first flared up. It had been in the papers for a while, of course, big news in its day and scandal enough to destroy Cook's career, yet by Oscar's time no one knew but the descendent participants that the dispute simmered still and sometimes boiled over long after history had set it aside. They talked a good game among the musty oak panels and threadbare armchairs of their club downtown but the Cookies never went anywhere close to the Pole, no closer than BIP (which was, officially, in Peary's camp, not that it mattered much day-to-day), because exploration costs money and the Arctic was a hard sell to those with deep pockets and purses, unlike in Peary's day when business scions and industry's leading lights had been eager to attach their names to each expedition.

Even space had become a hard sell though you'd never know it from NASA's brave face, shameless as the men of BIP found it. Retroactive discovery and prognostication were more cost effective, exploring backward rather than forward by deciding what was already discovered then laying a paper trail to it. If the records say a campus was already constructed, that a sawmill or shipyard or even a beachfront resort with a volleyball court on frigid Ellesmere Island is there and already paid for, if the paperwork is all in place then it's so. As far as anyone knows. And in a region where it's unlikely anyone would venture to check, saying so had always been enough to ensure the next year's budget.

That's what Oscar and Alexi were told weekly by Director Lenz and no doubt it's what he was told by whoever told him what to do. Maybe the Suit and the Stars.

After all, the argument had gone at the founding of BIP and each time Director Lenz refreshed his underlings' motivation, who ever goes to the Arctic? Who but the great men who discovered great things and died out a long time ago? Those great men and now, for some reason, the two of them. Oscar and Alexi. They may not be great, and were often reminded by their director they weren't, but think of the money they'd saved with their work. Think of the places they'd prevented the country from spending its taxes and resources and manpower to visit, by proving we'd already been there and so had no need to go back. Perhaps they'd even saved lives.

There were days Oscar's discoveries felt so important, when he felt so successful, he wanted nothing more than to tell his wife what he'd done. He'd rush home picturing how proud she would be but it was an exercise in futility: he never told her and he never could because secrecy was rule one of BIP. Secrecy even from spouses. So instead he'd get home and when Julia asked, as she always did, how his day had been, he'd have nothing to tell her but, "Fine." On regular days, days when he hadn't done what felt like great things, he could make up a story about color coding or some especially challenging new filing system required by the Division of Aquatic Categories or whichever agency first came to mind. He could even conceal what he'd really done with a code of his own, telling his wife he had come up with a breakthrough alphanumerical system allowing twice as many files to occupy the same space when what he was actually talking about was discovering a lost colony on some Arctic spit.

But on the best of his days, days like the one when he discovered Symmes' Hole, he had nothing to say; the gap between the truth and the best possible lie he might find to hide it was simply too great. So those days he most wanted to share with his wife were the days he could tell her the least and the days Oscar felt loneliest. He worried this would be one of those days, because how could he tell her he was off to the Arctic? What made up story about filing systems could communicate the wonder of that?

He and Julia would arrive home at the end of a day, ask each other how their day had been, and each of them would say, "Fine," leaving nothing to talk about next. He'd even started to wonder if the work in a subdivision of Transportation Julia sometimes told him about—sharing funny moments from the Registry of Approved Tires and Treads—was in fact what she did all day or if she had an unmentionable job of her own, because hours at home with the familiar made strange by their silence were often as quiet as hours at BIP.

As quiet as he and Alexi were for a few hours that afternoon, each at his own terminal, but Oscar's head whirled with possibilities about the expedition Director Lenz was sending them on as he waited for the appropriate obsolete building permit template to load on his screen. BIP's computers were slow and the joke that went back further in that office than Oscar was that each time they asked a document to load or a query to run the bits or bytes or whatever they were had to mush all the way to the Arctic to pick up the file from Northern Branch, then mush all the way back. And there wasn't much to do while they waited because those computers weren't online, not really: BIP had its own intranet containing all its records and work, so Oscar could access what Alexi was doing and what Slotkin had left behind and even electronic versions of everything older, but he couldn't check email or read websites or—worst of all—check the North Pole web cam for hours at a time. They were cut off with only each other to talk to, so at least they had that in common with the great men of the Arctic. They had their own jokes and their own secret stories, as Parry had his expedition's newspaper, or they'd had those things until the past couple of weeks because Alexi wasn't yet up on the lore of the office so there wasn't much to talk about.

But when Oscar couldn't keep it to himself any longer, and assuming his partner, too, had been wondering all afternoon, he asked Alexi, "What do you think we're being sent for?"

"Sent where?" his partner replied, distracted by the list of names he was inventing for the technical college's honor roll of three years back.

"To the Arctic! The job Director Lenz talked about. It was only this morning, Alexi."

"Oh, right. That. I don't know, maybe a convention or something? I kind of forgot. What do you think? What was it before?" The lightbulb above them swayed with sudden vigor and in the same seconds Oscar's monitor flickered—the power cord socket was loose and had been for years, and it always suffered when he bumped or kicked the wrong spots in the frame of his desk—and in those two simultaneous wavering lights his eyes swam. He felt dizzy and not quite himself, more a sailor at sea; he felt a bit like Franklin adrift in the ice for those slightest of seconds, not to make too much of it, and gripped the arms of his chair with eyes closed until the waves passed and he sailed again into the calm harbor of BIP's basement office, guided back by the gibberish morse code of Alexi tap-tapping his keys.

"There never was a before. BIP's never sent anyone north as far as I know so I can't begin to imagine," he said. "The Arctic, though. We're going to the actual Arctic. That's what he was saying, right?"

"I hope they give us a decent dining allowance."

Alexi's obsession with food, his one track, digestive tract mind was almost charming to Oscar for the first couple of hours they worked together but soon it began to annoy him, and how could it not? But he was trying to get used to it, trying to accept it as the way of the world or at least the way of the work while he worked with Alexi, because they would likely be partners for years to come. That's how things go, how they must go, when men work in the close quarters and isolation a region like the Arctic necessitates. But there had already been moments when Oscar wished his new partner had a little more to him than impulse and appetite, even if it was for the sake of competitions which, by his own account, Alexi was pretty good at.

He'd asked a week or so ago how Alexi came to join BIP but all the answer he got was, "Oh, you know, I've moved around," and in government work that was a hint not to ask any more questions—either the story wasn't interesting enough to dig for or was more interesting than the inquirer wanted to know.

"When do you think we'll go?" Oscar asked. "Director Lenz

said we'd receive more instructions."

"Whenever we're meant to, I guess." Alexi had stopped naming students and was reading the entertainment section of a newspaper he'd brought from outside after lunch.

Despite himself, despite the protocols of government work and the honor of Arctic explorers, Oscar gave in and asked if Director Lenz had told Alexi anything in their second meeting.

His partner turned a page and said, "Hey, the new season of *To The Moon!* starts tonight."

Oscar groaned. "I can't stand that show. Who cares about space? Who's impressed by all that? I mean, if the idiots who win that show can go up, how hard can it be? It's not a dog team to the Pole."

"Five o'clock," said Alexi, already standing and in motion toward the door and the end of the day. "See you tomorrow."

Oscar said goodnight and shut down his computer, then he cleaned up the papers spread on his desk and filed them in the right drawers, sighing at the left behind chaos of Alexi's own desk. He checked that the drawers were all locked, his own and Alexi's, in case someone came wandering in; Oscar assumed and had for years that somebody ran through the office at night with a vacuum because the carpet had maintained a consistent level of dingy without giving over to filthy for as long as he'd worked in that basement. He checked the drawers in the archival cabinets where neither he nor Alexi ever had cause to roam, nor had Slotkin in the course of most weeks and months. Once, though, a few years earlier, Oscar had consulted that cabinet and its crisp, yellowed pages for details on brick manufacturing trends from Bylot Island—he needed to explain why the region's largest brickworks had relocated to North Cornwallis—and in the course of that journey into BIP's material past had discovered something surprising. In a fat, brown folder of pages, maps and records and lists and diagrams, he found a full accounting of the *Jeannette*, of her ill-fated voyage in search of Adolf Erik

Nordenskiöld and his own vanished ship *Vega*. The details of the voyage didn't surprise him; like any Polar enthusiast he was long familiar with DeLong's abandonment of *Jeannette* near Wrangel Island after she froze into the pack ice. He knew how her crew had been scattered, wandering over the ice, but also how they had first tried to drift, to let themselves be stuck fast and slide toward the Pole on slow currents, only to have their ship sink and leave them stranded.

He knew because it was the unexpected drifting of DeLong and *Jeannette* that gave Nansen his vision, to build a ship intended to freeze and to drift, a ship meant not to fight for its own motion or set its own course but to equip its captain and crew for a long, patient wait. The kind of deep patience the Inuit call *quinuituq*, another word Oscar tried to work into conversation whenever he could. And for Nansen it had worked out so much better; rather than lose his ship he brought *Fram* safely to port with such stories to tell about months doing nothing in ways that meant everything.

He knew because *Fram* and her patient journey, her passive quest, was Oscar's own favorite of all the Polar excursions. He admired Peary and Franklin and all the others, of course; he admired his American forebears with the pride of any government worker of any grade, but Nansen was the explorer who meant the most to him, the one whose words echoed loudest in Oscar's mind from all his re-readings of *Farthest North*.

But that wasn't the point of what he'd found in the filing cabinet, in that old folder full of old pages left behind by Wend, according to the handwriting inside. What he'd discovered was an account of the *Jeannette*, yes, but not quite the way things had happened: Wend had rewritten the voyage and the aftermath of its loss to the ice. He'd created records to show all the crew had come home, those who drowned in a launch and those who wandered to their death on the Siberian tundra alongside DeLong. Wend had filed tax returns and love letters written after the fact, he'd made accounting claims and real estate deeds and applications for library cards, as if none of those men had been lost on the ice. As if they'd all come back for long lives. Wend had filed obituaries for each of them, deaths by cancer and car crash and fire, but not one of them frozen up north.

Oscar had never mentioned those files to Slotkin or to Director Lenz or to anyone else. Certainly not to Alexi. He'd checked the database, though, to be sure Wend hadn't put all his rewritten sailors in there; old paper in the back of a drawer was one thing but in the database, in electronic form with the long reach of wires, someone might notice and who knew where suspicion might fall. But sometimes, like that afternoon while locking up for himself and Alexi, he checked to make sure the folder was still where it belonged, whether it really belonged there or not.

Finally, using an old handkerchief kept for the purpose and left behind by a predecessor of his predecessor, so long ago the handkerchief itself sometimes came into productivity lectures as an inspiration in its own right—the subservient ego, the selfless sidekick and all of that; the bulb's Matthew Henson, perhaps— he reached up to straighten the lightbulb left swaying by his partner's departure before leaving the office himself, though he wondered, as always, if it would start swaying again when he'd gone. Would the residual heat left behind be enough to keep that faithful underground sun in motion?

Oscar climbed the dark stairwell from BIP's basement into the lobby of an unremarkable building housing government departments unknown to all but the interchangeable bureaucrats working in them, and in which he'd spent all of his working life beginning with an internship during college. Weights and Measures upstairs, BIP in the basement, the Division of Agricultural Categories on the third floor, and some others he didn't know because in all those years Oscar had never once taken time to read the whole orientation board in the lobby. He was content to keep his knowledge of the building and its occupants on a small scale. To stick to what he already knew.

If the basement of BIP was stuck in a bygone era of quasi-Soviet green and gray with all its whites yellowed, then the building's lobby above was capitalism's future as seen by the past: glass cubes, soaring ceilings sliced by odd architectural angles so whispers bounced until they were shouts, and steel tube furniture with plush pleather square cushions that squeaked and exhaled when you sat. But no one was sitting when Oscar emerged from the basement and no one was standing still, either. Every body in that bureaucratic cathedral was in motion from the elevators and stairwells en route to the exits: brown suits, blue suits, jacketless shirts and black skirts, all flowing together toward the revolving glass doors and bright street outside.

Cell signals and wifi couldn't penetrate the fire doors and blast ceilings down to BIP's basement, but once in the lobby Oscar pulled out his phone and went online to check the North Pole cam as he always did. The ice was calm, with only a slight wind across it stirring clouds of snow every so often, and as he watched he relaxed, his fingers at ease against the grained texture of his phone's case; he'd seen cases of actual wood and had nearly bought one, but the plastic wood seemed more practical, more durable, yet more palatable—closer to the compasses and map cases of real wood the great men relied on—than the dull, gleaming alloy of the naked object itself. A lens flare in the far off northern sky trailed purple and orange orbs like a comet and pockmarks like footprints led away from the camera toward the haze of horizon. They weren't actual footprints, just cracks and holes piled with snow and slightly lower than the ice sheet around them; they appeared often within view of the cam and Oscar knew why, but they still suggested footprints as if he'd just missed someone up at the lens before he logged on. He liked to imagine he had. He liked to imagine his own checking in had almost coincided with the arrival of some expedition though he would have known if a real expedition to the Pole was underway—it would have made the blogs, or shown up in the automated news searches that emailed him whenever the Arctic was mentioned.

Still looking down at the screen of his phone, Oscar merged with the building's bureaucratic foot traffic and was ejected into the glare of Washington, DC's lingering Indian summer and the heat hit him hard. The ice sheet went spotty, awash with dark stars for a few seconds as he stood blinking on the sidewalk, surrounded by his fellow government workers all blinking, too, many of them looking at their own phones—perhaps at the Pole cam, who knows, but more likely squinting at email or text messages or traffic reports; they all worked upstairs where cell signals reached and wifi worked so they weren't catching up on a whole day's passage as Oscar was. They weren't taking their first look at the ice sheet in hours.

A text message popped up on his screen, from Julia hours before, telling him she'd be late after work, don't wait up, some of her friends from a karate class she'd been taking were going out. It happened more and more often, whether karate class or late meetings or last-minute trips, and Oscar suspected he and his wife had more conversations by voicemail and text than in person. He'd begun to keep track one month but after a couple days' record keeping the data were already sufficiently dispiriting to make him stop.

Oscar liked texts and voicemail. He liked the way he could come out of work, step into a signal, and they'd all come at once. Like it had been for Peary and Nansen and all the others, sailing into port after months or years in the ice, or running into a whaling ship carrying letters, and catching up on what had happened elsewhere only after the pressure of the moment had passed. A welcome soaking after a drought, all those letters and all that lost time at once, though the possibilities for failure were deepened: to be the crewman with no letters waiting, the days Oscar emerged but no messages pinged on his phone.

Beads of sweat ran from under his hair down his forehead and into his eyes, and he wiped them away with a sleeve without taking his gaze off his handful of cold northern desert. He held the phone at arm's length and almost horizontal to lessen the glare as the shadow of a bus stopping in front of him fell upon both his eyes and the screen. The ice gleamed white as the marble of the city around him, the monuments, the columns, the glare of the Capitol dome, and each car window and side mirror flared silver as it grabbed every available particle of light from the air and condensed them, concentrated, into a thousand small suns that made walking down the street a minefield for the eyes. Everyone spilling out of those buildings, himself included, did their best to avoid any reflections and every few seconds a glistening government employee walked behind the extended screen of Oscar's phone, picking at his or her sticky clothes or wiping sweat from a face, partly hidden behind the snowfield as they passed, a partially disembodied explorer passing across the top of the world and it jolted his eye when they didn't appear at the Pole.

A souvenir vendor stood by his overloaded shopping cart hawking inflatable Washington monuments and cheap sunglasses and T-shirts bearing logos for the CIA and FBI and NASA and, in a stack that had either started out smaller or sold very well, for the IRS, too. Often, daily even, Oscar forgot there was so much light in the world while working in BIP's basement under that singular bulb. It was easier in winter, when the Pole cam on his phone was dark after work and all day, when the sun had already set over Washington by the time he emerged for his commute home. But regardless of season, regardless of light, it was disorienting no matter how often he did it—and he'd done it for years—to pop out of the past back into the present at the end of a day, from a department where nothing changed and time passed backward and in the abstract, always alterable after the fact, into a present where the past existed only as a sales pitch for the future.

Eyes adjusted, he walked toward the Metro in the same direction as everyone else save the few who hailed taxis and the fewer still headed for private cars in parking lots and the odd duck from Agricultural Categories who day after day hauled his bike up and down the stairs to his office rather than lock it to the bike rack outside like all the other cyclists who worked in the building. Oscar held his phone close at an angle that let him keep one eye on the street, watchful for curbs and crosswalks and fellow commuters, while the other could watch the ice sheet for action, until he descended into the station.

His shot sliced only an inch or two wide of its mark, close enough to kill the creature regardless, in time. But off by enough to keep the caribou bleeding for hours which he couldn't stomach. So when it staggered away the hunter crossed the distance between their two bodies and pushed into the brush on its trail, following breadcrumbs of blood. He hadn't come north to leave things undone.

He heard stunned legs stumbling, an off-kilter body not heeding commands, bumping trunks and tripping over itself. Despite injury and blood loss and no doubt confusion the caribou managed to stay ahead, to always be on the far side of a gully when the hunter arrived or up the first leg of a switchback with him at its foot.

The day dragged on like that but he followed. Each extra meter or mile made him feel worse for the creature, let him borrow more of its pain, and the notion he was preventing its suffering by driving it on a long chase became more absurd the longer it went. But this was his mess, his mistake, and he would make things as right as he could.

He was thirsty but didn't drink because the caribou hadn't stopped to drink either.

He was hungry but the trail mix and pemmican remained in his pack.

He walked while the creature kept walking.

And there it was, close enough to take a new shot—not a retake, never those, but a chance to finish what had taken too long and what, had he known, he would not have begun.

The caribou wobbled below him on a scree slope then buckled onto front knees; the side facing the man was matted and running with blood. Its tongue draped low from far back in the mouth and the auburn chest heaved as the hunter took the clean shot he should have taken before.

It was done.

He slid sideways through the loose stones, stopping himself beside the carcass, then looked back up the slope wondering how he would haul that still-warm weight to the trail. He took hold of one foreleg and one hind, dug in his heels, and tried to work his way up by pushing with one foot at a time, alternating as if pumping some awkward machine, but the animal had hardly shifted before the hunter was spent.

He drank, taking water slowly to ward off the cramps and the dehydration headache he knew he deserved for dragging this out.

He tried again to haul the caribou up with no greater success. Now his arms were bloody, his boots and pants, too, and the animal's thick, sticky fluid had soaked through his socks and run into his boots and oozed now each time he put weight on his feet.

One final attempt, pushing with both heels at once plus the boost of a keening yell that bounced back at him off the opposite slope. The weight of the animal dislodged all at once but instead of climbing toward him it slipped, freed from whatever had held it fast on the scree, and it pulled the hunter down with it; he let go just in time, barely keeping his own bloody body from following the other, the body he'd killed, off the edge of a cliff and onto the rocks far below.

The falling corpse carried with it the waste of a life, the waste of a day, weeks of meat lost for the hunter, his family, his village. He would return from his hunt empty-handed and his wife would tell him it was okay, they had enough in the larder to last, but the fan of wrinkles at the edge of each eye where for so long she'd squinted against harsh northern glares would tighten as it always did when she worried but wouldn't say so.

This place. All its promise. Too much to leave now they'd come close to achieving what they came north to do, so close to cutting their ties to the world and untangling themselves from its net, but still. If there was something, just something, this place would give up to them more easily… if they found some resource they could sell back to the world, minerals or diamonds or gold, uranium or oil or even a way to send south the steam from the ground that powered their few contrapted machines, he wondered if the villagers would be willing to do it despite their ideals and the pronouncements they'd made upon packing up and heading north.

It was fortunate, in its way, that their excursions all over these mountains had given them nothing but berries and meat. Nothing to tempt them back into the web of the world. The decision was always already made for them.

The hunter leaned his head to his knees, cursed, and sat until his breath returned. Then he crawled up the slope, regained the trail, and walked back in the direction he'd come from toward where the mountains gave way to the coast and to home.

But it wasn't a waste for everyone, that falling corpse. When caribou struck ground at the base of the cliff organs ruptured, bones cracked, and flesh tore. Before the thunderous waves of its impact reached the far point of their rippling across yellowed grass, flies lit on the syrupy blood of the wounds the hunter had provided them with and among the dark runnels congealed in the animal's fur after walking so long with its heart pumping hard.

Those flies were already laying their eggs in rich layers of fat and of flesh before the body had cooled. Microbes descended out of the air and rose from the soil to penetrate every delectable niche. Foxes crept closer; a bear raised its nose into the wind with a snort and a sniff and shifted course toward the corpse; mosquitoes as large in actual fact as their southern cousins only sound in a dark, quiet room drew blood from the carcass and its four-legged diners alike.

How long would it be until every scrap of that carcass was broken down and devoured, and how long after that before every vestigial scrap of its generous energy had been exhausted in smaller bodies then in concentric tiers of even more bodies that fed second-proboscis through those? Generations of bacterium and black fly would rise and fall on that caribou's haunches and a civilization of maggots and worms would reach the proportions of legend, an empire of gristle and blood in those vast dormant lungs, persisting through skirmish and snap-freeze and epidemics of food poisoning, perhaps someday half-remembered in wonder as another species might speak of Atlantis.

Elsewhere icebergs were crumbling. Elsewhere all signs were the Arctic was dying but here in the bloat and decay of a corpse there was life after death as millions of miniature stories were written in blood, an overflowing database of past, present, and future on the broken bones of a man's failure.

4

Underground again and out of the heat so more comfortable for it, on the platform and shoulder to shoulder with other government employees at his own grade and above or below, Oscar awaited a train. Across the tracks on a wall hung a huge poster advertising the TV show Alexi had mentioned, *To The Moon!*, with its big silver slogan, "Who will conquer the greatest frontier?"

He shook his head, sighed to his scuffed shoes, and wondered how anyone could get so excited about something that's all automated, the work done by computers, while women and men who could be anyone or even no one sit in a box and wait to arrive so they can turn around and go home. There's the science, of course, he wouldn't disparage that, the behind-the-scenes unsung work of professionals like himself, but why pretend there's more to it? Why pretend it's real exploration when it's mostly a video game? The astronauts mere avatars for self-directed machines.

But the show was a hit. It had turned out to be the solution NASA needed for its falling budget, a way of reinstating itself in the public eye to a degree BIP could never withstand—if taxpayers knew what they were paying for... if taxpayers knew BIP existed at all. Sure, NASA had sold the country on space all over again with their reality show, but it wasn't the work of explorers, just moderately attractive showboats who made good television. Oscar would have liked to see any of them try to steer a dog sled or hack ice from the hull of a ship with only an ax to avoid being crushed. There's no autopilot to bring a lost sledge back to camp and no computerized temperature control in a parka or boot accidentally plunged into a subzero sea.

He'd said all that to Julia the evening before, when she mentioned being excited about the new season of *To The Moon!* while watching a recap of the last, and the night ended with the two of them in separate rooms. It hadn't come up in the morning but later, on the subway to work, he'd texted, "Sorry." She hadn't replied, not directly, but she hadn't not replied either—she'd told him she'd be out that night, after all, so she seemed to still be speaking to him, more or less—and it wasn't the first time one or the other of them had been wrong about something at night, had been stubborn or stupid or angry and taken it out on each other, then gone on the next day as if nothing had happened. They'd been married long enough for that to work.

Still, Oscar had expected her to text back with "PF," their own private code for when he'd gone too far and forgotten not everyone shared his own polar fever. Julia had picked up the habit in college, shortly after they began dating, of letting him know he'd become awkward and was alienating the people around him by dramatically announcing, "Pee-EEEH-eff." They'd laugh, no one else knowing why, and he'd make an effort to talk about something else. Later, at dinner parties and work events she brought him to, she might pass a slip of paper marked "PF" across the table or flash the sign language for those two letters (the only sign language they knew). One Christmas he had the two letters embossed in gold on a durable card as a stocking stuffer, so she could hold it up in his direction whenever necessary without drawing too much attention. But more than once her subtle gesture across a table or amidst a group conversation had backfired into the two of them laughing together and making things more rather than less awkward for everyone else before they slipped away for some time to themselves, to act on the energy of that inside joke.

Lately, more likely than not it wasn't a card or a note but Julia saying, "P fucking F, Oscar," and leaving a room as she had the previous night. And Oscar not knowing if he should follow her to say he was sorry or stay where he was, unsure which she would want, if either, and which choice would just make things worse.

The train arrived in a blast of hot air and hissing, jerking to a stop between his eyes and that awful poster. He stepped into the tube of the car and was lucky enough to find a seat. The doors snapped closed, the next stop was announced, and he waited along with everyone else.

Space travel might as well be the subway.

Diagonally across from him, in the sideways seats by the door, a newspaper fluttered and over one folded corner he caught a pair of dark glasses, a dark gray fedora, a trio of curled fingers pulling back the page but as soon as he looked in their direction the fingers released and the paper wall was rebuilt. A moment later he looked again and the page had been pulled back down and the lenses were again looking, only to vanish once more.

Someone's seen too many movies, he thought, and looked instead to the heating and cooling vents near the floor of the train, dented, scarred steel cut with square patterns of alternating horizontal and vertical lines. If he looked back and forth between them quickly, flitting his eyes, latitude aligned with longitude and both vanished as the lines become a hole for a second. It was a game he'd been playing all his years on the Metro and even in other cities when he'd had occasion to visit and their own subways used the same models of car. He passed time by trying out different ways he might combine sets of absence or presence, different ways to group data, until his eyes couldn't tell them apart. It gave him the same down-the-rabbit-hole feeling as when he got sidetracked in the BIP database or reading about the Arctic in his magazines and books or online. He'd follow some reference or footnote or hyperlink then follow another until he was far from what he'd intended to read, his original direction abandoned so many sidetracks ago he could never return, but all those sidetracks and diversions along with his initial intent adding up to something whole in his head.

He thought about Director Lenz and the mission, wishing he'd heard more about it by the end of the day as the director had promised. It might be anything or nothing at all; he had so little to go on, so little to speculate with, Oscar couldn't imagine what the mission might be—he needed something to work with the way he worked with a blank map but not a blank wall to get the day started. It was hard to get nervous about the assignment when he couldn't be sure it was true, but he daydreamed and saw himself and Alexi in fur hoods and mukluks, skiing across the ice sheet and waving to the Pole cam as they passed. Then daydream Alexi stopped skiing and pulled a sandwich from under his furs, pulled off his mittens and started to eat while Oscar stood waiting with his skis sinking into the powder. Undefined animal shapes appeared in the distance and crept slowly closer on the scent trail of his partner's lunch, and that brought him back to the train. He checked the web cam again and he wasn't there and neither were Alexi and his sandwich, so that was something at least.

It was a shame he'd go to the Arctic with his new partner instead of the old. Slotkin's polar fever had perhaps rivaled even his own and the older man could talk for hours about the details of any expedition Oscar brought up, recounting the progress of Peary's first attempt on the Pole with precise latitudes for each day's events, or reciting long lists of supplies included in some explorer's memoirs. If anyone at BIP deserved a trip to the Arctic, it had been Slotkin. It wasn't that he didn't care for Alexi, or didn't like working with him, more that he hadn't had enough time yet to decide. From what he'd seen in those first couple weeks Alexi didn't care one way or the other about the north. Working for one agency was as good as another to him as long as he got paid and built up his pension, but Oscar wanted to give him a chance. Even the most unlikely members of an expedition prove crucial when the moment is right, when their unique skills and experience are what a tense situation demands.

Avoiding another glance at the creep with the newspaper and

glasses, he looked down the length of the car. Two benches away a redheaded woman sat wrapped in a brown trench coat despite a heat in which everyone else had taken off jackets and loosened ties and unbuttoned collars. Plaid lining showed where it flapped open at her crossed thighs; Oscar knew the brand's pattern from buying Julia a scarf for her birthday one year. Each leg ended in a glossy red shoe and atop a slender, unadorned neck she, too, wore dark glasses. From behind he could see in at the side of her face to the flame of her hair caught in the lens, and he was probably staring but had never seen such vividly reflective sunglasses before—not reflective on the inside, that is. He wondered how she could see anything but her own eyes.

She caught Oscar's reflected gaze and turned to face him, and before he could react or turn away she'd raised a tan wrist and laid a finger tipped with the same shade as her shoes across her lips. He could have sworn she nodded her head the slightest bit in the direction of the creep behind the newspaper who was looking again, then wasn't, again. Oscar felt certain she couldn't be telling him to be quiet because he already was being quiet, and even if he had been speaking she'd never have heard him from two rows away over the noise of the train and other passengers talking and playing their chirping and beeping and buzzing games, over so much music too loud in headphones designed to share sound with the world whether the world wanted it shared or not. Still he felt scolded, as if she'd shushed not his voice but thoughts he hadn't had about her—he might have, in time, if he'd kept looking for a few stops, though whatever women crept into his passing public transportation fantasies more often than not morphed into his wife as the scenario developed, into a body he actually knew well enough to imagine though he'd done more imagining than knowing the last couple years—and Oscar turned back to the vents near the floor a bit shamed.

He'd seen her before or at least thought he had but he couldn't place where. Did she work in his building? Was she a train regular? Many of the riders were familiar by then and he'd ridden with some of them for the better part of the years he'd made that commute. He noticed when they were gone for a while; in summer, he hoped they were enjoying a vacation and in winter he worried they might be sick. And when someone vanished—when Oscar realized, for instance, he hadn't seen for some time the woman with the big bag of knitting or the man who carried two insulated lunch bags each day—he hoped they'd retired or moved and not died. For a few years he and Julia had commuted together, before she transferred across town to Tires and Treads, and they'd often talked about who had or hadn't been on the train the way other couples might talk about old friends they'd run into or family members who called. He'd felt the loss of their riding together as keenly as the disappearance of any other long-time regular; it always took a few weeks or months to get back to normal when someone was gone.

Theirs was a silent communion, a twice-daily band of brothers and sisters. More like Vilhjalmur Stefansson's team of professionals in it together to get the job done but not to make friends, a far cry from the phonographs and light opera and group entertainments of Franklin's expeditions or, for that matter, Peary's. Shared purpose but still aloof, cohesion without camaraderie. They watched out for each other, the regulars, but kept themselves to themselves; they weren't about to publish the subway car's own *North Georgia Gazette* or toast one another's birthdays.

But the redheaded woman: Oscar didn't think he knew her from the train or from work, so maybe he recognized her from someplace else—where else did he go?—or maybe she just had a look the way some people do. Whichever it was, however he knew her or not, his station was next so he stood up and moved toward the door in plenty of time, maximizing the efficiency of entry and exit, his own and everyone else's.

He flowed with his fellow riders up through the station,

between the turnstiles and onto the street, where he refreshed the web cam on his phone. The ice was still empty as he walked two blocks toward his apartment, past a trio of boys on a corner fighting over who got to wear the toy space helmet next, who got to be the astronaut and who had to settle for mission control in their game.

Doused in blood, sore from the weight of the caribou and its loss—sore, too, from his own failure—the hunter's day felt very real. The kind of day he'd come north to find in these strange, steaming mountains for better or worse.

As he reached the pass from which the trail led out of the mountains and down to the shoreline and home, the thundering churn and chop of helicopters led him by instinct back into the trees. Black metal wasps came from all sides, some over water and some over land, all enormous and all closing in on the log cabins and bright-hued houses with roofs of sod or dull, rippled steel, on the small geothermal plant that powered the village, and what remained of a failed attempt at at some kind of mill abandoned long before his own time, now an industrial ruin with crumbling walls and overgrown windows and some of the tallest trees in the region growing up through its floor where they were sheltered from the worst of the wind.

He watched his family and friends and neighbors come out of their homes at the sound overhead, as distant and indistinct as figurines on a tabletop railway display when they took to the village's single dirt track to cluster and point to the sky.

Almost as soon as the helicopters flooded his sight their rockets were launched, their guns rattled and blazed. The hunter saw the flashes, the flames, the explosions and ruptures of his neighbor's houses and of his own but the sounds took a second to reach him so his senses fell out of synch.

Bodies of all sizes scattered in every direction, rushed in and out of their homes as flashes of fabric and color, and the guns did not discriminate as they tore apart children and adults and rain barrels alike. It happened in a fiery blur, beyond the reach of his rifle—and with all those helicopters, all those shots fired and shells exploded, who could he possible shoot to stop anything if he had been close enough for a shot? He could watch, that was all.

In what felt like seconds but might have been minutes the village was leveled and the helicopters alit in a ring on its edges more gracefully than they deserved.

Through the impotently powerful scope of his rifle, designed for longer range than the rifle itself, the hunter watched men and women in pixelated grayscale camouflage rush from those helicopters one after another and charge through what remained of the village, guns drawn and occasionally firing.

Their uniforms bore no insignia, not one single ribbon or stripe and not even a flag, and the helicopters' hulls were pure black apart from matte, ashy streaks where the rockets had fired. The hunter swung his sights from one anonymous enemy to another, lining up their heads, their heartless torsos, but who could he shoot? Felling one target wouldn't remove all the others. He might have crept forward to squeeze a shot off before they knew he was watching and turned their attention to fire on him but at this distance, alone, he couldn't prevent anything and in short time the firing was over. The blood had been spilled.

As the village burned in flames whipped up and around by strong wind off the water, those men and women in gray worked in pairs, one always covering the other with a rifle as the partner pulled bodies from rubble and embers, laying them out along the dirt road. A man in an identical uniform but without a rifle walked up and down the line holding a clipboard, counting the corpses with a wave of his pen and checking off items on a sheet.

The hunter zoomed in as close as he could with his scope but couldn't make the list into more than a blurry white square, no more distinct than the clean-shaven face of the man wielding it.

The wind picked up, making uniforms stand at sharp angles where extra cloth hung, and before the man with no rifle could grab it a pink sheet blew away from his clipboard. He chased it and some of the others did, too, but it was too fast on the gust and cleared the village and got into the brush without being outrun. The man stood with his clipboard up to shield his eyes, watching the sheet blow away and looking—not that he knew it—right in the hunter's direction with his face in the crosshairs of the scope.

The man with no rifle had come close enough for the hunter to watch his mouth shape two soundless curses, one after another, before the gray body turned and walked back toward the violence he seemed to be in charge of.

The hunter could have fired. He almost did. But his life in the village was already lost and he was outnumbered by dozens, so he waited and watched them instead. He trusted his own time, his own vengeful moment, would come.

He watched the destruction for hours. At near-dark they set up a circle of high intensity floodlights on poles around the village while tearing down every last scrap of cabin and house. They burned the boats and then burned the pier, and what couldn't be burned was scattered or gathered into bins and hauled aboard helicopters or into huge cargo nets.

When they were done it was morning, or daylight at least in those timeless hours of the Arctic. They took down the lamps by early sunlight as if they had planned it that way. The first four helicopters lifted just high enough for the cargo nets containing those last scraps of life to be hung from their bellies, then they flew away across the water. The remaining men scoured the ground, scraped or stamped out every trace, and when the man with the clipboard had been satisfied they boarded the last of the clattering beasts, lifted off, and were gone.

Only then did the hunter descend.

There was nothing for him to go through. Nothing left to cry over. His cabin, his family, his whole life in that village erased. They'd left him only a gun.

He scoured the scrub at the foot of the trail, parting branches and briars, crawling through tangled growth, until he found that pink sheet blown away from the rifleless man. He sat with the base of his backpack taking his weight, the gun strapped to it lending support, and read a list of his family and his friends and his neighbors, every life lost in that village. He read his own name and was silently grateful, though sorry, for the stranger who had arrived in the village a few days before—too recently to have been on the list but there to make the body count seem accurate.

Hashmarks to one side of the page counted the dead, the recently living, and though not quite every victim was accounted for by those ticks he knew it was only due to the wind's interruption. That they were dead in life if not on paper, and on the original if not the pink copy.

The hunter looked at the purple duplication of the other man's handwriting pressed from one page to another. Angular. Rushed. Businesslike. A man who only has time for results.

And he looked at some other markings near the top of the sheet. Marks that weren't letters or numbers or names but the faintest outline of a logo, a stamp, applied to the top page of the form. When he held it to light the hunter could almost make it out and with a stub of pencil drawn from his pack he darkened the shape: an unfilled, indistinct circular outline of the north. A map in wait to be filled.

5

Work was being done at the end of the street as seemed to always be the case. Oscar and Julia joked sometimes about roving bands of road workers wandering the District and trying to look busy. Especially in summer it seemed you could go to work in the morning and come home to a whole different landscape, the digging and paving and constant rerouting were so much a part of routine.

Sidewalks had been cordoned off and a yellow tent erected over a manhole while men and women in hardhats and reflective vests crowded around. A thick, corrugated blue hose ran from one of their trucks down the hole and under the street, vibrating and jumping in the arms of the workers while a machine of some kind roared and rattled on the back of the truck. At his approach, one of the workers waved Oscar off, jabbing his finger at a folding signboard nearby reading DETOUR with an arrow pointing away from the building his apartment was in. Oscar pointed toward his front door, visible on the other side of the trucks and cordons and workers, but the interloper shook his hardhatted head, scowled, and gestured down the block. "Detour!" he mouthed, or perhaps yelled; it was hard to tell over the roar of equipment. "Go!"

Oscar liked his routine: the same path from BIP's basement to the Metro to his apartment. He stood at the same spot on the platform each day while awaiting his train because he knew that particular car would line up with the stairs when he reached his stop, and he noticed the same sidewalk cracks everyday when walking home: which ones were growing weeds and how tall they'd become, which had been filled with tar or embossed by lichen or moss. So as he turned left and headed around the next block down a street more or less like his own—the same brick row houses, the same magnolia and dogwood trees growing in sidewalk cutouts, the same types of cars parked at the curbs—it wasn't unfamiliar, exactly, but he felt out of sorts. Thrown off. So after he'd walked all the way around the far end of the block and approached his building from the other direction he had to stand on the stoop for a moment not to catch his breath but to catch up with himself and regain his bearings. At least it had happened on the way home, because a surprise like that in the morning could throw off the day's prognostications. It would have shown in his work, because it was hard to explore the unfamiliar realms of the north without knowing things remained unchanged at home. Peary brought his wife and their furniture all the way to Greenland before setting out for the Pole so the comfort of domestic routine would stay as fresh in his memory as possible for the remainder of the expedition, and all Oscar wanted was to walk down the same street every day and come home to the same apartment and TV and marriage.

From the stoop he checked the Pole cam where nothing had changed—not the light, not the snow, not even the footprints that weren't—and Oscar relaxed as he watched. The rumbling equipment at the end of the block, emitting low tones that burrowed into his body and up through his feet, shaking the street and the buildings upon it, couldn't intrude on the quiet and calm—the great, reliable sameness—of the North Pole, safe in the small space of a screen.

Oscar and his wife often arrived home at about the same time, running into each other there on the steps, and he waited a few minutes expecting her to come down the street along the same detour he'd taken before remembering her text. So he climbed three flights on his own to their green door, swollen all summer in the humidity and stuck in its frame, where he dug out his keys and wrestled his way into their home.

He did his everyday things: changed out of his work clothes into a T-shirt and shorts, checked the mail (nothing much), read the news on his laptop and watched the same news again, more or less, on TV. Ate a dinner of leftovers from takeout they'd gotten the evening before because neither of them felt like cooking or like eating other leftovers they already had. And through all of that, the routine he and Julia went through any evening but tonight on his own, Oscar thought about the day's news. Not the news he'd been watching but the news of his own: that he was going to the Arctic. If he was going, if Director Lenz hadn't changed his mind after their meeting and that was why there had been no more information as he'd expected in the afternoon.

He stood in the living room he shared with his wife, surrounded by three yellow walls where his built-in bookshelves of *National Geographic* reached floor to ceiling: every issue since his birth and most of the earlier ones, though not quite all the way back to 1888. Any issue with even the briefest bit of Arctic lore was marked by a red sticker dot on the spine so he could find them when needed, though he probably could have pulled down whatever issue he wanted to find a specific passage or report from the Pole just by remembering where in the room he'd found it before. He was lucky, he knew: Julia didn't mind his magazines or at least she didn't complain. She'd never once asked him to get rid of them or even move his collection, perhaps because it was a big room in a big enough apartment and between the two of them there was nothing else to fill up the space, busy as they both had always been with their jobs. Apart from his magazines and her cookbooks in the kitchen—which she read but rarely cooked from—and her karate trophies (if it was karate: he had a hard time remembering which martial art she actually studied and she'd never invited Oscar to watch her compete; she just came home with a new trophy sometimes) in a display case above the TV, there wasn't much to their home. The usual things, of course, the furniture and clothes and shoes. A few photo albums, but most of those they'd scanned and stored on hard drives and discs instead, the way they'd ripped all their CDs and cleared the shelves of jewel boxes. So they'd given themselves plenty of room for storing the things that needed storage and even for hiding what they wanted out of the way. The evidence of their lives both apart and together were nestled in one database, their choices and memories and tastes, and they only had to ask that database for what they wanted via laptops or phones or menus summoned on their TV to get back just what they were after and leave all the other, unwelcome choices tucked away out of sight, out of mind, without the guilt Oscar used to feel about listening to the same CDs and watching the same movies over and over while so many others stared him down from the shelves that once filled the fourth wall of the room. He couldn't enjoy one direction when all the others he hadn't chosen insisted on making themselves known.

He'd been against that consolidation at first, the stripping away of relics he'd always thought grounded their lives, but after the compromise of letting him keep his magazines—making more room to display them, in fact—he'd given in and soon admitted Julia had been right all along.

A whole extra bedroom hadn't ever been slept in for more than a night or two at a time when some friend passed through town and Julia had done what she wanted to with that unoccupied space, making its emptiness her own. So Oscar's century-plus of magazines had the run of the front room with only the sliding glass door to a small balcony breaking into their yellow expanse, letting in genuine light all afternoon and through the evening though at times it paled beside those bright spines.

He pulled a beer from the fridge and had to stop his other arm's muscle memory from grabbing a second for Julia as it often did, though less consistently lately since her promotion and increase in karate nights. Then he stepped outside to that railed-in rectangle hardly large enough for their two folding lawn chairs without a lawn and a small, square table between them, where Oscar stood his bottle before sitting down.

They were a quiet couple, he and Julia. They didn't talk much and they'd always been that way or else had slipped into their quiet so gradually neither one noticed the change, like a bath you're sitting in cools but you don't realize you're shivering until you've turned blue or—let's hope not—have died.

He drank his beer slowly and whenever he set it down between pulls habit made him check to avoid knocking over Julia's absentee bottle. Below on the street one car ran into another. Neither was traveling fast, one was pulling away from the curb and the other was pulling up to it, but the crunch of plastic-on-plastic and the "oohs" of kids and adults on the sidewalk and stoops rose to the balcony like a much bigger accident had taken place. The drivers got out, exchanged papers, shook heads and eventually hands, and went on their way without waiting for the police. Across the street, on the far side of the smash up, a man in a hat and dark glasses ducked backward around the corner of the Chinese takeout that had provided Oscar his dinner. The strangeness of it, the absurdity, reminded Oscar of the man on the train, too conspicuous behind his newspaper to mean anything, and he even wondered for a thin second if those two men were in fact one but dismissed the idea: it still felt like summer and was still sunny so hats and dark glasses should be expected on an evening like this, a more likely explanation than, what, spies watching him drink a beer on a balcony without his wife?

He spotted his phone on the table and thought of the Pole cam and what it might be showing—the clean simplicity of the ice sheet, nothing superfluous as the sun set almost in sync with his own farther south, the equinox only a few days away. Soon after the swathe of sky visible between the underside of the balcony above his own and the flat roof of the more or less identical building across the street had taken on the faintest purplish tinge, and soon it was dark. Leaving his empty bottle to the flies Oscar headed inside after holding the door open for a ghost or a wife to go first.

He turned on TV without optimism and the first thing he saw on a channel left behind by his news earlier was the opening sequence of *To The Moon!*. Oscar snarled, and he sneered, and he slapped at the remote but, predictably, worked up as he was he wasn't precise and probably watched that infuriating show longer than he might have done had he calmed down, kept control, and carefully pressed a button to shift the channel one way or the other. A single stroke would have sufficed but instead he flailed across all the buttons at once, blindly hoping for change, and half the buttons he managed to push negated the other half and it took longer—a few seconds at least—until the change he so longed for could come. Which we shouldn't belabor but isn't it always the way?

He tried watching a show about food and a show about dogs, and he tried watching a news magazine about murders or celebrities or celebrity murders (he couldn't quite tell because none of the celebrities or corpses or celebrity corpses were polar explorers so he wasn't sure which ones were meant to be famous and which were just meant to be dead) but after the unfortunate episode with the remote he saw astronauts everywhere and gave up on TV. The screen going black, first at the edges then closing in toward the center, came like a breath for his eyes and his ears the way winter's night comes to the Pole.

Instead of TV Oscar turned to his shelves and after a moment's consideration—finger poised, scanning the red-dotted spines—he ventured forth with a surgeon's precision and withdrew volume XVIII, number 7, July 1907 and it fell open within a page of his destination, one of his favorite passages of Arctic lore: Max Fleischman's account of July 4, 1906 at Virgo Haven with the Wellman expedition, fireworks bursting over their half-built but American houses so far above the 49th parallel, north of another continent altogether, of course, but... no, he'd forgotten, there weren't fireworks, no room in the hold for such extravagance. The men had fired their rifles and pistols into the sky of that bright northern night in Spitzbergen, at Major Hersey's command, "Make a noise!" and it's a good thing they did, too, Oscar thought, because within a few weeks their airship was grounded, its engines burnt out, and the expedition was forced to abandon. They had little enough to celebrate right there at the moment they at last thought the Arctic was theirs so it's good they'd found time for that earlier impromptu party. It's that kind of region, the north: wearing down men on one hand and machines on the other but always leaving enough breathing room for dreams to survive, and of course Wellman tried again the next year to no greater avail.

Oscar shook his head and laughed at himself for once again remembering that bittersweet scene with actual fireworks, a false image he couldn't shake however often he returned to that page, as real in his memory as the Arctic's own illusory islands always waiting on the horizon, driving sailors onward and into madness at times.

He read those pages for who knows the how many-nth time, lingering on favorite passages he knew by heart but loved to see set in the heavy black print of an earlier age, an age with more confidence than his own. He meditated and daydreamed over Fleischman's photos, especially the left behind huts of the 1882 Austrian expedition on Isle of Jan Mayen. He wondered, he had always wondered, what state they were in by his time. It was so hard to tell from the grainy old photo and Fleischman had snapped it from such a distance. Oscar had always meant to visit the *National Geographic* archives across town, to see the original image up close for himself or at least to know it was there. He'd always wanted to know how the huts had held up in those twenty-four years of abandon and after. Were they still there? How long could they stand on their own, a steadfast afterthought, their obsolete purpose long since served? Maybe they'd been occupied by later travelers or even natives, as labs or houses or shelters for animals getting out of the wind. Someone, he thought, should go back and find out, should follow up for the magazine and the many readers he could only assume were left wondering as he himself was.

After two then three yawns crept up on him, Oscar slipped the magazine back into its space, leading with a fingertip to separate the neighboring spines so he wouldn't bend any edges. How could anyone not be amazed at the Arctic and what men had done there? The winters and frostbite endured and the ingenuous inventions survival required. Work they could do on their own, on the ground, not the adjustments of scientists in their shirtsleeves thousands of miles away, safe at home. Even Julia, who had been always been willing to listen even if she gave him a pitying look that was, frankly, a little bit sexy and had often worked out that way, seemed to lose interest these days when he pointed out passages in his magazines, when he gave her the most amazing details about expeditions and icepacks and the illusions of land that appeared over vast Arctic seas to make sailors think they'd arrived when they were still as adrift as they'd been all along.

And she laughed when *To The Moon!* drove Oscar out of the room.

"But it's so stupid!" he'd said the night before as she watched reruns intended to warm up the audience for a new season.

"Of course it's stupid!" she countered. "It's a story! If it was complicated, it wouldn't be a way to relax. If they were really in danger, what fun would that be to watch? If it was all life and death we'd have to worry instead of enjoy it and I get enough of that at work, thanks."

He almost asked what was so life and death about registering tire tread patterns, but wasn't optimistic about the way that might go.

"But you used to hate this sort of thing," Oscar said. "We never watched shows like this."

"I didn't hate them. I just didn't want to listen to you complain about them and ruin the show. Oscar, I'm tired. I had a long day. I just want to watch something dumb. It doesn't make me a bad person. Just because you're obsessed with one thing doesn't mean you can't take an interest in others."

"But it's always the same. It's practically scripted. Where's the surprise?"

"Where's the surprise in reading the same magazines over and over? Or in watching another PBS show about the North Pole? You've seen them all. They aren't going to change."

That one left him speechless so she went on. "And besides, everyone watches this show. It's fun to have that in common, to laugh about it together. And to *know* you have it common. You can take it for granted, like if you just mention the show people know what you're talking about and it calls up a whole bunch of other things to talk about even if you don't know the person you're talking to all that well. I mean, sure, you could do that with politics or something instead but that's so exhausting. And who wants to fight with a stranger just because they ran out of things to talk about? That's why they call it *popular* culture, you know— everyone likes it." She turned back to the TV and said, "Everyone except you, I suppose," before turning it up.

He'd tried many times to explain that the Arctic was popular, that *Nanook of the North* was the first great blockbuster and spontaneous parades erupted in the streets of great cities when explorers came home, but… well, saying so felt a bit too much like one more party where no one else in the room had read *Farthest North*. He'd been to enough of those for one lifetime already and he suspected Julia had, too, which was why most of the time he didn't mind when she went out alone and why she seldom asked if he wanted to come.

Oscar didn't like to think of himself as out of touch. He

preferred thinking he'd stayed in touch longer, his attention a long polar day instead of the brief flash of sun a TV show or movie or space flight might earn. He wasn't so willing as most people to talk about nothing, to spend his time keeping up on things that might not in time matter, when there were already much better things to be learning and talking and knowing about. When there were already centuries of Arctic lore to discuss. But it was hard to get into all that without telling the truth about BIP, which wouldn't much help his case, anyway.

He stood with a hand splayed on his magazines wondering where Julia was and what she was doing with her karate friends; he pictured them out fighting crime, all those mild-mannered bureaucrats by day bringing the District to justice at night, and he smiled. Then he brushed his teeth, had a pee, and went off to bed after a quick check-in at the Pole, which had already faded to black as had the sky outside his own apartment; only a narrow spotlight from above the camera lit a swathe of snow as the streetlights did for the sidewalk below.

Hours later Oscar was awoken by his wife climbing into their bed and opened his eyes to her back curved before him, covered only by the ribbed white tanktop she preferred on hot nights and her hair pulled into a high ponytail off her neck. In the half-light, shadows that might have been bruises lay on her shoulder and upper arm, and a dark quarter-sized smear on the back of her shirt looked like blood. Oscar wondered again what her karate class had gotten up to or if it was all a trick of the light.

He set out to stroke her, to lay his hand on her side or run fingers down her spine, wrap a hand around her shoulder, perhaps, but the white tundra of bedsheet between them, the fabric mounded into a scale model mountain range, proved daunting. He remembered the night before and so many nights before that when he'd touched her, stroked an arm or a thigh or reached around Julia's back and under the edge of her shirt, wanting to touch her and know she was there, hoping something might come of it, only for her to roll further over or scrunch herself into a shape that left so little skin exposed for him to touch. They'd go months sometimes without sex or anything like it, months without touching each other in bed, her body closed off to him however warm she'd been over dinner, over drinks on the porch, even on the couch a few minutes before. Some nights the result was an argument after dark, more or less the same one every time.

Him saying she'd changed and her saying of course she had, they were older, their lives busier, insisting the question to ask wasn't why she had changed but why he had not.

And Oscar insisting sex wasn't the point but the effort was, her being willing to rise above being tired, to muster some last reserve at the end of the day for his sake. To show him he mattered that much. Once he made the mistake of insisting that Peary's last push at the Pole, when his team finally reached it, wasn't only about wanting to but about honor and debt and what partners owe to each other, and she'd stormed from the room to sleep on the couch, mutters of "P goddamn F," trailing behind her and Oscar left alone in the bed, wide awake, knowing he'd gone too far but with no route of return that didn't lead through the living room where his wife steamed.

Another time he'd raised the specter of Peary's wife Josephine and how game she always was for adventure in the dark of their bedroom, and Julia said, "For fuck's sake, Oscar. There's no North Pole in our lives. Stop trying to turn everyday life into big, dramatic moments and important moral dilemmas. It's not like that. No one's life is. That's what we watch TV for. I'm just tired, okay? That's all there is to it. Some days you're just tired and it doesn't have to mean anything. Now shut up and let me sleep."

More often the argument ended with Julia yawning, clamping down on her anger and telling Oscar not to get so insulted, not to take it so personally, that the last thing she wanted at the end of a long day was more expectation—she came home to get away from demands for a few hours and to put her body aside.

"Your body sits at a desk all day, same as mine," Oscar said, or some variation on that. "How can it be so much more tired?" And she would ignore him or tell him to sleep and roll herself farther away toward the edge of the bed. Or they would fight until neither of them got a night's sleep at all.

But after going through all of that too many times, enough times to realize nothing would change and this particular latitude couldn't be reached, after too many hours spent angry and ashamed on his side of the bed knowing Julia was angry on hers, each of them pretending to be asleep or to think the other one was, after playing and replaying too many worst case scenarios in his head—separation, divorce, disruption of his entire life for the sake of what, of sex, of demanding something his wife didn't want, of feeling cruel and ashamed and weak for it—Oscar had taken to leaving the bed to let Julia sleep and to burn his desire off elsewhere without even trying, without risking a touch before removing himself.

The twin beds of old movies began to make sense, that deep empty distance made literal instead of his imagined icefield of unoccupied sheets stretching toward the lonely north of a long marriage and a lost expedition.

He spent many nights, half the dark hours of each week, up late among his magazines. Returning to favorite moments at the Pole or at home—often quite close to his home, in fact, nearby in DC, at the magazine's own offices or the Smithsonian—in accounts of explorers making preparations for expeditions or captains of government and industry praising expeditions returned, praising the steadfastness and stoicism that brought men to the Arctic or, perhaps, to the couch.

He read about hardships, of months and years spent in the company of only men—whatever rumors of half-Inuit offspring may have followed Flaherty and Henson and even Peary home from the ice—and of sacrifices made for the team: frostbite endured, new depths of energy plumbed, new reserves of strength and willpower summoned to drag oneself and one's partners the long way to the Pole, and he soothed himself to think he had some kinship with them on those frustrated nights. And when he awoke in his chair the mornings after and Julia emerged from their bedroom a little while later as if he'd simply left their bed a short time before her, they said good morning and nothing else larger than small talk. They carried on as if the night before had been washed away or had been long enough to forget how it started as nights could be so often up north.

So despite thinking his wife might be awake after just coming to bed he stayed poised with a hand held mid-reach between his own body and hers, halfway to the graceful white slope of her shoulder and back and the crescent of her breast glimpsed in the armhole of her shirt. The distance proved greater than Oscar could will himself across on that night's expedition. Or morning's, as it turned out, because who knows how long Julia had been home and how long she had been beside him in bed or if she really had woken him coming to bed a few minutes before because it was only an hour until his rising time and alarm, by the nightstand replica of Nansen's ship's clock she'd somehow found for his birthday one year. So Oscar rolled over and swung his legs out of bed, ready to equip himself for the next charge, leaving Julia to her dreams on the far side of the mattress.

He padded toward the bathroom but paused on the way to take in the last moonlight blending with the first rays of dawn on his magazine's spines, a luminous glow in his living room, something he'd noticed before many times but never tired of just as no one—not even the most hardened explorer—could fail to be awed by the Northern Lights overhead.

6

Oscar's shower began a few seconds sooner than anticipated as it almost always did, his wife being the person in their marriage who left the knob turned to shower instead of to tap when she finished; Oscar, for his part, was the spouse who reliably took out the trash without putting a new bag in the can.

Then out of the shower and into the kitchen, barefoot in pants and T-shirt, no belt, his phone on the counter (a quick look before breakfast, too early for sun at the Pole) and scooping coffee into a brown paper filter. There was a knock at the door—one-two-(pause)-three—and he froze, a scoop of ground coffee hovering midway between vessel and maker. But the knocks came again so he dumped the coffee into the basket, swung it closed, and turned on the machine before answering the door.

Two men, one tall and the other one wide. They were no one he knew, no one he recognized from anywhere. Both wore dark suits, dark ties, and dark glasses though the sun was barely into the sky. It was still invisible, in fact, from his apartment because its windows did not face that way.

"It's time," said the taller man, standing in back and speaking over the head of his silent companion. "Your car is outside."

"Time for what?" Oscar asked, but the shorter, wider man was beside him, then behind him, somehow both pushing and pulling him at once through the door, still barefoot, half-dressed, still waiting for his coffee to brew.

"Time to go," said Tall. Wide pulled the door closed without struggling against it despite the humidity of the past several days and even, already, that morning.

"Wait, stop. Go where?" Oscar asked as each man took one of his arms, not firmly, not in a grip, but enough to let him know he was being guided somewhere and he had better go. "I don't understand, I…"

"You will, sir," said Wide, whose voice turned out to be a higher squeak than his icebreaker of a body suggested.

Oscar looked around all the way down the stairs, frantic, confused, hoping for help but not sure against what. "My wife," he said to no answer. "I have to work."

"Sir, this is work," squeaked Wide.

Outside the front door of the building, two wheels over the curb and on the sidewalk, back door standing open, a long, black SUV waited, engine running, and Oscar was whisked inside—someone's hand on his head pushed him down as another hand shoved his back—and the car was in motion before he saw a driver, a license, an indication of anything.

There was someone in the glare of the passenger seat, an anonymous silhouette of head and shoulders, but when those shoulders turned the head belonged to Alexi, his partner, a familiar face. "Good morning, Oscar," he said, smiling. "Off we go!"

"Go where? I don't understand!"

"The Arctic! Off to the Arctic! Didn't they tell you inside?"

"They didn't tell me anything! We're going now? I didn't tell Julia, I didn't pack… I'm not wearing shoes or even a shirt! Wait, I need to go back."

"No time, sir," Wide said. "It has been taken care of." Then he handed over a stack of clothes expertly folded and, as we might expect under the circumstances, in Oscar's size. And one of the thugs, whether it was Tall or Wide, had carried Oscar's most comfortable shoes to the car, shoes he'd thought had been by the bed but he hadn't seen either of the men go that far into his apartment.

"Are we going to see the Director? Is that it?" he asked, struggling in the small space to get dressed.

"No time for that either, sir. Your train departs in a few minutes. You'll be briefed then."

"Could we stop for some coffee?" Alexi asked. "And maybe a breakfast burrito? I know a place close to the station."

"Sir," Wide replied, in the tone of a warning but also a plea, as if Alexi had already asked for food at least once before Oscar got into the car. Had already asked and had already been answered by men who weren't willing to answer again.

There was no more talking, there wasn't much time, because already the SUV had arrived at the station and Oscar had only just tied his shoes when it stopped. They pulled into the pick-up/drop-off circle outside the front door and Tall ushered Oscar out one side while Wide climbed out the other and walked around. Alexi, for whatever reason, was allowed to get out by himself and neither of their escorts seemed to pay Oscar's partner the least bit of mind.

Tall handed each of them a train ticket in a blue envelope and said, "This way. Platform three." The prognosticators followed him into the station, through revolving glass doors and angles and curves of gleaming brass hardware into the cavernous space of the main lobby—cavernous, and also a cathedral of towering ceilings and windows so tall no one knows what the view is at the top. Oscar had been there before, dozens of times, hundreds perhaps, but this morning was different. Perhaps it was the hour, perhaps a fluke, but despite the early crush and crowd of passengers coming and going, despite the coffee and donut kiosk thronged with customers (including Alexi, who had rushed away from Tall and Wide as soon as he came within reach of the queue and was already pushing his way through the scrum) and the newspaper stand humming with chatter and clinking with change, the station seemed silent somehow. Suspended and waiting for something.

Iktsuarpok, Oscar thought.

On the front page of all the newspapers apart from the serious one with no photographs was an image of the would-be astronauts from last night's show.

"Sirs," squeaked Wide, pulling Alexi back by the shoulder, away from the kiosk and crowd, but he was already clutching a steaming large coffee and greasy white donut-stuffed bag.

"All ready," he said, holding his bounty aloft. "Fast as a light-bulb, I told you."

"What about my wife?" Oscar asked. "I didn't leave a note for my wife, and she'll wonder. She wasn't awake yet when you took . . . when I left."

"No time, sir," Tall said in a tone that made clear it was the last he wanted to hear about that. Say what you will about Tall and Wide, they were excellent and efficient communicators. Model government employees, if that's what they were. Model kidnappers, too, for that matter, if they were meant to be those instead.

The prognosticators were led onto the platform and all the way to its end, past the regular commuter cars to a stretch of strange cars without logos or signs, just sleek silver sides unbroken by image or text, unlike all the others with stripes and warning labels and notices where to step up and watch out. Tall and Wide guided them into a car and opened the door to a cabin, nothing fancy but there were bunk beds and a table and chairs, a rack of magazines and a basket of fruit. And a dark brown envelope, unmarked, pinned to the table by the weight of the bowl. The envelope was a shade of brown unfamiliar to Oscar: not the yellow of BIP's interoffice communications or the caramel manila of confidentiality, a darker brown with more obvious fibers, a visible grain that to Oscar's eye looked like wafer-thin wood.

No sooner had he entered than the train was in motion, pull-ing out of the station and away down the track. "Okay," said Tall, "we'll be back soon to keep an eye on you two."

"Shouldn't one of us stay?" asked Wide in what may have been meant as a whisper to his partner but it's hard to keep a voice that high-pitched hidden. "He said we should…"

"I'm not getting your coffee. You want to stay, go ahead."

"We'll be back soon," agreed Wide. "We'll be fast."

"Like a lightbulb," Alexi said, drawing an exhausted look from Tall and another from Oscar.

And without another word the kidnappers or escorts or whichever they were left the cabin, the dark clouds of their respectively tall and wide black-suited broad shoulders gliding off into the train.

Alexi was already eating, coffee in one hand and a powdery donut in the other, snowing all over the carpet and table and chair. A dislodged triangular chunk bounced onto the envelope, a rogue pastry iceberg adrift.

"What the hell's going on?" Oscar asked.

"It's been a while since breakfast," his partner replied, hoisting the coffee as if it held all the answers Oscar might need. "I'll get my metabolism all screwy if I don't keep to my regimen. Discipline."

"What I don't understand," Oscar went on, "is why the director told us we were going if we were just going to be hauled off in disorganization. Why tell us at all?" He thought of the chapters upon chapters devoted to preparations in the great Arctic accounts: Nansen and Peary and all the others had been meticulous about planning, cataloguing each detail of rations and weight in their journals and later their bestselling books. Charles Francis Hall spent years traveling the United States to raise funding for his expeditions, and Oscar couldn't help thinking all that—the waiting and planning and slow, thoughtful packing—was an important part of any good expedition, of an excursion on course to succeed, not to mention part of all the best stories and a part he had looked forward to in his own. A good explorer spent time building connections and stockpiling supplies, not just those sure to be needed but preparations for the unexpected, those minor and major disasters that lurk in the long polar night. Even a crew, no less than a store room, should be assembled with care: take time to build a foundation, to see how they mesh on warm ground, to ensure a blend of personalities, a crosscut of strength and weakness so when one man falters another steps up, when one wobbles there's a shoulder at just the right height.

An expedition was a courtship as well as a marriage and he felt a bit robbed by this one night stand despite the romance of a train.

Alexi fought one-handed with the cabin window, trying to slide the lower pane up to let in some air, but that hand was still holding what remained of his donut—not much, but enough to compromise his dexterity—and struggled to get a firm grip and leverage. "Right," he said with a bit of a grunt from the effort. He squinted one eye and got right up close to the frame, looking for the cause of the jam.

"Maybe he wasn't supposed to tell us," said Oscar. "Or maybe he was supposed to tell us the men would be coming this morning. Maybe it wasn't meant to be a surprise when they came to my door. I should have been ready, I guess."

Alexi removed his shoe to hammer the dull metal window casing and the sock revealed was a rusty shade of brown with a hole at the heel the size of a camera's lens. The banging of the shoe and the clatter of the train were so loud in combination that Oscar's voice grew louder to keep up with them until he was practically shouting.

"It doesn't make sense, does it? There are procedures to follow. There are ways of doing things in BIP." Then he realized how loud he was talking and that his partner wasn't paying attention so gave up the conversation to sit at the table instead, absently picking at grapes.

"Unless this isn't for BIP…," he wondered aloud. "Maybe this is something else?"

"Oh," said Alexi, but to himself, or to the window perhaps. Then he gave up on trying to force the lower pane of glass upward and instead, with smooth ease, slid the upper pane down. A blast of cool, dusty air rushed into the room and both men shivered. The noise of the train became louder, drawn in now through the window instead of just felt in the walls and the floor of the train, making the motion and the departure both real in a way they hadn't been yet. Outside, the stumps of the city ceded to the occasional house and in the distance a shopping mall or massive furniture store or a nondescript row of warehouses like ground down teeth on the horizon.

Oscar tore open the brown envelope left for them in the cabin and that simple gesture, something familiar, calmed him down some—he'd opened envelopes hundreds if not thousands of times, he'd done it in the BIP offices among others and at home and now on this train so even in his confusion it carried the welcome weight of routine and of work. Not quite the big map on the wall to start his day off but close enough to his usual actions to bring that strange day down to earth.

Alexi pulled at the hole in his sock, unraveling the fabric from inside out as thread spiraled around and around; if he kept on that way there would be nothing left but his fingers holding the string.

"We're going to Boston," Oscar announced after reading the page. "We'll be told more there."

"Boston's nice. Clam chowder. Chowduh. Have you been? I took bronze—too much bulk from the potatoes."

"It really is all food with you, isn't it? Do you think about anything else?"

"Hmm…," Alexi said, tilting his face toward the window. "Hmm," he said again as the train passed over a raised section of track with four busy lanes of traffic below. "I do like food. But you know, Oscar, I've never had a great memory. It goes in, it gets jumbled, and I don't know what I've done or who I was with or... but if I eat. If there's a meal. Well. Then I remember. If I go somewhere and eat something, the more it stays with me, the better it keeps in my head. Clearer. It's like... I think it's like a backup, if you know what I mean. Like at BIP all the records are backed up, right? And if someone could erase all of that..."

"Why would they? And anyhow there isn't a way."

"There must be some way but that's not my point. If they could..."

"But why? Who'd erase BIP?"

Alexi paused, mouth open, giving Oscar a funny look. He said, "Never mind that. Okay. It's all backed up, right?"

"Of course. But..."

"It's the same with me. If a memory's in my head it gets... it gets corrupted. But if a moment is in both my head and my body—in my stomach, I mean—I can recall. It helps me keep track and the more I eat, I guess, the better I can remember."

"Oh," Oscar said. His partner hadn't spoken so much across the entirety of the short time they'd worked together, never mind all at once.

"You know, and I like food. I like eating. And I guess I'm good at it. Like that chowder: sure, I only took bronze, but I did okay. I mean, I ate a couple of gallons and it was a pretty hot day." Alexi closed his eyes, apparently recalling that chowder. "Boston is good for chowder, though. Have you been?"

Surprised but also relieved to be back where they'd started and wondering, now, if Alexi had consumed enough donut to remember the moment just passed Oscar said, "I've been through for one thing or another, but no, not really. I haven't spent any time there. Anyway, the paper"—he rattled it—"says someone will meet us at the train station. And we aren't supposed to leave this cabin. At all. We need to keep the door locked." He looked up, reached toward the door—he had to stretch and had to lean his chair over, but he reached it without rising—and tested the knob. It was locked; they were following orders so far.

"Fast as a lightbulb," Oscar said.

"Where are you going?"

"Nowhere. Weren't you listening? It says we're supposed to say here."

"But you said, 'fast as a lightbulb,' like you were going somewhere."

"No, like 'fast.' Stuck fast. Staying put. That's what it means, Alexi. That's why we say it. Steadfast. Solid. Like all great explorers."

"Huh. I thought it was fast like, get there fast, do this fast, and all that. Like, get to Director Lenz' office fast."

"No, it's stand fast in front of my desk. Right away."

The difference lingered between them, an awkward cloud, before Oscar held the single sheet from the envelope up to Alexi. "Does this look like BIP stationary? It doesn't, does it? The paper weight's wrong. And look at the fibers. The watermark. This isn't our paper, Alexi."

His partner made a show of inspecting the page, leaving powdery fingerprints that snowed to the floor as the paper hung in Alexi's hand. His other hand remained busy worrying threads under the table, pulling his sock apart, though he screwed up his face and nodded just enough for Oscar to think he was paying attention, concerned with the unusual paper stock, too. "How long until Boston?" he asked.

"I don't know. A few hours, I guess."

"Enough time for a nap," Alexi decided. "Not a bad start to the day." Then he climbed into the upper bunk and before Oscar could ask if a nap was a good idea under the circumstances, or could remind his partner that technically speaking they were on the BIP clock, snores rattled along with the clack of the train and the humming vibration of everything else carried on it. Oscar pulled the glass up to seal the window again and the room was a bubble unburst.

Sitting at the table he called his wife but went straight to voicemail. Her phone was still off, she might still be asleep, and he didn't know what to say in a message—how much could he tell her of this, how could it make sense with the distance between what he could say and what he couldn't too great for words to bridge the gap? He'd show up as missed in her phone's logs and sometimes that was enough: Julia would know he'd reached out.

He watched the Pole for a while and the cramped berth of the train felt a bit more like home once the white sheet of ice was inside it, once all the sweat of that frantic morning had dried from his body in the cold air of daydreams.

Oscar ate a banana from the fruit bowl and read again the paper left beneath it, brushing off the last flurries of Alexi's donut. He felt the smooth stock between his fingertips and recalled the paper mill and attendant mill town he'd discovered on Prince Patrick Island a few months before, around which had grown up the town of Symmes' Hole, where the hunters lived who had made contact with the new settlement during yesterday's prognostications. First there had been a forest, an unexpected, serendipitous forest of hardwoods and soft: oaks and maples, spruces and pines. And once reports of that forest reached the lower latitudes in an official letter to Forest Management dated 1932 but written by Oscar one Monday morning last winter, it wasn't hard to develop a paper mill there: file the permits, record the plans, log their production one year to the next. The mill was state of the art for its time—it opened in 1939—but over the years, as we'd expect, environmental problems arose, acid rain in particular. It had been updated as technology and knowledge allowed, within reason. It's hard to keep things as current up north as might be taken for granted down south, but he planned to take their whole paper operation clean and green before long. He'd been making notes and conducting research on his own, after hours, reading online to figure out what kind of paperwork it would take to fulfill the town's destiny.

More than the mill, Oscar was proud of the town: he'd

named it Symmes' Hole after something he'd read in accounts of Charles Francis Hall's expeditions, some idea of what the Arctic could be; it was a name that had stuck with him for years until he seized his chance to use it, to plant its flag on the map. The mill itself was in the files as Prince Patrick Paper, the alliteration lending itself even to Oscar's meagre logo design skills, and rather than the run-of-the-mill milltowns he'd discovered elsewhere in the Arctic or the other factory towns he'd filed or updated after discovery by other prognosticators, he'd made this one special. Not for any particular reason he was aware of except he'd felt like it that day. Symmes' Hole was committed to education, to health, to the environment despite its sole employer pumping enough sulphur into the air to strip paint off the walls of its workers' homes. It was as progressive a town as you'd find in the Arctic (not that you could really find it, not that anyone looked). He'd taken them off the grid, powering the town—village really, but they had aspirations—with geothermal and biofuels produced locally to run the snowmobiles and outboard motors, an inspiration of sustainability he'd taken from Nansen and the windmill erected on the deck of the *Fram* to provide electricity and light during a long winter spent frozen into the ice.

There were even rich veins of uranium in the foothills edging the town, a detail he'd been surprised to discover. More than enough to make the town and its inhabitants rich for decades to come, more than enough to make Symmes' Hole into a boomtown instead of a quiet, coastal settlement, and it was that prospect of boom, the unwelcome image of bustle and sprawl, that led Oscar to amend his discovery of those rich deposits with records of a vote taken by all adult residents and added to the town's charter that they wouldn't exploit or announce what they'd found. For better or worse, Symmes' Hole and its citizens—who had, briefly, toyed with calling themselves Symmesians before agreeing the word sounded awful—would rise or fall without the risky rewards of uranium mining. A hard-fought, complex, consequential decision known only to the BIP database, so far as he knew.

Oscar was proud of the town and, truth be told, of himself.

It was the kind of town where he might settle himself if he someday moved to the north, unlikely as that seemed. The kind of place he'd have sought out had he gone as a young man still looking for a place to set himself down in the world. A place like Symmes' Hole. If he had ever been a man prone to travel or change, whose biggest changes in life had covered greater distances than from one floor of a government office building down to another.

Oscar's work on Prince Patrick Island, his empire of blank paper, had been noticed and admired in the small but significant circles who notice and admire such things. He was given a plaque for his work, awarded at the annual awards banquet for government employees, although the plaque read only *For Excellence and Inspiration* and the citation in the evening's program and in his file said only the same; no one knew—no one but Oscar himself, and Director Lenz, and Slotkin who had beamed like a proud father at graduation, and whoever the Bureau reported to—the truth of what he had accomplished, the invention and population of a truly excellent town, and what that award was actually for. His crowning moment, the highlight of his career, and he couldn't tell anyone why.

Not even Julia, who came to the banquet and sat right beside him in her brand new gown, looking incredible, toned and muscular in ways she'd never been before taking up karate a few years ago, and more than once Oscar caught men above his grade looking and he never saw her looking back. He didn't see her dressed up very often, or even in skirts, no more often than she saw him in something grander than business casual for work or a T-shirt at home and he'd held her hand under the table in a way that let it rest on the slick cloth at her thigh.

During the presentations, over the nineteenth or twentieth

round of polite clapping for awards to other departments and agencies, she'd leaned close and asked Oscar to tell her, again, what he was being honored for. It soured the night and the award to keep the truth from his wife, to know she was proud of him without knowing why, clapping and whistling and beaming when he approached the podium to accept his own plaque after waiting through dozens of others. But he had an answer worked up with Slotkin about a new filing system breakthrough he'd made, a way to enhance the familiar method of tagging a folder with three letters of a last name plus three from the first, and a spiel for explaining it guaranteed to bore anyone out of asking too many questions. All that to keep the secret of the Bureau's own work, the secret of the Arctic and of how its discoveries are made.

In other words, that they aren't.

He wondered what the word was for those paths through the ice. Sidetracks or streams? Rivulets, strands, or diversions? There was a word and he'd read it, but what?

And where?

Whatever the words were the ship slid among them, one un-chosen path after another, all those possible routes that would close up and vanish as the ocean piled itself into ice. Changing the shape of that land without land. Each crack of the ice, each scrape and screech of bergs calving and charging ahead came as question and answer at once: confirmation a chance had been missed, confirmation a chance taken, too.

Perhaps he could backtrack. Perhaps change his mind, the minds of his navigator and map, but no, there wasn't the time. Never time. In the moments it took the ship to change course those paths could already be gone; his choice had been made, had been made before the Captain realized he had chosen, and any path taken erased every other on ice as on land as in life.

But such thoughts. He was melancholy that day and laughed at himself while packing a pipe with almost the last twists of Virginia. The morning's slaughter still rang in his ears, the crack upon crack of the men and their rifles killing time by killing bears—looming white silhouettes in a row, no more than bottles lined up on a fence. The cub he'd remember. The already broad paws batting its felled mother's grayed face and glazed eyes, those mewling cries that might have been kitten's or might have been child's carrying to their red ears on the wind, and the faces of the men, his men, as they heard. Rifles were stowed, eyes dropped, all hands were at once full of work and they sailed on until that path, too, had been swallowed and closed in the ice at their back.

He wondered, the Captain, about that cub. That left behind bear. If it was old enough to fend for itself and if it would. And, too, if it would find them again—ice bears, he'd read, covered ranges as wide as his own and if winter closed the ship in its teeth they could be waiting for months if not longer. Plenty of time for a bear grown strong by then to close paths of its own and to find a single black ship in the white.

He shook out his head, shook out a match, and the ship at his feet ground over the ocean to a chorus of whistles and cracking and creaks. A long streamer of Virginian smoke unwound in its wake, unwound into the air, and was torn apart in the wind but the scent reached dark nostrils already planning ahead.

A short walk south of the village, of what had been the village, the hunter pulled aside a rough canopy of branches and brush and an old moldy net to reveal a open motorboat resting low in the water with two oars across its thwarts. He set in his pack, then his rifle, and several jugs of fresh water and gasoline and sealed pouches of food retrieved from the emergency food stores his neighbors wouldn't need any longer. That wind off the water continued, had worsened but it blew south and the hunter would head in that direction so he took it as a good omen. An endorsement of his expedition.

He settled himself in the hull, pulled the starter cord on the motor, and slid away from the shoreline even before the propellor had time to catch water. The wind was with him and he did not look back at what had been the village and had been his life, only ahead toward his next destination.

His small engine churned black water through daylight and darkness, in the benevolent grace of southward winds and against razors of icy horizontal rain. He steered with one hand and bailed with the other, steered and ate, steered and drank, steered and leaned sideway to piss in the sea but always the hunter steered south. The water jugs and gasoline canisters piled empty around him. His face caked and tightened with salt, chapped and burned, split and bled and that blood, too, was dried by the salt into stripes of warpaint.

And when all his spare fuel for both body and boat were exhausted, he rowed. Even in half-sleep his raw seeping hands worked the oars and that pink sheet, that list of names with its traces of some unknown seal, rested dry and safe in a watertight pouch deep inside his shirt.

He hauled his boat ashore in pre-dawn darkness, up a graveled beach thick with the dreaming bodies of walrus. Only one animal opened its eye at the hunter's approach and just long enough to close it again. The air was green with the stench of fish and he fought a cough, pushed his body's natural response deep into his gut and out of his mind for the sake of the task at his hands.

He shouldered his pack, slung his gun, and chewed on a pemmican breakfast as he picked a path through the snoring and snorting bodies up to higher ground. And when he had climbed a short rise from the shoreline a cluster of buildings and vehicles stood before him, mostly dark. He moved toward the largest with its sign announcing those buildings as a research station and as a joint operation without specifying between whom. The door was unlocked and why wouldn't it be; who was there to worry about so far north?

The hunter crept into a dark, vacant office and closed the door then woke a sleeping computer and launched its browser—several versions updated since he'd last used one but its functions were still the same. It only took a few minutes to track down the logo he'd reconstructed on the pink paper, to pull up screen after screen of conspiracy theories and accusations about false exploration and forged documents, about wasted taxes and betrayed legacies, but none of that distracted him. He knew what he'd come there to know. He knew the who and the where and he had no need for the why.

The hunter made camp in the leeward side of a low hill where he carved an indentation deep enough to sit and lie down and stay out of the wind. Over a small flame of scraped lichen and scrub and broken up sections of pallet he'd found in a pile at the research station, he cooked a rabbit shot earlier and hung from his pack. It was halfway through its molt from summer brown to winter white and its pelt made him pine for coffee and cream instead of silty water with iodine pills.

He sat for hours with his eyes on the ribbon of the aurora

borealis. Everything burning, the sky burning and the hunter's mind burning, both earth and water reflecting the movement above. Then he slept just long enough to rejuvenate himself and no longer.

The next morning the hunter walked south. The cold wind from his island, the wind that had lifted the paper and showed him this road, found him here when his energy flagged and urged him on with a firm hand at his back. In the later hours of morning he saw motion up high, first a speck in the distance then an airplane, low enough to see the blur of its jets. It arced above him, turning from north to south as it began a descent that took it almost to the limit of his sight before he turned in the direction where the plane had vanished into the ground.

7

Oscar was stirred from his memories of Symmes' Hole, golden memories embodied in paperwork properly filed, by a long, loud whistle somewhere else on the train—not a train whistle, not the kind he had never heard hanging in the distance on romantic country evenings as he'd always assumed they did somewhere, but an ordinary, high-pitched whistle you might expect from a referee or a cop. Alexi slept on, undisturbed and perhaps even snoring a bit louder in response to the noise. Oscar picked up the brown envelope to return the page of instructions to it but something else fell out first: a smaller envelope, a lighter brown shade, stark as a desert against the pale gray carpet of the train cabin.

He retrieved it and read on its face *CONFIDENTIAL DELIVERY—to be opened only by authorized representatives of Northern Branch.* Was this the point of the mission? Was delivery of one envelope why he'd been whisked away without breakfast, without putting on shoes or pulling up plans, why he was on that train, why he was going to the Arctic at all?

Perhaps. Perhaps not. He didn't yet know. But if that was his job he would do it: expeditions need support staff as much as heroes, and the great men—the Pearys—need their Matthew Hensons who put their own egos aside for the good of the work to be done. Oscar could be that envelope's sidekick. He could be its Matthew Henson though he wasn't sure what that made Alexi—the sidekick's sidekick? Something else altogether?

He flipped through his mental filing cabinet of expedition logs and *National Geographic* accounts, looking for some label to apply to Alexi, some way to tag his role in all this, but before he'd worked it out the cabin door rattled as someone tried the knob from outside. It shook then stopped, shook again then again stopped. This happened a few times while Oscar stood silent, breath held, too startled to answer and unsure of what he should say—if his mission was a secret, his presence on the train, too, should he announce himself? Then the rattling stopped without restarting and Oscar exhaled. He rose and moved toward the door for a glance through the peephole, but before his eye reached the lens the door shook once more. Differently this time, not from a grip on the doorknob but instead something inserted between door and jamb.

"Wrong door," he said in little more than a whisper and almost a question at that. The rattling stopped but briefly, as if whoever was outside thought they heard something within then decided they hadn't. The jostling of the door in its frame was more aggressive when it came back.

Oscar hissed, "Alexi! Wake up!" but his partner slept on. He'd turned toward the wall at some point in his nap so Oscar pleaded to his back, "Someone is breaking in!"

The door shook and the cabin's walls with it. There was nowhere in the room he might hide, only the lower bunk which would be as obvious and exposed as staying where he was. He could climb into bed with Alexi, against the wall with his partner's body between his own and whoever was about to burst in, but how would that help? He'd be better off trying to stay behind the door when it opened, that old movie trick. Or that other one, to climb out the window and hang from the frame then climb to the roof where he wouldn't be seen—unless the would-be intruder followed him up for a cinematic car-to-car chase, leaping across gaps and ducking barriers, passengers inside wondering about the clatter above as the train bore down on a tunnel and the wind-whipped combatants squared off, taking each other's measure and waiting to see who would give first—but no, he wouldn't do that.

Oscar was no action hero. And it was his berth, after all: he wasn't the thief. He wasn't the one who should hide.

Finally, with no other choice, the danger at a head, he announced in an almost loud voice, "I think you might have the wrong door."

The rattling stopped and a voice muttered, "Shit." Loud, heavy footsteps rushed away and Oscar, before he could second-guess himself, before he could think, jerked the door open and leapt into the corridor. Adrenaline? Instinct? Who knows, but he acted in time to see the back of a man running away down the tight space of the train, a man in a dark trench coat and hat. The man from yesterday's ride on the Metro, the man behind the newspaper, he was more or less maybe sure—perhaps the same man who'd stood across the street at the Chinese takeout after all—and Oscar yelled for the intruder to stop before surprising himself by giving chase.

But only until reaching the small vestibule where two cars came together and a tall, empty luggage rack faced a bathroom from which someone exited in time for Oscar to plow face-first into the door. Whoever had come out was knocked back inside with a grunt and Oscar grunted too as his nose burst and he was thrown backward onto the floor.

Half-conscious, shirt sopped with blood, he tried to keep his eyes open and tried to stand up but was washed away in waves of nausea and pain. He was sure—almost sure, he thought he'd seen something—the bathroom door opened again and a flaming bright head of hair rushed away in the other direction, but it may have been the fireworks in his eyes as he passed out in a sticky red pool of himself.

He came to on a bed not his own nor the bed in his cabin and not an especially comfortable bed, for that matter. He blinked. He struggled to lift his head and look around at the bright room where he found himself. An infirmary from the look of it, and he knew he was still on the train because as his body sorted out the rattle and clack of the tracks from various aches and pains of its own he felt the external motion of the rails as distinct from his internal dizziness.

"Don't try to move," said a male voice, quietly, and a young man in an ambiguous gray uniform leaned over Oscar and held him down with a hand on his shoulder. "Are you in pain?"

"My face hurts," he said and reached up to touch it, setting lightning bolts bouncing inside his skull. His fingers found a large bandage stretched over his face, the gray edge of which intruded into his range of vision. He recalled running into the door, recalled why he'd run into the door—chasing someone down the train's corridor, as if he was some kind of spy!—and felt foolish. "My whole head."

"I'm not surprised. You knocked yourself out pretty good. But you seem to be okay apart from a bloody nose and some bruises." A tiny flashlight bobbed before his eyes. "Follow that... good. No, I don't think there's any concussion. It's your lucky day."

"I don't feel so lucky. Do you have any aspirin?"

The doctor—was he a doctor, or just the railway employee who'd happened to find Oscar first?—laughed and said, "Sure. Sure, we have aspirin. But I can give you something stronger than that, if you like."

"Oh... no, I'd better not. I'm working. Business trip. I should stay alert."

"Suit yourself," the doctor(?) told him and a moment later handed over two tiny white tablets and a plastic cup full of water. Oscar lifted his head to swallow and saw he wasn't in a real infirmary at all, only a cabin more or less like his own but with a single bed, not a bunk, and everything was very bright. Sterile, he thought. There was nothing, however, to prove that particular cabin was meant for medical uses. Or, for that matter, was not.

"Okay, sir. Feeling better? Why don't you sit up for a moment, maybe swing your legs over..."

Oscar let the doctor help him and after changing position it took a few seconds for his head to catch up with his body, a few seconds of everything swimming and of swirling black lines at the edge of his eyes.

"I'm okay," Oscar said.

"So you're on a business trip? What line of work are in you in, Mr..."

Oscar gave his name and the doctor typed on the screen of his phone. "I'm not seeing you on the passenger list. Did I spell that right?"

Oscar realized he hadn't booked the ticket himself, hadn't even known he was going, and he wasn't supposed to have left his cabin. His name probably wasn't on the passenger manifest because on paper he might not be there. "It might be booked under my employer."

The doctor looked up quickly from his device and leaned a bit closer to Oscar. "And who's that?" he asked, voice bright and rising in tone.

"I work for the government, for an agency. BIP. The Bureau of Information Policies." Despite the pain, despite the confusion, Oscar's training kicked in and his lies were ready: keeping the secret of BIP was his instinct, the good of the bureau before his own, and he was glad he'd been hit by that door instead of Alexi who might not yet be able to withstand such a challenge without spilling the truth. Oscar couldn't help but be a bit proud of his own professionalism and cool under fire. He wished Slotkin could see him in action.

"BIP," said the doctor or whoever he was. "Didn't I just read about them? Some big news in the paper?" He leaned even closer as he asked, holding his phone near Oscar's mouth.

"Oh, I doubt it. We don't make the papers. Pretty dull stuff," Oscar said, that last line the official deflection he'd been made to learn on his first day, the unwritten, unofficial slogan of BIP, not the real BIP but the fake, boring one Slotkin had taught him to pretend he worked for. "Nothing you'd want to read about, just regulations for other departments, deciding on acronyms for interagency projects, that kind of thing. Pretty dull stuff, I suppose, unless you're in on it."

"And how'd you get 'in on it,' if you don't mind my asking?"

Oscar's head was still throbbing and swimming at once and he couldn't tell if he was nauseous or feeling the train's motion more acutely because of the pain or if it was his adrenaline winding down after the action. He blamed TV for putting in his head such a moronic move as chasing a stranger on a train.

He said, "I fell into it, I suppose. That's how most people end up in their jobs, isn't it? You need a job while you decide what to do with your life then there you are a decade or two later and what you're doing has become what you'll do whether you meant it to be that way or not." He remembered what Julia had said during one of their arguments, about everyday life not being made of big choices. That Oscar was unrealistic if he expected his life to be a story composed of great moral dilemmas and one defining moment after another. Maybe she'd meant the same thing as the lie he was telling, the BIP party line, and maybe she'd been lying, too.

"That's a bit bleak, isn't it?"

"Don't get me wrong, it's a good job. I enjoy it. But… I didn't write about designing file systems in elementary school essays on 'when I grow up.' Did you always plan on being a doctor?"

"A what? Oh… yes, always. A doctor."

"Well, medicine is that kind of career, isn't it? The kind you're driven toward by a dream." Oscar almost smiled, knowing how he'd been driven by his own dreams to BIP, how he'd reached the minor heights of Arctic exploring, but experience—experience and professionalism—kept him calm and kept the lie real. His nose throbbed, the bandage itched, and his nostrils were stopped up with mucus and blood so he breathed with a whistling wheeze and occasional snort.

The doctor leaned in as the train rounded a curve which tilted his body even nearer to Oscar, almost on top of him because he couldn't lean away with his back already against the wall of the bunk. The doctor's phone was in Oscar's face, as near as a gangster might hold a gun, a trigger finger on the touchscreen.

"But I'm sure I read something," he said. "About a new site for mining, perhaps? Something with mineral rights? Yes, I'm sure of it. Where was it… where…"

"That doesn't sound much like BIP. I mean, unless maybe the Division of Mining and Minerals needed some new acronyms or an official assessment regarding the format of their documents… that's the sort of thing we'd get into, that's all. Like I said, dull."

"No, I'm certain it was something else, something…"

"I'll take him back to his cabin now," another voice said, a woman this time, quiet but forceful. A strong wind that could drown out other sounds without being loud.

The doctor jerked away and turned toward the voice, and Oscar turned too, on the bed. She was in the doorway, still in her dark glasses, still framed by the flames of her hair. But how, Oscar wondered. How could the woman from the subway be here, why would she be here? Was she following him?

For that matter, her being there was no stranger than the man in the trench coat being on the train, too, and what had happened to him? One of them, maybe. That Oscar could have believed. But seeing them both he knew was absurd so decided the man must have been someone else altogether, if this was the same redheaded woman. Otherwise the coincidence was too great, like two expeditions reaching the North Pole at once. Impossible odds.

The doctor took another step back, against the wall as if he would have passed through it to the outside if he could. "Fine," he said. "Fine, if you know where he's going."

Before Oscar could even say thank you, the redheaded woman stepped all the way into the room, took his hand, and pulled him onto his feet in the corridor. The last he saw of the doctor he was dialing his phone as Oscar's new escort led him into the hallway and along the length of the train too quickly, too no-nonsensically, for his unasked words to catch up. Each step sent a fresh wave of pain through his body and he felt a bit like that carnival game where a hammer sends a weight chasing up toward a bell but today with his own face standing in for it.

The corridors were too narrow to walk side by side so Oscar slipped in behind his guide, who seemed to know where she was going while he had no idea. He felt at his hip for his phone as they walked and panicked when his pocket was empty—the Pole! —but remembered setting it down on the table while dealing with the rattling door and hoped it would be there, unharmed. Somewhere ahead of them, somewhere else in the train, a high pitched scream sounded and was cut off sharply; mechanical, Oscar assumed, even if it did sound a bit like a person. Brakes.

"Do I know you?" he asked his guide, or the bright orange back of her head. "You look... familiar. From the Metro yesterday? In Washington?"

"Not me," she said over a shoulder. "I got on in Philadelphia." Oscar couldn't recall the train stopping but didn't ask, and she said, "I saw you come out of your room and run into the door. I wanted to make sure you were okay, so I waited. That's all."

He might have been wrong about the subway, Oscar supposed (he might have been, but he wasn't, because what kind of story would that leave us with?). He didn't ask if she'd been the person behind the door when it swung open into his face. His nose itched beneath the bandage.

When they passed from one car into another, Oscar could have sworn he saw a pair of thin, dark-suited legs being dragged through the far exit but the edge of the bandage creeping up his face toward his eyes made it hard enough to see what he'd seen let alone what he hadn't. He could barely stay focused on the woman before him, never mind what was that far away.

"Here we are," she said, stopping in the corridor beside an

unnumbered door like any other. She turned the handle but paused before opening it. "I hope you'll be more careful on the rest of your trip. I'd hate for you not to arrive safely, wherever you're going…"

"Oscar," said Oscar, and he extended a hand which she took in a way that let her fingertips send lightning bolts up and down his body, a much nicer sensation than the ones in his head, with only the slightest touch of his inner wrist.

"Oscar," she repeated but did not offer a name of her own. He almost filled in the silence with his destination, the details, the truth—even with sunglasses on she had the kind of gaze that made him want to stop lying—but before he could speak she'd swung the door open and gestured him in with that electric hand. "I'm sure you'd like to rest before we arrive. To feel better."

"Thank you," he replied and was about to ask her name but she'd already moved away along the wall of windows, beyond which trees melted into a solid green blur, too busy for Oscar's eyes so he closed them and pictured the clean white space of the Pole cam instead. Then he stepped into the room where Alexi still snored with his face to the wall though most of the fruit in the bowl had been reduced to stems and cores while he'd been gone.

His phone rang, rattling hard against the table and its vibrations moving it toward him as if eager to be answered. It was Julia, responding to his unleft message.

"What happened this morning?" she asked. "You were gone before I woke up."

"Something came up for work. Sorry. It was… it was very sudden." It was hard to angle the phone to his ear and mouth at once around the bulk of the bandage. He had to tilt it back and forth between listening and speaking, and every word buzzed and stung his nasal passages. His own voice sounded strange and far away.

"Are you okay? You sound funny. And there's a lot of noise behind you."

"I'm on a train. To Boston. A work thing, I… like I said, it was sudden."

"Boston!" She seemed about to say something else when something like thunder interrupted her, followed by what sounded to Oscar like yelling in the background.

"What was that?" he asked.

Julia didn't answer right away and Oscar thought she was talking to someone, maybe holding the phone away from her face. "Hm?" she eventually asked.

"What was that? That noise. What's going on?"

"Oh, nothing. Just noise. Just... somebody dropped something here in the office. Oscar, I have to go, we're pretty busy. I'll talk to you later. Have a great trip."

"Well it's work, so...," he started but she had hung up.

He set his phone back on the table then settled himself into the lower bunk with a groan. He lay flat, trying to ignore the jackhammer excavating behind his eyes; maybe that was the noise he'd heard on the phone, coming from inside his own head.

"Are we there?" Alexi asked from above, but Oscar was already asleep.

From behind the crosshairs of his rifle's scope the hunter watched a nondescript man in nondescript clothes—a shirt, trousers, shoes that would have made more sense in an office than on the ground beside a subarctic airstrip. He watched the man rifle through a large black duffel bag, pulling out a parka and pants and goggles and boots, trying them on and striking poses. Then he watched the man pack those things away and sit on top of the bag, shifting position every few minutes and occasionally poking a phone.

The hunter slung his rifle back to his shoulder and walked toward the airstrip and its occupant.

Soon the man noticed him, looking in the hunter's direction and giving a wave, but the hunter had no time to return it. He was walking. He was on his way.

But before he reached the airstrip and the man and the bag, an ATV in multiple colors—mismatched panels and parts in orange and red and green and rust—approached from another direction, bounding and bouncing across the landscape, grabbing air as if on the moon. The hunter dropped into a gully and raised his scope to watch a bear of a man in an awful Hawaiian shirt and shorts, of all things, climb off the ATV to usher the waiting man and his bag on before the two of them sped away back in the direction from which the four-wheeler had come. The driver's clothes were bright scars seared onto that drab vista, left behind like contrails of color on the hunter's eyeballs and it took a long blink to erase them.

The ATV was easy to follow after its wide tires clawed across thickened gray mud. The hunter walked between the parallel lines of the vehicle's courses toward and away from the airstrip, pausing only to take a curious fox for his dinner and hang its gutted length from his pack. And it wasn't long before he saw the four-wheeler again, parked now outside a low cinderblock box with a sloped metal roof and long entryway. A tall antenna rose between it and the steel curve of a prefabricated structure nearby.

He moved closer, walking then crawling on elbows and knees with the rifle in his hands, and he stopped when his scope had a clear view of the building's front windows. The bear from the tropics stood by a table inspecting a phone; the other man, the one from the airstrip, sat at a table with a third man who was eating something out of a can. The hunter lined up each of them in his crosshairs in turn, rotating through the men one after another and sometimes pulling back the zoom of his scope to watch all three at once.

The bearded one in the loud shirt walked away from the table and down some stairs the hunter couldn't actually see; the bobbing descent of a shaggy head gave them away. In a moment the other men followed and the hunter moved in. He kept low. He kept quiet and he kept one eye on the window with a partial view of the stairhead.

When he reached the front wall of the structure he ducked under a window frame at the far end from where the three men had been, from where the stairwell descended, then he raised his eyes over the sill to take in the room.

It was unoccupied.

The hunter crept across the front of the building, past the long entryway and its bright orange door, to the four-wheeler parked with its nose toward the tall radio mast in a cinder block footing. A single key with no chain, only a blue elastic tied through its hole, stood up from an ignition cylinder below the handlebars but he didn't start the engine, not yet.

He rolled the vehicle backward in neutral until he had room to swing it around, away from the antenna and buildings flanking it. Then he pushed a bit farther, looking back over his shoulder, and once he'd put enough distance between himself and the windows the hunter swung a leg over and turned the key and rumbled south into the gloom of an expiring day.

In the crystalline quiet where no one watches an iceberg calved with the shrieks and growls of any birth. A part of her shivered then rumbled then slipped, splashed into the ocean to announce an arrival with ripples of frigid blue waves.

From the raw edge of ice that remained a cylindrical tin of preserved meat emerged, a tooth cutting out from a gum or left behind by a bite taken badly. A blue stamp on one end had been smudged by time and the elements, and whatever label there had been removed or erased, but the metal itself was unpunctured; the canister still held its shape since being dropped by some expedition long gone. It pulled free with a scraping exhale audible only to a lone skua resting at the peak of the berg—its body a graphite smudge like something almost but not quite erased—but the bird didn't react as the weight of what had been exposed of the can towed free what was still in the ice. That second splash was nearly lost in the still-flowing wake from the heavier fall of the calf now floating nearby. The can dunked under quickly and bobbed as if it, too, might float, a third iceberg in miniature, then it sank—more slowly this time—to the seabed where it came to rest.

The gray and the quiet resealed the rent. Fish fed in bubbling shoals from the stirred swirls where calf and can met water while two icebergs, one large and one small, glided apart, pushed by the force of their own separation, broken but still somehow whole. Oceans away, days afterward, weeks, water lapped the smallest bit higher on some far off beach and none of the tan, dangling toes come to eke out the last scraps of summer were the wiser when a chill of northern water washed across southern skin. In the north those icebergs glistened with meltwater runnels and the slimmest suggestions of cracks that would, someday, become fissures then splits as those frozen wedges of time sweated through seasons they weren't meant to see at temperatures they'd never known. The can rusted below in the dark and the cold until one day it burst in a thick cloud of old meat, a strange feast for scrabbling creatures who feed from the bottom and were only too glad to take it all in while what remained of the metal rusted into no more than specks in the sand and then into nothing at all.

8

Alexi shook Oscar too hard by the shoulder, saying, "Up and at 'em. We're here. Let's get to work."

Oscar groaned and rolled over. He spent a few seconds to take it all in and remember yes, he was on a train, with Alexi, and they were on their way to Boston and to the Arctic beyond. He sat up, rubbed his eyes, and yelped when his hands found the bandage instead. Then he remembered how it had come to be there and made a more human sound. The gauze and adhesive itched where they were already pulling away from his face and his nose felt clenched as if frozen mid-sneeze. Oscar eased a bit of the bandage away from his nostrils, pulling a few hairs along with it and bringing tears to his eyes, all before he'd made it as far as the floor of the cabin.

Alexi was already half out the door but had left both the outer large envelope spent of its contents and the smaller brown inner envelope, too, on the table. So Oscar took both of them, slipped one back inside the other—and, yes, that paper, the weight and the weave were still wrong: not BIP and too nice to be government issue at all if Oscar's fingers knew anything which, by this point in his bureaucratic career, they probably should—and followed his partner along the empty train corridor. He turned toward the exit he'd spotted earlier by the bathroom door he'd lost a fight with, and the hatch that had been sealed stood wide open with steps extended to the ground outside but no conductor there to watch them descend. And no Tall or Wide either but perhaps their assignment was only to put the Prognosticators onto the train, not get them off.

In fact the whole platform was mysteriously empty. Only a few other passengers made their way from the train toward the doors into Boston's South Station. Oscar was at the far end of the platform and the next passengers were several cars closer to the building, beside the regular train cars with their stickers and stripes. Alexi had vanished already, no doubt in line for a snack within seconds of leaving the cabin, and yes, that's where Oscar would spot him once he was inside the building himself: almost to the counter of a sandwich kiosk. So he sat yawning on a conspicuous bench, yawning and pulling the bandage in uncomfortable ways when he did, while he waited for his belly-led partner to purchase some lunch and join him.

A small girl holding her mother's hand almost tripped while twisting her neck to gawk at Oscar's mummified face for as long as she could and no wonder: his face was a mess, though the bloodstained bandage made it look worse than it was. After a couple more stares like that he was fed up and, pain or not, doctor's orders or not, couldn't stand the unprofessionally conspicuous attention that bandage was getting so he grabbed one side and yanked it off before he could think.

It took all his experience, his full years of training and the committed focus of a lifelong government employee to prevent himself from screaming in that crowded train station. Though the pain dissipated after the bandage was off.

A white paper bag dropped in his lap. "I got you turkey," Alexi said, handing over a bottle of water.

"Oh, thanks, I… thanks, Alexi."

"And napkins. And… for your face." A flood of scratchy brown paper napkins spilled on top of the bag followed by a single wet wipe in its sterile pouch, so Oscar cleaned up as much as he could without a mirror and without looking up from the floor to see how many strangers were watching. He appreciated his partner's thoughtfulness at not asking what had happened while he'd been asleep. And if it was disinterest instead of politeness, that was fine, too, as long as he didn't ask—and, frankly, Alexi was already tearing into his own lunch and hadn't seemed the least bit interested i the bandage when Oscar awoke on the train or by the dried blood and swelling now.

Which was okay with him as he dried his face with a handful of napkins and reached out to drop the whole soiled wad in a trashcan at the end of their bench.

Oscar wondered what time it was, anyway, and looked up and around the vast hall of the station now that his full range of vision had been restored. Up on the bright board of departures and delays and arrivals, amidst other numbers, he found a clock hiding—he found a four digit train number first and was amazed the day had gotten so late until he realized—and it was indeed about time for his lunch so he ate.

"Do you remember," he asked Alexi, "the telecom outpost we discovered on Baffin' Island your first week at BIP? The startup, trying to bring cell service north?"

"On Baffled Island? It isn't ringing a bell."

"No, Baffin. Qikiqtaaluk. You know—69°N, 72°W?" Oscar recalled Alexi on one of his first days at BIP complaining he hadn't brought enough to eat for lunch, but couldn't be certain it was the same day.

"Oh, right, Bafflin Island. Wasn't there an amusement park, too? With the big wooden roller coaster that froze so badly it had to be torn down after only a couple of seasons?"

"No, that was at Repulse Bay. This was…," but Alexi's attention had wandered, he'd begun flipping through a discarded newspaper, so Oscar gave up on that expedition and set a new course.

"What do we do next? Where do we go? The memo said we'd receive more instructions once we got here, and I'd assumed our kidnap… our escorts would be here, too but…"

"No harm in starting with lunch." Alexi craned his neck to

look around the concourse. "And maybe dessert."

"Should we call Director Lenz?"

"Do you know the number?"

"Well... no." Oscar thought of their office, per policy without a phone and only the yellowed intercom for communication. "I've never had to call him."

"There we are then," said Alexi, dusting the ghost of a sandwich from his hands as he stood. "Coffee?" he asked but was already too far off for Oscar to bother replying.

Oscar looked at the envelope in his hand—and at the other envelope inside the envelope, too; he couldn't see it just then but he knew it was there—wondering if it might hold a clue to their next move. Taking it out here in public didn't strike him as a brilliant idea. It had official stamps and seals on it, after all, that inner envelope did, not to mention the conspicuous paper, and someone might ask. It was need-to-know information and a good civil servant and explorer alike takes pride in discretion, nearly as much as in efficiency and perseverance. He sat with the envelope(s) across his lap, palms flat on top, thumbs together.

This was a moment for action. A moment for decisiveness yet here he was on a bench, the envelope closed, the path closed before them... hardly the moment of a great man, Oscar admonished himself. But he thought of Franklin, of his heralded slowness and brave insistence—whatever others might call it—on taking as much time as he needed to make a decision. To act if and *only* if he felt ready.

Franklin wouldn't be hurried, he wouldn't be led by faster men's whims, and if patience worked for such a man surely it could settle for Oscar who sighed as the weight of that paper decreased in his lap.

His phone buzzed in a pocket, delivering a text from Julia: "Forgot to say if you're going to Boston hope you packed your kite!" And though he'd told Alexi he had never been to Boston except passing through and had believed it himself, Oscar now recalled a long weekend in that city with Julia when he was still in Weights and Measures, before they were married but already living together. Julia had a Friday meeting to fly to and he'd gone along. He had even taken a day off which he hadn't done once since starting at BIP. They hadn't done much with the weekend, mostly wandering around the old brownstones of Beacon Hill and window-shopping in the stores of Newbury Street. Their hotel had a balcony overlooking the Common—or the Public Garden, in fact, Oscar recalled, though he still wasn't sure what the difference was between the two—and they spent a lot of time on it, just sitting, together, the same as they would have been doing if they'd been at home on their own balcony in their own chairs.

On the Saturday they took the subway, the cars of which had the same alternating horizontal and vertical cut-outs he was used to despite a different layout of seats, into Cambridge where Oscar thought a collection of Peary's letters were on display. But it turned out they were kept behind lock and key and he would have needed to ask permission to view them months in advance so they had lunch and took a long walk back to their hotel. On the Esplanade, a long strip of green by a river, they were walking and talking about nothing and holding hands when a pair of large mallard ducks stopped them in their tracks. The birds had been grazing on opposite sides of the path one second, beaks down and tails up toward Oscar and Julia, and the next they'd stepped in synch onto the pavement and had turned toward the humans.

"Do they look angry?" asked Julia and Oscar had to admit the ducks did—something in their eyes, the turn of their beaks or the particular hackling of their neck feathers. Without asking each other, without dropping the other's hand, Oscar and Julia each took a step back only to discover two more ducks, also mallards but female, had taken up the same pose to their rear.

"Go away, ducks," Oscar said and Julia laughed, and not one of the ducks made a sound as all four waddled closer, making that waddle somehow seem menacing. Oscar squeezed Julia's hand or Julia squeezed Oscar's—one or the other, who can tell now which came first and it doesn't matter—then three shrieking children ran by dragging an unhappy kite on the ground and the ducks flew off as if nothing had happened, except for one male who flew toward the kite as it lifted a foot or two off the ground only to drop once again with a duck tangled in its sunfish shape.

And that duck extricated himself right away and flew after the others and the kite bumped along after the kids.

Julia looked at Oscar and asked, "Did we just...," and he said, "I don't know," and the two of them walked toward their hotel. Once, a year or two afterward, they tried telling that story at a dinner party but couldn't get it all to make sense: how ducks could look angry, how strange and hilarious and menacing the encounter had been, and Julia and Oscar ended up laughing together on one side of the table while their audience of three other couples exchanged looks of concern and confusion across the remains of chicken Kiev.

How had he forgotten all that? How had he forgotten the ducks? They hadn't talked about it for years though it had been one of their strangest and most private moments, a running joke between them for so long afterward: all one or the other had to say was, "Ducks!" and both would collapse into laughter followed by lust.

How had he lost track of that, and when had they stopped saying "Ducks!"?

Across the concourse Alexi stepped away from the coffee kiosk with an enormous white cup in his hand and moved across the room toward the bench. Oscar watched his partner's smiling approach and behind him, over Alexi's right shoulder, a man in dark glasses and a dark suit stood half-hidden behind a squared pillar. It looked like Alexi turned and spotted the man at one point, perhaps even gave him a nod, but Oscar took that for an illusion of coincidence. After Alexi had advanced a few steps the man moved from one pillar to another, waited a few seconds, then did it again. Then he stopped because Alexi was sitting down. Oscar tried not to look as he whispered, "I think someone's following you."

"Mm?" his partner asked from behind the plastic lid of his cup. "You think so?" He turned around to scan the station.

"What if he's looking?" Oscar whispered, pulling Alexi's shoulder and head back toward the front of the bench while trying to work out where the lurking man was. "We need to get going. We need to move. Let's get up."

"Off we go!" said Alexi, coffee cup in the air like he was running with the Olympic torch. "Fast as a lightbulb," and Oscar was too nervous to correct him this time.

And they did move, off the bench and through the station and onto the street; Oscar tried to watch for the man following them but his subtle looks backward involved turning his whole body around and practically stopping so any tail worth his salt would have stopped, perhaps even to laugh.

They weren't all the way down the bland concrete stairs from the station's doors to the street before a voice called, "There you are! We've hardly got time!" and hands ushered Oscar into a car but more gently, more kindly, than Tall and Wide had done that morning and once again they were in motion.

And a few minutes later they weren't, when the car pulled up outside a different train station and the driver pulled Oscar out of the car and steered the prognosticators through another set of double doors, to another train platform, and stuck another set of tickets into their hands.

"That would have been my neck," said the driver and he probably looked like something or had a presence that made some kind of impression but who had time to notice while he was pushing his charges toward a conductor who took the still unread tickets and pointed the travelers onto a train—a commuter run this time, no sleeping cars—upon which they took seats side by side with a view of the back of the next row of seats.

Oscar's mouth hung open almost that whole time in the car and onto the train, like he meant it to speak but it was as speechless as the rest of him in the confusion and speed. Alexi's mouth was full of coffee behind which it was humming a bit. As the train pulled out toward Portland, Maine (as they would learn a few moments later when announcements were made) Oscar sat with the brown envelope in his lap, palms flat, thumbs together, with Alexi beside him consuming the rest of his lunch as if they'd never gotten up from their bench in the other train station.

They'd hardly rolled out of the city, past a wiry white bridge and some office parks, when Alexi said, "Hmm...," and was up and away down the aisle.

Oscar slid the envelope into the seat pocket facing him then worried and pulled it back out to remain in his lap. Fingers crossed, he checked for a signal—three bars!—and loaded the Pole cam to calm himself down. There it was, the ice sheet, the almost footsteps, the nothing. He watched, he waited for an expedition to come, he gazed into the Arctic long enough to watch the light change; not a lot, nothing drastic, but the shadows shifted a bit, he was sure, as the time between Boston and Portland passed and the northern afternoon dropped as his own did down south. Something flared on the ice and he jumped, ready for an animal or human to cross the camera, but no: it was only the sun, his sun, not the Arctic's, coming through the window at an adjusted angle as the train turned to follow the track.

He thought of calling Julia again, she might still be at lunch, but the ice kept his attention through the whole ride and he was reluctant to turn off the camera to make the call so he texted instead. "Reached Boston," he wrote. "No ducks." He was about to say he'd gone on to Portland but wasn't sure how he'd explain without telling her he was headed still farther north which he couldn't do—there wasn't much Bureau of Information Policies work to be done in Maine, never mind beyond that—so he added, "Time to get myself to a meeting."

But a moment later that felt so distant, so cold, that he wrote again, typing no more than, "Moo." It was an old joke, *Knock knock, Who's there? An interrupting cow. An interrupting cow w… MOO!*, one Oscar had told Julia the night they met back in college. Not a good joke nor the funniest by a long shot but it was their joke because she'd laughed in that way you can't stop, a way that almost becomes scary because your body is taken over by something— an invasion of mirth, an infestation of joy—and though she kept wheezing, "Stop! Stop!" through her red face and laughter, no one else in the room, neither Oscar nor Julia's roommate, was doing anything but watch her, amazed and amused, then snorting themselves at her remarkable laughter until the whole room was out of control over a joke that wasn't, let's face it, so funny.

It was their first shared joke, their first secret code, and all it took was one of them to interrupt something with "Moo!"— anything, a movie or TV show or lecture in class, a kiss about to be laid—and both lost control like clockwork, bodies and minds rendered useless for anything other than joy as long as the laughing might last. A few years later a bad day at work or bad news on the phone or tragic events on TV could still be undercut with a moo, the worst days of their lives undermined and undone by an admittedly dumb knock knock joke. But they'd left that joke and its cow behind somewhere with the ducks, they had stopped using it until Oscar thought of it again on that train and wondered if Julia would remember it, too.

No sooner had he hit *Send* than a very short man in a very dark suit and with a very bald head took the seat beside him. Oscar said, "I'm sorry, but that seat's taken. He went…"

"You're into something," the bald man interrupted without looking at him. His dark eyes stared straight ahead at the back of the seat with its orange, red, and brown pattern of dashes and blots. A bad fireworks display, Oscar had thought earlier. "You have no idea."

"No idea about what? What do you…"

"I know about BIP. I know what you do."

"Well, sure, the Bureau of Information Policies isn't a secret, it…"

"I know what you really do. I know about Symmes' Hole and why you won that award—I know what you're excellent at."

Throat tight, Oscar strained upward to take a look over the seats and toward both ends of the cabin, hoping Alexi was on his way back. He wondered what had become of Tall and of Wide on that day's first train and found himself wishing they'd show up again. After hours of motion, this far from home, at least those two felt almost familiar—old acquaintances if not quite old friends, an unwelcome routine which might be better than having no routine at all.

"Oh, sure," Oscar said, "but it's pretty dull stuff. Their filing, you know, was…"

"I know but you don't," the bald man went on. "You don't even know what you know, what you've found. They know, though. They know." He turned quickly, screwing his eyes up and getting right in Oscar's face as his voice, already quiet, became a whisper so sharp he could feel the smaller man's breath in his ear.

"Listen. Oscar. You were right. Right enough, anyway, to cause trouble. Enough trouble to get yourself here."

"Right about what? I don't know what…"

"Let us help you. Keep you safe. Tell me how you found it, how you knew where to look, and you have my word. Believe me, other people are looking. Watching you. They won't be as generous. They'll try other ways to get what you know. Our ways are better. You don't want to know why."

Oscar tried to resist but couldn't help eyeing the envelope in the seat pocket before him. The bald man noticed and cocked an eyebrow.

"Mineral rights. A lot of money in that. Think about it. Enough for you, enough for the village." He paused. Smirked. "Enough for us, too, of course. Believe me, we'd be discreet. The others don't love the north the way you and I do, Oscar. They won't care, they'll destroy everything to get into that ground, to grind out every cent, but not us. It's the best choice. Remember that, before you tell anyone else."

"Tell anyone what? You must be looking for somebody else." His stomach squeezed itself like a washrag in anxious hands. It was all he could do not to piss himself in the seat, but Oscar's training kicked in—his hours with Slotkin—and he held up the lie. "I design filing systems. Like with three letters of your last name and three of your first, then a number, that sort of thing? Colored stripes? I don't think I've done any filing design for a project with mineral rights but I could... well, I could check my files when I get back to the office, if you have a card."

The bald man's face sank, his mouth turning down and brows dropping and eyes darkening all at once. "You're going to tell someone Oscar and it should be me. It's the right choice. The safe choice. Do you think no one else will come looking? Who do you think your escorts were this morning, dragging you away from your home? You can thank me, thank us, for dealing with them. Who else can you trust, your new partner? Do you even know him?"

Oscar concentrated on his poker face. His "public" face, as Slotkin had called it.

"The word is out. Your face is out. Watch your back." Then a conductor announced the train was arriving in Portland and the bald man stood up though his head hardly rose over the backs of the seats. Leaning into Oscar's face, nose to nose, he said, "You'll make the right choice. We'll convince you one way or another." Then he turned and rushed toward the rear of the train but not before Oscar, standing to watch him go, spotted a small silver C pinned to his lapel.

When he turned to face forward again, Alexi was coming back to their seats and it was time to get off the train before Oscar had time to tell his partner about what had happened or to decide if he wanted to. They lined up at the exit with their fellow passengers but the bald man was not in the crowd.

9

In Maine they left the station expectant. Oscar felt he'd picked up the routine of arrival and departure through the course of his busy morning and even that slight familiarity put him at ease, though his encounter with the bald man and the bizarre nature of the day overall kept that ease ill. He focused on work, on the task in his hands, and pushed aside worry and doubt and everything apart from his mission. He was professional. He'd trained for this. He had practiced hard at lying to everyone else so lying to himself came easily now.

He considered telling Alexi about the encounter but the bald man had been right: how well did he know his new partner? Not much better than he knew the bald man, in fact, so perhaps it was best to keep those details to himself for the time being, one envelope sealed inside another.

But no car awaited them at the curb as it had in Boston. No dark SUV, no men in dark suits, no indication of what to do next. He fingered the envelope in his hands and asked Alexi, "What do you think?"

"Oh, Portland's nice enough. There's a good bar down…"

"Not the city, the mission. I'm talking about work. What do you think we should do? I thought someone would meet us again."

"What can you do?"

"That's what I'm asking you!"

"Huh."

A green car slowed as it approached and Oscar almost

grabbed Alexi's arm to show him but realized the vehicle was only slowing because the two of them stood in the road. It went around them, the inconvenienced driver even gave them a smile, and they were back where they'd started. Oscar turned the envelope in his hands, as if looking for something he'd missed or shaking a fresh Polaroid to make the image appear, but he would have found it already if it had been there, right?

"I don't like this," he said.

"What can you do?" Alexi repeated so Oscar knew he'd lost his partner's attention. He closed his eyes, had a breath, and pictured the calm of the ice. He listened in on the deep northern quiet behind the clatter of station and city, the cars, the children, the seagulls lurking for scraps, the salty bouquet on the air with its tangy piscatory notes.

"We might as well look around," Oscar said. "Maybe we've missed something." And without waiting for a reply he walked away from the station. It was out of character for him to wander away from routine, to step out on his own, but this whole day was a break with routine and here they were into late afternoon with still no idea what they were doing or why they were doing it but trying to stick to the task they'd been given, whatever it was. Fast as a lightbulb, of course. Efficiency and perseverance. Take too long and they'd be on vacation and all of that.

"There was a man on the train," Oscar said as they walked, deciding he needed to give Alexi the benefit of the doubt. He'd been vetted by BIP after all, and by Director Lenz. "He knew about BIP and what we do. I think he was a Cookie—he had a pin—and he said we're 'into something.' Something big, and I think he meant something dangerous. He was talking about Symmes' Hole and I couldn't tell if he really knew what it was or not. He seemed to think it was real, that I'd actually found it. Mineral rights. Alexi, is there something going on we're not seeing? Is there something wrong with our mission?"

"I met a man on the train, too. He recognized me from the

hot dog contest at Coney Island. Not one of my better showings last year and I think that's why he knew who I was. The puking, remember?"

"You told me. Yes." It had, in fact, been one of the very first stories Alexi told Oscar, not long into their first day working together. "But listen…"

"He came up and started talking about it. Asked me why I kept eating when I already looked green. A lot of people said I looked green that day. A lot, Oscar. Seriously." Alexi slowed down, almost stopped, to fiddle with a button on his shirt so Oscar slowed, too, and people walking behind them had to step off the narrow uphill sidewalk into the street to pass around. The sidewalks were precarious enough already, laid from bricks but rippled into waves over time, a stalled mirror of the rolling ocean beyond the edge of the town, so two men standing still didn't help anyone get where they were going.

"Sorry," Oscar said to the dirty looks of fellow pedestrians squeezing around, and he shrugged with a tip of his head toward Alexi who was looking down.

Once Alexi started walking again, after taking both his own time and Oscar's, not to mention the time of those strangers, he went on as if he'd never stopped talking. "And the truth is I didn't feel so great that morning when I got up. And I thought, hm, Alexi, maybe you shouldn't eat forty-some hot dogs today. I knew I wasn't really in contention—dogs aren't my thing—but it's a good time. The peak of the season, you know? The main event."

"It is the only eating contest I've ever seen on TV," Oscar said. "But we need to think about what we're doing here. Can this wait?"

"Exactly. So I decided, what the hell, what's the worst that can happen? Maybe shoving a few dozen hot dogs into my belly would be just the thing to perk me back up. Feed a cold, isn't that what they say? I didn't have a cold, but… well, you know. I mean, sure, I puked all over the table and the front row of the crowd.

And the judges, a little, but I might not have. It could have gone either way. So that's something. I went along with the day and that's where it went. A long weekend in the hospital. Very restful."

Oscar, a bit green himself from picturing the competition, mustered a lackluster, "Aha."

"*And* I know exactly what happens if I eat too many hot dogs on a sour stomach. That's a bit of useful information I can file away for next time. So."

Oscar waited for the rest of Alexi's story but nothing else came as they passed a children's museum behind the wide front window of which stood a complex contraption of plastic and metal and wires, a Rube Goldberg machine complete with parachuting ball bearings and waterwheels and a miniature crane scooping the same few cubic inches of sand into the same conveyor belt baskets time after time. There was a path that led all the way from start to finish—useful motion—but there were also dead ends, components making no clear contribution to the larger machine, like the toy dump truck set moving by a passing balloon only to bounce off an elastic and end up back where it started to wait for the balloon's next excursion. Nothing gained but the motion, nothing but a distraction from the machine's actual task of performing the eventual mechanical event that set off a buzzer and bells and flashing lights at the end of the run and told the machine to reset and do all that again.

They stopped to watch, both at once without asking the other, and try as he might Oscar couldn't work out what all those moving parts amounted to. What, in the end, they accomplished, apart from drawing eyes to the spectacle of motion itself, a motion repeated over and over *ad infinitum* or at least *ad someone turns off the power*—unless its motion was powerless and perpetual, permanent movement with no lasting change and no drain on or gain to the world, nothing to be taken away except having watched. Yet he did watch and so did Alexi, as did several other passersby drawn in by the machine, so maybe motion alone was enough. Perhaps simply keeping parts moving—balls in the air, so to speak, or dump trucks on a track—was a satisfaction in its own right. An achievement of sorts.

They watched the whole procedure from start to finish several times, but Oscar never managed to discover what the final celebration-invoking element was: each time the end seemed near he was distracted by some other motion, some other dead end he hadn't yet noticed, and looked away at the right second to miss what he was trying to see, and the buzzers and bells were already at it when he looked back and the machine had already reset.

It was Alexi who stepped away first and kept walking, leaving Oscar to rush and catch up then overtake his meandering partner.

They walked past restaurants and banks and nondescript offices with Oscar in the lead and Alexi humming behind as they strolled into the square of a four way intersection. On one corner was a boutique of some sort, the same sort as several others in sight from that very corner, but Alexi, after a quick look at something across the street and a funny little one shoulder shrug, said, "Oh, I've got to go in here," and ducked inside.

The shop's windows were full of the same sea glass mobiles and woven beach bags they'd spotted all over town, especially by the water, and Oscar couldn't see why this shop among shops had captured his partner's attention. He was tired, though, he'd had a long day, he was beyond working out Alexi's whims so he stood on the sidewalk and extracted his phone. But before he could cast his eye to the North Pole someone caught his attention from across the street: the man, the trench coated and sunglassed man from the Metro yesterday afternoon and perhaps the sidewalk last night and, Oscar suspected, both the first train this morning and the station in Boston. All of which would have seemed ridiculous, impossible, except there he was: across an intersection in Maine looking like a spy disguised as a more conspicuous variety of spy to avoid being spotted, which wasn't a bad approach, if you thought about it, because who would expect a spy to be dressed like that if he was really a spy which this man couldn't be, dressed like that? But after the bald little man on the train Oscar was nervous. He clung to routine and was committed to keeping the day as ordinary as it could be under such strange circumstances, but the bald man had him concerned there was more going on than he'd been told back at BIP, and more was the last thing Oscar was after in life.

The man raised a hand from his pocket and rolled it toward Oscar in a dramatic, somehow dark pointing gesture then stepped into the street to walk in his direction through a break in the light flow of traffic. His other hand was still in a pocket but it, too, withdrew and was holding a gun, a real gun, or something very much like one and Oscar wasn't about to wait around to find out; he hurried off in the other direction, around a corner and leaving Alexi behind in his shop—most likely, he hoped, the man hadn't seen Alexi go in so his partner had nothing to worry about whereas he, Oscar, very much did.

After a block or so he looked back for a tail—a little more smoothly this time than his earlier attempts in the train station, to give him his professional due—and there his tail was, the trench coat, the dark glasses, the gun no longer visible but presumably tucked away again in a pocket. His pursuer spotted him looking and called out, "Sir," in a voice not quite a shout but not friendly either and Oscar quickened his step. Past more souvenir shops and a display window full of T-shirts with unfunny slogans, on menacing brick sidewalks past doors that opened right onto the street with almost no space and a hill sloped away to the water so down Oscar went—not by choice or intention so much as gravity, he'd gotten himself going and it was easier to go down than back up. And never mind gravity because going back up would be toward the man with the gun, and why would he want to do that?

He hit the hill's bottom, a wider main road, and on the other side warehouses, a fish market, a few restaurants, a marine supply store with inflatable beach toys gone soft but still hanging from the walls after summer was over. And a pier with fishing boats tied up beside it—lobster boats, really, but the difference wasn't noted by Oscar—and on one those boats stood a squat, blockish man in a red baseball cap and green rubber bib and tall boots. The lobsterman waved an arm, then both arms, and he called out what sounded like Oscar's name in a funny accent.

"Ovuh heyuh, down the gangway!" and who was Oscar to argue with that, someone who knew his name even if they talked funny versus someone following him with a gun despite calling him "Sir?" So he rushed down a wooden ramp inlaid with crossbars in case someone slipped—good thinking, that, because he did—and the man in the cap helped him onto the boat which wasn't so big but had a cabin and a bit of a deck and a large man who knew Oscar's name and did not, so far as he knew, have a gun.

Oscar turned and looked back up the ramp where the man in the coat stood half-concealed behind a streetlight—which might have worked better had it been dark—and holding a phone to his ear. Already the rumbling engine of the lobster boat pulled Oscar away from the pier. He held the envelope tight to his body and out of the wind as he checked for the lump of the phone in his pocket, and he watched the man in the coat and sunglasses shrink. Then he remembered Alexi and turned to the old salt at the steering wheel with a cigarette stuck to his lower lip but not actually in his mouth.

"Wait, my partner, I've left my partner."

"Ayuh, no time for that, fella. You've got a boat to catch."

"What boat? I'm on a boat. But Alexi... my partner, Alexi, he's..."

"He'll find his own way, Awskuh," his rescuer answered, and how much could Oscar—or Awskuh, for now, in that accent too overblown not to be real, too unbelievable not to be believed—argue with that? The lobsterman had whisked him away from a man with a gun, and had kept Oscar moving, which seemed to be the point of this day that had gone on forever: being in motion had come to feel more natural than sitting still.

Though he was sitting still or standing at least while the boat moved around him and so did the water. It seemed like it should already be nighttime. He'd been up since before sunrise and while he hadn't changed timezones he had traveled north, into unfamiliar angles of sunlight and shade so while the clock on his phone called it late afternoon Oscar's body wasn't convinced.

The lobsterman flipped a plastic bucket with his foot without looking and said, "Have a seat. Y'look fuckin' exhausted," and Oscar sat. Despite himself, despite his left behind partner and mysterious mission and everything else, none of which was enough to fend off the hum and vibration of a big diesel engine and salty breeze, Oscar fell asleep with his forehead against the bloody edge of a blue plastic bait bucket sloshing back and forth with chopped up hunks of fish.

But not for long—the sleeping, that is: the sloshing went on all the time, whenever the bucket was full—because his seaborne chauffeur nudged Oscar awake with the same foot that had flipped over the bucket and said, "Wake up, fella. Ya ship has come in." Oscar startled to life with couple of lines indented on his face from the bucket, and a patch of dried scales glistening pink from fish blood caught beneath, a distracting shine he'd catch at the edge of his eye for hours to come, and where the bucket had pressed on his still tender nose (which had, after all, only been bloodied a few hours ago), his sinuses throbbed. The lobsterman hustled him onto his feet, over the gunwale, onto the much larger ferry they'd tied up beside where a man in a dark sweatshirt, hood up and hiding his face, helped Oscar aboard and pushed the smaller vessel away with a boot to its old tire bumper. And now it really was getting dark, so he'd been asleep at least long enough for that to happen.

Here he was on another boat altogether while the lobster boat steamed away, so with the envelope as a flag he waved goodbye to his rescuer's red baseball capped head, whoever he was. And he noticed, to his career bureaucrat's shame, that one corner of the outer blue envelope had been stained and soaked through with blood; a fish's blood, not his own, but he wasn't sure if that was better or worse, more or less professional, as it were.

"Come with me, sir," said the man in the hoodie, who—to judge by the voice—was a woman.

10

The woman in the hoodie led Oscar into the maze of the ship, passing through narrow oval doorways on which he invariably bumped his head and up slippery stairways upon which—no surprise here—he slipped. Lights were dim, tinted red on lower levels then lightening to pink as they climbed, a gradient that might have looked nice from outside if the boat had any windows at those lower levels which, so far as Oscar could tell, it did not.

"Where am I?" he asked the dark green back of the hoodie but it didn't answer and neither did the body within. "What boat is this?"

Three or perhaps four levels up she finally stopped and turned with a hand on the door before them. "This is you," she said, then reached out to adjust Oscar's shirt collar—not his, really, but the shirt given to him by Tall and Wide an ice age ago—in a strangely warm gesture, domestic even. It was something Julia had done for him many times, though never to a shirt so vile with accumulations of sweat and fish blood and distance and time.

Those fingers flitting at his neck felt like his wife's the last time she'd turned him out—for the awards ceremony, he realized, *For Excellence*—and he thought again of that gold dress and her body inside it. Oscar tried to peek at his guide's face, into her hood, but before he could get a good look she had opened the door with one hand and pushed him from behind with the other so he was out of the stairwell and the door had clanged shut at his back.

And he was in a bar where the lighting scheme reached its pink apotheosis. Tufty heads of white hair flared rose as old women hunched at slot machines raising a terrible din, one machine bleeding into another and another so the noise never stopped, there weren't any gaps, just a single long godawful note: the aural equivalent of those files a dentist bores a root's canal with to make sure he has really scraped all the nerves clean, that pain you can still feel in your jawbone years later simply by thinking about it, even by accident, like when someone reminds you of it while telling a story.

It was that kind of room.

A room that made Oscar yearn for the stairwell and bumping his head, for the fish blood and even for the man with the gun, but before he could run after any of those a barman in black vest and old-fashioned armbands took his elbow and said, "This way, sir. She's waiting for you," and led him not quite gently across the room, through the vortex of aged ladies panting in anticipation of a third lemon, the rare clatter of coins, the cursing of mouths they kissed grandchildren with. Through the clatter and clang he grabbed fragments of conversation in languages he didn't know; behind banks of slot machines bodies tilted together, two men in dark suits, their heads close, and in another corner a man and a woman in the same secretive pose. And another pair looking in Oscar's direction as a woman at a mirror-faced machine caught his eye in its reflection.

On TVs overhead in every direction, turned at all angles so every eye could see one though few seemed to be looking—only two old men with their heads on the bar, and an old lady in a neck brace who seemed unable to turn away—an episode of *To The Moon!* was playing, whether a rerun of last night's premiere or a new episode or some older one he was glad not to know. It seemed to be the only television program the world watched anymore.

The barman brought Oscar through a door into a much brighter room and, once the door closed, a much quieter one. This was a classier bar, decked out in dark wood like some old establishments Oscar had been to in Washington, DC, but also like bars he'd seen hoping to be mistaken for pubs in some other country, aiming to endow themselves with the comfortable weight of tradition by spending enough on design and old, battered objects of decor. The barman led him past tables and stools to a far corner and a wide booth with a circular bench almost surrounding it and the redheaded woman he'd seen on the train (and, he still suspected, the other train, too) sat in the far corner of that far corner, the farthest part of the booth and so of the bar, a glass of red wine before her and—the incongruous thing, what made it all strange—a half-eaten but still enormous platter of nachos.

"You made it," she said, dismissing the barman with a smile and a wave. "Sit, please, sit down. You must be exhausted. You've had a long day."

And whether it was the power of her suggestion or the length of his day or just how comfortable that barroom booth suddenly looked, he did sit, sinking into the padded bench with a simultaneous exhalation from his lungs and the thick cushion. He laid the envelope on the table but right at the edge with his hand still on top, ready to grab it but also not very effectively concealing the stain of fish blood.

"I'm sure you have questions," she said, then slid the plate a few inches toward him on the table. "Nacho?"

"Where am I? I need to talk to my wife."

"You're confused. Exhausted. And there will be time to call your wife later. Don't worry yourself about that." She paused to select just the right chip from the pile, one with a balance of toppings and cheese but not soggy from too much salsa settled in the bowl of the plate. Chip selected, hanging from her hand at an angle that boldly risked the slide of an errant jalapeño slice, she said, "But right now we need to talk." Then she crunched into the chip, gone in two bites, a crisp bit of punctuation to stress what she'd said.

She urged the plate on him again and Oscar gave in, pulling

what he thought was a firmly built nacho out of the stack only for the chili and beans to fall off, leaving him merely a thin thread of cheese. But he ate it to avoid looking as if he had made a mistake; Slotkin's advice had always been to act like you know what you're doing no matter what happens, to make the lie stick.

Oscar rubbed his eyes and despite himself—despite his training—he moaned as his hand brushed his nose, low but not quite as low as he meant it to be. "I don't know what... Where... I don't..."

She laughed, bright but sharp, a twist of lemon in water. "I'm sure, Oscar. I'm sure. Okay, I'll start. You relax and have a drink."

He opened his mouth to ask what he could have but a tall, pale wheat beer with an orange slice was, somehow, already sweating its glass at his elbow so he drank several inches of that in one go. He ate more nachos as she spoke, trying to pace himself though the first bite had unlocked his hunger and it was all he could do not to climb on the table and wolf them down.

"You're on your way north. On an errand for Director Lenz." She paused. "Yes, I know, BIP's a secret, all of that. There aren't any secrets, though, are there? Not really. So." She took another chip, a bit haphazardly this time at first glance, but no, she'd chosen well without even seeming to choose.

She was that kind of woman, this redheaded one.

"I trust that envelope"—a nod toward where it lay on the table—"is the mission. No, no, I won't ask you to open it. What's inside doesn't matter to me. To the people I work for. That's not our concern. What we're interested in—what *I'm* interested in— are the circumstances by which such envelopes are produced. The machine, Oscar. It's always about the machine. Not the product but production's means. The movement, the chain of events. Do you see?"

Oscar, for his part, from his side of the table where his beer was nearly empty by now, struggled to follow. And why not? He really was tired. He'd lost his partner and he'd come a long way, by car then train then car then train and of course a boat to a boat to a bar on a boat... all that's enough to tire anyone out. Just reading all that would be tiring, and disorienting, and Oscar had lived the real thing. He heard those redheaded words, through those lips... he heard them just fine but they didn't mean much, so he asked, "The machine?"

He thought of the lightbulb far away back at BIP, fast on its cord, fast in its cinderblock windowless basement, and he wished he was still in its small Arctic glow. His fingers crept more or less on their own to the touchscreen of his phone on the table. They called up the Pole cam with the single-tap shortcut he'd created to save himself time, and though the angle was awkward he found a view of the ice. It was as dark in the north as it was on the boat through the big windows ringing the bar so he couldn't see much in the weak lamp of the camera and the darkness beyond, but he took comfort in knowing—in assuming, at least—everything was as he had left it: the footsteps that weren't, the tiny hummocks and hills of blown snow and heaves of ice, the occasional lens flare on the reliable screen that delivered him every day to the ice.

He took a deep breath and a deep drink all the way to the end of his beer, but another had taken its place on the unbranded cardboard coaster before he'd even set the glass down and the waiter whisked away the empty right out of his hand.

And the redheaded woman waited through all of this, through his check of the cam and his breaths and his beer. When he'd finally settled, when Oscar was ready, she went on with what she was saying.

"Yes, the machine is what matters. I'm sure you see that, a man of your expertise."

Oscar blinked and would have asked, "Expertise?" if his mouth hadn't been full of beer (but he pretty much asked anyway, without words).

"Your speculations. Sorry, your... *discoveries* have been invaluable, Oscar. To all of us. We can't thank you enough for what you've done. The opportunities you've made possible. Truly."

On his phone, a shadow still visible somehow in the darkness drifted across the ice; not all of it, not a large shadow, but enough to be visible along the bottom of the screen as it moved. It rolled, so to speak: from one side of the ice to the other, rounded in the center where it stuck out further, and Oscar's heart leapt—something was coming! An expedition. An icebreaker, maybe, plowing the sea up before its thick bow. An airship... he counted quickly, in his head, and yes, it was close to an anniversary for Andrée and his mission. Excited, suddenly wide awake, he leaned forward, hunched over the phone and the table, and the shadow moved forward, too, farther onto the ice, farther into the dark. And when Oscar sat back the shadow retreated.

He sighed, looking up at an inset lamp over his head.

"What is it?" his companion asked. "What did you see?" She leaned over the table and though it was too far across the dark, glossy circle of wood for her to see the screen she did give Oscar an unexpected—let's be fair, he wasn't purposely looking—but impressive view down the front of her low cut blouse.

He forced himself to look away, more or less. He took a sudden interest in the orange slice afloat in his drink. "Nothing, I... like to look at the Pole. There's a webcam."

"Ah," she said, leaning back. "Where were we?"

"Opportunities?"

"Yes. But the problem, Oscar, the problem..." And in a swift but fluid motion—so much so she hadn't seemed to be moving until she'd arrived—the redheaded woman propelled herself almost all the way around the booth's circular bench and was beside him, her hand, her fingernails, weaving a spiderweb on the back of his neck, her breath in his ear, his eyes glued to the screen of his phone, to the ice, his imagination working as hard as it could to feel that chilled air, to summon an Arctic blast—he pulled from his mental filing cabinet Nansen's account of a crew member who despite frostbite already on two of his fingers refused the warmth of a wolf-skin suit while on watch, telling his captain, "It does not do to pamper oneself"—and Oscar tried to feel that cold in his body as hard as he could. He recalled that same crewman—Hansen, the name came to him now, and the rhyme between captain and crewman had always seemed to diminish the work those men did, to make a cartoon of it all—rushing on deck in his shirt and drawers with the temperature forty below, no time to put on his clothes: the science, the job must come first. He willed that wind upon his own skin to steel his commitment, to firm his resolve and nothing else, knowing if those great men had endured such sharp cold he, Oscar, could endure this unwelcome moment of heat.

"Listen," he said, "all this is nice… the boat. The drink." He held it up. "But I just develop filing systems. I can't help you with anything else. It's pretty dull stuff."

"We know what you know, Oscar. We know what you found on Prince Patrick Island and what it means. What it could mean to who gets there first. There's enough for all of us Oscar, have no fear of that—we, the people I work for, have no intention of cutting you out. What we need to find out is how you know, how you found it. The problem is we know just enough that we need to know more. The leaks have been a trickle. An enticement. Your superiors have done their jobs. Plugged the leaks. But it's too late," and here one quintet of fingernails raked through his hair while the other strolled up his leg under the table, "because word is out. Rumors have started. The north is in play, Oscar."

On the ice a ribbon of snow kicked up in a dance from left to right in the small patch of light on his screen as wind crossed the camera's view. He followed it with his eyes, imagined that wind, saw himself opening layer upon layer of GoreTex and fleece, tearing apart velcro fasteners to let the wind render his whole body numb. He willed it. He willed his body to feel it and it almost worked.

"How did I find what?" he asked. "What do I know? If you tell me, I…"

His phone cut him off, rattling and buzzing toward him across the high-gloss wood of the table.

As swiftly as she'd arrived the redheaded woman pulled back, sliding around the bench once again with a parting pat of his thigh. "Go ahead," she told him. "Answer your phone."

It was Julia but he could hardly hear her because something thumped rhythmically in the background. "Where are you?" he asked, too loudly he realized because the woman across the table winced and turned away. "Sorry," he mouthed.

"I'm, uh… I'm on the train," his wife yelled, then, "It's the train," or maybe not—Oscar couldn't quite tell. He covered his other ear.

"I can't really hear you. Why is the train so loud?"

Julia only got as far as, "It…," before there was a louder thud, distinct from the regular and repetitive thumps, then some kind of siren in the background.

"Are you okay?" he asked. "What is that? Why are you so late going home?" The redheaded woman widened her eyes and leaned closer, giving Oscar another view which he tried, again, to ignore.

"Fine, Oscar. I'm fine. A, uh, power problem or something. I'll talk to you later. Guess it's not a good time," and she was gone so he set the phone down.

"My wife…," he told the woman across the table. "Something was going on with the train, a power outage, I think. Sorry. What were you saying?"

"The north is in play," his hostess repeated as if the interruption hadn't occurred. "And we hope you are, too, Oscar. We very much hope you are, too."

He finished his drink, splashing far less than might be expected in light of how vigorously his hand was shaking, and he even managed an, "Oh."

"The secret is out, Oscar. The uranium. The possibilities! It's all over the internet, the papers are bound to catch up and notice, the Russians... do you want them there first? We aren't so far from the Soviets, are we? Not so far from those days we can afford yet to pretend they never occurred, and I'm not the only one who thinks so. I'm not the only one looking for you, or who knows about the work that you've done. Everyone knows or will soon. But you," she slid back around the bench to his side, as liquid as she'd been the first time, "are the only one who knows how to find it. You"—her lips moved so close to his ear that her voice seemed to be inside his head—"need to choose the right side."

Her hand moved up his thigh and his body, after almost forgetting what it was to be touched, burst to life and no daydreams of Arctic air could stand up to that. But his training, Slotkin's wisdom, his bureaucratic professionalism kicked in with the instinct of an extra limb and Oscar insisted once more he only worked with filing systems. He calmed his body and rampant mind with visions of six letter codes and color schemes and specialized cabinets for maximized efficiency. He drilled deep, writing long strings of idiosyncratic database queries in his head, numbers and letters and coded commands, ranges and sums and exclusions.

"I can see you're a man who knows what he's doing," she said, backing off but remaining on Oscar's side of the bench. "A professional. So I'll be straight. Everyone's after those mines. Those deposits. Everyone knows you're the man to get them there. That will keep you safe, for a while, but in the end... in the end, Oscar, we all have to choose. I'm sure a man of your talents has noticed the others on your trail as easily as you noticed me—and yes, you were right, I was on the Metro, of course. I knew I'd been spotted. There were too many ears on that train to Boston for me to say so. But mark my words, you will have to choose, and I'll do what I can to keep you safe until you have chosen, provided you consider my offer. Provided you make the right choice."

Had there been an offer? There had been vague threats and seductive hands and nachos and beer but Oscar hadn't noticed an offer, per se. He yawned and trying to hide it behind a hand made him yawn again, and she laughed.

They were interrupted by her own phone, her ringtone a shrill bleat. From the side of the brief conversation he heard, Oscar got the impression something was wrong, a problem somewhere on the ship in need of her attention, and he wondered what her role was exactly on board.

"Okay, let's get you to bed," the redheaded woman announced. Oscar's body tensed until she waved the waiter over and asked, "Please show the gentleman to his cabin, won't you? He has a busy day ahead of him." Then she slipped out a back door, on her phone.

And Oscar, perhaps a bit past half asleep at the mere mention of bed, made no notice of how he got there, the trip to his cabin, the cabin itself, the pillow, the blankets, the bed. He thought he'd seen guards, men with guns, and sometime in the night he may have been awoken by the sound of a one-two-(pause)-three knock working its way down the hall then what sounded like gunshots and shouting and fleeing feet, but all that may have been no more than a bad chili pepper.

Either way he awoke in the morning with two porthole eyes staring him down from from the wall and a seagull's tufted ass in one of them before it crapped on the window ledge and flew out to sea.

So a promising start to the day.

Despite the freeze going to plan, despite the ship's thick wedge of hull rising as the icepack squeezed in as it had been designed for, the captain felt a moment of panic as the Arctic seized the vessel once and for all. The creaks, the cracks, the howls of ice twisting and straining on wood—like voices, like wolves in the distance, like left behind polar bear cubs. The one thing of all things he had never quite gotten audiences far south to understand of the north: the ice is alive, always speaking. The ice is every ghost left behind, all densely packed on the top of the world. The bottom, too, he supposed; why should that other Pole be any different though his own eyes had always looked north.

The men in that hull, spirits as buoyant as the captive ship they'd call home for the next months or years, still sang and still laughed and blew fluttering rings from their pipes. They joked about the ice coming to bear on their vessel, about the bears coming to bear across the packed ice, and they joked about the dark months to come in close quarters. He, their captain, believed as he had to believe that all their good humor was real. He had to believe it so they might, too, months later when they'd forgotten and his most vital job was to offer what weak reminders he could.

A man walked into a bar.

Somewhere, someday, for whatever reason, into a bar decorated with nautical relics: anchors and life preservers and bells from old buoys, harpoon tips and a narwhal tusk that looked real enough to fool drunks though it wouldn't have snuck past a cetologist worth the salt on the rim of her margarita. Behind the bar, suspended between the top shelves, a fur trimmed parka hung under glass with a framed photograph of Fritjof Nansen below on the wall; there was probably a story about how it came to be there but no one in the bar—the owner included—had any idea what that old story might be.

Our man took a seat beside another man who looked more or less like him; not in the manner of long-lost brothers or cousins or clones (they weren't in a science fiction novel or melodrama, about to discover themselves tied together by family secrets or mysterious experiments carried out in the past), just the way most men in most bars look more or less like each other. He didn't order a drink because the bartender had seen him coming so had already poured and there it was now, his stout pint.

The man drank a long draught then set the glass down with a sigh and watched white rings of foam cling then diminish and slide. He drank again.

"Do you ever feel," he asked his counter companion, engrossed by a pint of his own, "as if you're part of something bigger, something beyond yourself? Some chain of events you can't quite piece together but are all connected somehow? Something important?"

Down the bar a few stools, a third man who did not look like the others—he was very short, and he was very bald, and he was drinking a martini (dirty) instead of a beer—heard those questions and turned his head slightly to listen in on the answer without making his listening apparent.

The other man finished his drink and didn't answer, and still didn't answer, to the point you'd have to wonder if he hadn't heard the question but no, he had heard, because at last he replied, "Nope. Never. The opposite, really: I'm certain I'm not. I wish I was sometimes, but no, it's just me, I know that for certain, in a world about as big as this bar." He raised a hand, about to order another pint, and the bartender noticed and moved toward the tap, but the man changed his mind, shook his head, and stood up.

"Goodnight," the man said, and another man nodded the same.

And a man walked out of a bar but not the same man who'd walked in.

Someone—one of the other men, the bartender, us—might have followed him but no, no one did, because there were other stories to tell. Other strangers to follow, their own routes through the world, and who's got the time for them all? It's hard enough just to know you've ignored them and anyway the bartender had turned on TV.

Something was wrong at the helm. Electricity could not reach the controls leaving the shuttle simulator unpilotable, so the ersatz pilot had been pushed to one side and handed a bottle of water while he waited for a young woman with tattoo sleeves of barbed wire and ivy to crawl under the console in her toolbelt and work out what was wrong. He hadn't met her before, hadn't seen her on set, but she hadn't blinked or shown any sign of knowing who he was or more to the point who he had been. She hadn't been starstruck at all.

She wasn't so young and he wasn't so old but in celebrity years he was a relic, one of those bodies found frozen in ice long after its era, perfectly preserved but hardly much use as more than a curiosity for morbid gawkers, reminded of their own mortality by that arrested decline made suddenly rapid once exposed to the air of a return to TV.

He'd been on marquees, his own name as large as King Kong's or Nanook's in their day. He'd been everywhere, to the ends of the media earth. He'd broken new ground in promotion and paychecks and fame and after that ground had been broken more agile feet walked it and left him behind.

They'd left him with him this, a last grasp at the ring of… of what? Not celebrity because he'd never missed it, not once. Not money because it wasn't an issue; he'd invested more wisely than some of his peers, he had not lost a home or a boat or an overblown lifestyle he had never lived.

But something had once again led him onto the thin ice of TV, into the wasteland of reality and into that cockpit unable to fly, surrounded by other has-beens and never-quite-wases and a crew of professionals like that young woman under the dormant console with no time to care who the smiling heads were, sufficiently trained to get on with her job whatever distractions arose.

He wanted to win. It was that simple, really: he wanted to win that absurd competition and he wanted to go to the moon. He wasn't a big enough star to pay for it himself so this was his shot, his chance to do something, his chance to make matter all those trading cards and action figures and the *Voyager* lunchbox he'd spent so much of his childhood dreaming about before being convinced he had no head for science and no hope of flight. Before anyone had talked him out of himself.

If TV was his shot at spaceflight, his shot at becoming, he would endure all over again the humiliating sad scrabble of the press corps and paparazzi he'd left behind for so long. What would those matter from space, where he would be so far out of their reach?

He would endure the interminable downtime of making reality, the takes and retakes, the anxieties about elimination and the hours on set killing time at a window he knew was no more than a plexiglass sheet overlooking a studio wall but through which he could already see the whole planet so small and so far left behind.

He would endure those dull hours, the grind, the rumors already milling his name, if that's what it took to be great.

Some time later and much farther south, the hunter crouched on the roof of a building. Not a skyscraper, just ten or twelve stories, but higher than the building across the street and that was enough. He scanned the windows of that opposite building with his rifle's scope though the rifle itself had been left behind in the room where he'd been hiding his most recent days. He made notes on a pad at his side, resting on the asphalt of the roof and weighed down against a wind that hadn't come yet but still might by his knee.

It was lunchtime, not his but theirs, and he watched jacketless shirts and knee-length skirts and the occasional full suit or dress pass into or out of the revolving front doors. He thought of swirling eddies up north, back home, how quickly they grab hold of a boat and how firmly they can pin it down. How calmly they wipe out a whole family, as calmly as helicopters burn down a home.

The hunter scanned the grid of anonymous windows, crossing and recrossing those squares with his weaponless crosshairs. Sometimes he stopped if a body moved behind the glass: a head bent over a desk, typing fingers at the the ends of static wrists, a contorted woman with a sandwich in one hand and a phone in the other trying to pull some pages across the desk toward her with the bare heel of a foot. The plastic shells of monitors and laptops and telephones jaundiced or faded to gray in sunlight.

Bodies at work.

The work of bodies.

The hunter rolled his crosshairs from body to body. He saw how few of the screens on that building's many computers showed work being done, a mere dusting across the distractions of browsing and arguing and shopping online. A squat man in a suit showing both its age and his own browsed the catalog of the public library but the hunter couldn't tell what books he was after. There was sex, of course there was sex on those screens, but there always is and the hunter didn't stop at those windows because that's not what he needed from bodies that day.

It wasn't what he was after behind the walls of that building.

He was looking only for a way in and an indication of which way to go—he was looking for a map of the Arctic, left in outline as if waiting to be filled in by him. To be filled in by a man who had traveled a very long way after losing so much.

11

Oscar was up and already dressed in yesterday's new clothes, mysteriously but expertly washed and pressed while he slept. A twinge of homesickness had struck when he braced for the shower to douse him in cold water in the small seconds between turning the knob and remembering he hadn't checked, only to have the tap pour harmlessly onto his feet, but he'd pushed through that moment and was fiddling with the single-cup coffeemaker in his berth—a bit of *déjà vu,* he realized, remembering the previous morning a decade before, fussing with his own coffeemaker at home—when a knock sounded from the hallway which was even *déjà vu*-ier after the arrival of Tall and Wide.

"Sir?" called a very professional voice, carefully modulated to come through the watertight door without sounding like a shout. "It's time, sir."

Oscar opened the door with a sealed plastic tub of coffee grounds in his hand to find a slim young man dressed like a bellhop in a nautically-themed hotel on his doorstep. "Time for what? I don't..."

"No time for coffee, sir. We're about to dock. I believe you've overslept."

So Oscar checked for the phone in his pants pocket, took the envelope(s) in hand, and followed the steward out into the hallway, up a flight of stairs, across the deck, and to the top of a gangway where other passengers already waited in more of a clump than a line. These weren't the gambling old women he'd seen the night before but younger if not quite young travelers, working age folks like himself. Men and women in suits but also in jeans and and in casual skirts, briefcases and backpacks alike, some speaking to hands-free earpieces or into phones at their heads while others listened to earbuds and watched movies on tablets of various sizes or gazed out the window as the boat slid next to a dock. It could have been any morning commute, any day on the Metro or on some ferry in a city where that was the way people traveled to work, apart from being in the middle of nowhere or at least the middle of some place in which Oscar didn't know where he was.

The boat bumped the dock and crew members scrambled outside then a few seconds later the door swung open onto a metal ramp surfaced in gritty black grip tape. Oscar was halfway down before realizing he still had the coffee tub in his hand; there weren't any trashcans in sight so he held it for the time being.

On shore, beyond the heads and shoulders of his fellow dis-embarking passengers, he saw only a boxy white building and an official in a gray uniform. There was nothing beyond the building: no houses, no town, no sign reading welcome to wherever you are. What looked like a desert of blacktop spread from behind the bland structure and if not for that the whole nondescript place might have been lost in the nondescript landscape beyond.

At the foot of the ramp Oscar yawned and looked across the sea then at the sky, two planes the same weak shade of blue meeting at a border so hazy each vanished into the other. The sun seemed hardly above the horizon and he wondered why the ship had docked so early: couldn't it have waited at sea for a while to let people sleep? And how badly could he have overslept if dawn was just breaking now?

The steward who had summoned him from his room followed Oscar to the end of the gangway where the official in gray gave a nod. "All yours," said the steward, then he turned and rushed back up the ramp. Oscar watched him ascend and inside the door at the top of the ramp, before the steward closed it, he could have sworn he saw a low, bald head gleaming beside a taller dark trench coat under sunglasses and a third man just behind them who bore a striking if unlikely resemblance to the doctor who had patched up his nose on the train, which was absurd: all three of those men, all strangers he'd spotted miles away and spread across the eastern seaboard, somehow ending up on the same boat? It was early in the morning—barely morning, at that—and he hadn't yet gotten to drink the coffee cupped unbrewed in his hand so Oscar chalked it up to grogginess and his eyes playing tricks, and why not? What else would he assume, that he'd stumbled into a tangle of international intrigue and espionage on the waters between Maine and Canada, of all places? He'd have better odds of winning a trip to the moon.

It was cold, with a salty wind off the water, and this far north of the capitol Indian summer was apparently over. At least until sunrise had time to warm the world up. Oscar shivered in just his shirt, as clean and wrinkle-free as it was.

"This way, sir," said the official, one hand at the gun on his belt… wait, no, not a gun but only a walkie talkie where a gun might have been, to Oscar's relief. The other passengers had entered the square hut already so he hurried after his escort. Behind him the boat's engines grew louder, their low throb increasing to an almost shrieking thrum as it moved away from the dock. From shore, in daylight, now that he had a full view of its hull, it wasn't nearly as large a ship as he'd thought: it had felt like a cruise ship at night while he wandered through it and sat in the bar but now it had shrunk to the size of an ordinary car ferry.

He followed the official into the building where his fellow passengers had lined up to wait their turns at one of two customs counters. One at a time they advanced to the next available counter, showed a passport or papers, spoke briefly to the official, then were waved toward a door at the back of the room or else into one of two offices where other officials conducted longer, more private interviews with the arrivals. Oscar got in line with the others and realized he was the only passenger without any bags, without even a toothbrush or jacket, only a plastic tub of ground coffee and an envelope with another inside it, and the other passengers seemed to notice it, too. They turned to look at him, scowling, as if to say he was not one of them; those in pairs or in groups murmured to one another and he assumed it was about his own unbaggaged state.

The officials noticed him, too. One spoke into a radio clipped to his shoulder and gave what looked like a hand signal to a woman in the same gray uniform across the room, behind Oscar, watching the back of the line. She in turn spoke into her own radio while nodding in his direction.

Oscar looked to the floor, his face warm, then pulled out his phone and watched the Pole. The sun was as washed out there on his screen as it was outside the hut and he wondered how much closer he was to the Pole now than he'd ever been—he assumed the boat had gone north, it must have crossed into Canada considering how long they'd been on the water, but he hadn't the faintest idea of how far or to where and when he asked the map tool on his phone it spun its wheel before returning an error. But it calmed him to see dawn at the Pole and to know he was in more or less the same light as the camera at last, and he watched the ice as he shuffled a step or two forward each time the line moved.

The battery on his phone was getting low and with a twinge Oscar pictured the charger at home on his nightstand and its twin on his desk at work in the basement of BIP.

Ahead of him, at one of the counters, a small dark-haired man was growing agitated, insisting that someone he seemed to be looking for had come through this way, had passed through this station, and was still in the region somewhere. The woman at the counter shook her frown back and forth, uttered several variations of no, then summoned two men in gray to escort the upset traveler into one of those private rooms.

As they dragged him along the length of the line the upset

man said, "I know he was here! I asked online, I found people who saw him, aren't you listening to me? People knew he'd been here! He's working somewh…" but the office door closed on the tail of that sentence.

When at last Oscar reached the yellow waiting line painted on the floor, the final passenger in the group, the officials at both counters scowled and neither one waved him forward. Oscar looked back and forth between them, and again, before asking, "Which way do I…?"

The woman on the left, wizened and sour as a cafeteria lady or an apple left in the sun or a cafeteria lady eating a dried up old apple, sighed in a manner that was more of a groan and rasped, "Here." So he moved forward as she demanded his passport.

"I haven't… I don't… I wasn't planning to travel."

"What's that you're holding?"

"Coffee?" he said, holding it up. "And this envelope," he added, raising his other hand.

She glared at Oscar and at the coffee then reached for her phone, covering the mouthpiece and turning so he couldn't hear. When she'd hung up the woman barked, "Wait," then she sat down and swiveled her chair toward the offices at the side of the room.

So he waited and a few seconds later another official approached, an older man wearing a thin mustache and the same gray uniform as all the others but, somehow, wearing it better: whereas the other officials all looked generic, interchangeable parts in a whole, this man—the director, Oscar assumed, or whatever they called the boss here—wore his uniform while the others were all worn by theirs.

He cut through the room, clapped a hand on Oscar's shoulder, and said, "I've been waiting for you. Come with me." He led Oscar toward an open door, one of those two offices, and as he passed near he heard that small, dark-haired man who had been so upset not quite yelling but definitely still worked up, insisting on something about a server farm and a job and the person he was looking for, his husband he seemed to be saying. Then Oscar was ushered into an office himself and out of earshot.

The official urged him into a chair on one side of a massive green metal desk topped with a slab of dark veneered wood. A filing cabinet with a precarious stack of papers on top stood against the wall over his interviewer's shoulder.

"So," said the customs director—Apparently? Maybe?—"you're on your way."

"I guess I am," Oscar said. He set his coffee tub on the table but held the envelope in his lap. "Where am I right now? Where are we, I mean? Can I ask that?"

The official laughed and the badge on his chest, a shape and logo unfamiliar to Oscar, caught light from the window and flared. "Isn't that the question? 'Where' indeed!"

"But I really don't know."

"Hmm. Okay, sign…," the official flipped through a stack of forms at his side and slid one in front of Oscar with a black ballpoint pen, "this, please." Then he picked up the tub of coffee grounds and turned it over and over, inspecting its foil cover, its pull-tab, its flat plastic circular bottom, its tiny indentation either a vestigial mark of its manufacturing process or else some crucial component for correct operation of the machine meant for brewing the coffee Oscar had thus far been given no chance to brew.

"Hmm," he said again.

Oscar looked at the form, expecting something along the lines of a customs declaration—assuming he was in Canada somewhere by now—but it was only a table of spaces to fill in with his measurements: hat size, shoe size, waist and coat sizes, most of which he didn't know so he drew question marks in more than half of the spaces. When he was done he pushed it back toward the official who took it in hand without a look and in one fluid motion dropped the coffee, pushed back his chair, and stood up.

"So that's you taken care of, isn't it? Paperwork is destiny!"

"I knew someone who used to say that," Oscar said.

"He sounds like a very wise man."

They stared at each other for a few seconds, perhaps both considering the wisdom of Slotkin's maxim whether they both knew it was Slotkin's or not. Then the official said, "Okay, then. Let's get you going! This way." And he headed back into the big room where the woman at the intake counter glared again as Oscar followed her boss toward the other door at the back of the room where the director waited to pull it open until they could pass through together.

On the other side were racks of parkas and fleeces and boots and hats, skis and poles and goggles and socks with battery packs. High-tech dog sleds and sailboards hung from the ceiling in harnesses, and sleeping bags, tents, and all sorts of boxes and bins were stacked in every available corner. Men and women with clipboards bustled among the equipment, looking up briefly as Oscar and his escort entered, giving only the slightest of nods then back to work, whatever work was—some sort of inventory, maybe, checking pieces of equipment against a list. Other workers bustled around the last of his fellow passengers, holding one piece of gear or another up to various parts of their bodies.

"What is this?" he asked. "I thought it was customs. Immigration. You didn't even ask who I am."

The official laughed. "We don't worry so much about all that up here. We aren't so bothered about who owns what or who's where, just that they have the right jacket."

"But this is Canada, right?"

"You tell me," said the official. When Oscar didn't move the man urged him toward a window. "I mean it, go on. Look outside. Does it look like Canada?"

Oscar took in the flat, featureless stretch of pale grays and whites off to what would have been the right of the building—so, to the north—had he been facing it from outside. "I don't know," he said. "There's not really anything there."

"Exactly! Exactly, yes, there's not really anything here. So who needs a stamp in his passport from nowhere? But look. The borders up here have shifted so many times. Where the north begins, where it ends, who's laying claim to which part of it that week and swapping it for some other island the next... who can keep up? Who wants to? There's kind of an unofficial treaty to not give a shit. Has been for years, ever since... oh, what's his nuts, John Macdonald—you know, the first PM—and old Valhalla Stefansson gave everyone headaches fighting about how to carve up BC and grabbing up islands like kids in a sandbox with too many toys. I'm telling you, they cost us—both sides of the border, all of us—a fortune in misprinted maps and ruffled feathers so really, I mean it, who's got the time?"

"That makes sense," Oscar said. "I just... well, I always assumed there'd be more to the border. That there would be a border, at least."

"Oh, there is, there is. Don't get me wrong. You go on down to one of the "real" crossings and you'll get all sorts of stamps and inspections and they'll be more than glad to strip your car to parts and give you a screwdriver to fix it. I suppose I could do that for you, too, if you'd really like it, but, eh, you don't look to me like you've got a car and I don't know where my screwdriver is off the top of my head."

"No, that's fine. This is fine. Never mind."

"Okay!" he declared, getting right back to business. "This man needs to be equipped," he told one of the women rushing about the room, and held out to her the form Oscar hadn't quite filled with his sizes though now, at least, he knew why he'd been asked. "See to it, please."

Taking the form, the woman—a thin blonde who would have been waifish except her thinness suggested barbed wire charged with electricity more than anything so delicate—peered at it over her dark-framed glasses. "Not much to work with." She looked from the form to Oscar himself and added, "But I've seen worse."

"I leave him in your expert hands," said the official, leaving a too-hard pat on Oscar's back as he turned to go, and a coughing prognosticator in his wake.

The woman holding the form must have given some invisible sign—unnoticed by Oscar, at least—because another woman hurried over on clacking heels with a measuring tape hanging from her hand to the floor. Her fingers worked between Oscar's legs, her mouth calling out numbers the first woman wrote down, then around his waist for more numbers, the crown of his head, his ankles, his arms… Oscar waited to be asked to open his mouth and say *ahhh* but he never was.

"Got it," the first woman announced when a full battery of measurements had been taken and called out and inscribed, then the two of them divided across the room to return seconds later, arms laden with parka and fleece pullover and thick windproof overalls and everything else, and it suddenly occurred to Oscar— slow of him, yes, but he was tired and more than a little confused so let's cut him some slack—he was being outfitted.

For the Arctic. Equipped.

After everything, the cars and the trains and the boats, he'd almost forgotten his mission but there he was: being fitted for cold weather gear just as Peary and Byrd and Nansen and the others had been. Sure, most of them had worn layers of silk and wool and here he was being measured for Gore Tex and plastics and modern fabrics those great men could not have imagined and perhaps could have done things even greater than those they did do if they'd only had such high-tech convenience, but all the same he was being outfitted. For real. As fully equipped as his fur-collared Roald Amundsen action figure.

He tried things on, or rather things were tried on him because mostly he stood still and moved an arm or a leg as he was told or forced to by the firm hands of those women. They tried him with parkas too tight or too lose, boots that fit and did not, gloves and goggles and everything else, all going by in a blur either because it really did happen quickly or because his mind was now racing, envisioning the ice sheet in front of the camera at the North Pole, picturing himself standing before it and waving to whoever was watching. The pack breaking up and bobbing around in sharp chunks, the blues and greens and purples of ice seen up close in the Arctic sun and the sea... his body had travelled miles to get here and his mind was already more miles away.

As the women worked on and around him he saw other passengers going through the same thing then heading out a double door at the back of the room with their gear.

"Done," announced one of the woman; Oscar didn't catch which. As if he'd heard—and he must have, somehow—the official from the front room reappeared and said, "Excellent. As always, ladies," but the women had already gone back to their clipboards and inventory.

"Let's see," he said to Oscar. "You'll need something...," he trailed off, looking around the room. "Here we are," as he pulled a huge duffel bag off a shelf. "Let's get all that in here," and the two of them stuffed Oscar's carefully chosen equipment into the bag. "You won't need to put it on yet. You've still got a long way to go. Speaking of which, you should get going."

The official slung the bag onto one shoulder while his other arm wrapped around Oscar, leading him toward those doors. They pushed through together and were in a room full of chairs linked into rows and bolted to the floor. A television hung from the ceiling in pride of place, and a low table splayed with magazines and newspapers sat beneath it against the wall. A squat vending machine hummed in the corner with a windowless door beside it. None of the other passengers he'd seen pass through those doors before him were there.

The official dropped Oscar's bag with a muffled thump and told him to have a seat, watch TV, and wait. Someone would come for him when it was time to go.

"Go where?" Oscar asked, but the official was already on his way out the door. So fast as a lightbulb he sat.

Mornings with the light at its best and evenings when it would do, she rolled back and forth on the horizon. The swivel of the telescope her husband left for her entertainment creaked in its housing and stuck when it turned. From its southwestern extreme the brass shaft took a nudge, a firm bump of her palm, to set the device back into motion northwest. She never strayed from that range, never turned the lens skyward to take in the stars or inland to look back toward Europe or closer at hand across the blank slate of Greenland, that near-continent whose raw edge she occupied in her waiting.

The native boy and girl brought her breakfast with tea brewed from leaves long gone stale but so far from the shops and the mongers she had no other choice. And her husband, she knew, endured worse, was by then rationing the last dregs of weak coffee among tired men if luck had stayed on their side; if not they were scraping up lichen and stewing old leather for broth.

Or, dare she dream, they were already on their way south, toward her coast, toward those compounding lenses arranged one after another with her own eye at the far end of the world's gaze.

She had not spoken more than instructions in days: how to cook, how to clean, how to arrange her chair for the optimal frozen view of the sea from the windows of that lightly adapted— insulated, though you'd never know it, for God—fishing shack. She read but her books and her papers were old, threadbare as the castaway trousers she wore for warmth after the way her skirts lifted the hems of her husband's left behind parka to let in the cold during her first misguided days on that shore. If the women in the south knew what was out there, how cold it can be in the world, they would all wear trousers themselves; they would strangle the dressmakers with whalebone and hoops, even the most highborn and coldblooded ladies. And she could not help but wish to be reading instead her husband's own journal, the log of his excursion across the ice to the Pole. To know where he was and after a fashion to be there herself.

She had not spoken more than instructions to her makeshift household, her wish their command, but the rejection of her desire to join the expedition still stung: she was not man enough as a woman, her husband would not hear of it, would not take the request to his backers—he'd be laughed from the Society, he'd said to her face after he'd finished laughing in it himself. There was no room for women apart from those natives so often mistaken for men—or so she'd been told—on the vast empty span of the ice. No room for her stories in the serious white pages of the Society and its magazine, no room for the presence of a feminine touch, a weak female body, to diminish the pleasure of mounting the Pole. It means less, her husband admitted, if you can do it, too.

So she waited, marking the edge of the already-conquered, the no longer a feat. She watched the boy and the girl and their brown-skinned parents struggle with the mechanisms of her modern kitchen transported north, her parlor assembled as if she were in Philadelphia or Boston or Cleveland and the wives of other men might come calling at any moment expecting fresh tea. They knew how the gas cooker worked, her wild housemates. She'd seen them use it with the same confidence they brought to her phonograph, laughing and dancing and singing along in empty sounds she mused, despite herself, might in fact be purer music.

They knew but forgot or refused to employ it and served her raw fish tasting still of the sea and the ice and of the dark distance between the empty space of the Pole and her husband with a flag poised to fill it and the long shaft of his telescope left to her on that coast where foreign air trapped long ago between lenses held the world closer but still out of touch. She sent that fish back to the kitchen, asked them to scorch it until it tasted of dry land at least, and as she awaited a second try at civilization she turned the telescope southward until as always it stuck.

12

And he still sat, hours later, in that same sad departure lounge.

The television, looping a news channel in half-hour segments, inevitably offered updates on *To The Moon!* as part of its cycle but mercifully they—or it, the same update over and over—were short. Oscar rifled through magazines, hoping for a *National Geographic* but finding none. He considered logging into the online archive he subscribed to but wanted to save the battery on his phone. The magazines he did find covered fashion and travel and food, shopping and current affairs, which is to say affairs that had been current once but those magazines went back years and in some cases a couple of decades. All the way back to the Cold War, in fact, and there were covers of *Time* and *Newsweek* and *Condé Nast Traveler* announcing trials and trips on the far side of the Iron Curtain. There was even the November 1989 issue of *Time* announcing the fall of the wall—as if anyone hadn't heard by the time those pages hit print, though Oscar had to think back to remember how news traveled then—with its smiling young German faces framed by windblown hair and garish bright sweaters and scarves. Beneath the feet of those revelers the concrete itself, the wall, with its pebbled surface and spraypaint.

Oscar had seen it once. Not in place, he'd never traveled as far as Germany—until now, perhaps? Had he traveled that far albeit in a different direction, was he that far north?—but in Washington. He and Julia found a section of the wall at the Newseum, a surprise in a quiet courtyard where it snuck up on them; strange to say a wall snuck up on someone, but it did, that particular wall. It snuck up on everyone, practically overnight, and then it snuck down just when the world was used to it being there.

Then it snuck up on Oscar and Julia as they strolled past exhibits of headlines and award winning photos and interactive exhibits in which children could assemble a given day's news out of snippets of story and sound, a database of segments and contextless clues to a mystery that didn't exist.

The two of them stood in that courtyard, holding hands, the wall as immense in dissection as it had been in life. In their lives, at least, childhoods then young adulthoods in its long shadow, long enough to reach across two continents and an ocean. They didn't speak but they stood, and they squeezed. Later, at home after they'd eaten dinner, Oscar wondered aloud what had passed through that gap, that particular hole in the wall. Whose feet had stood upon it and whose legs, perhaps, had jumped over in the decades it stood in their way. Who had painted the letters and symbols and signs on one side, and who had daydreamed of painting the other, the empty gray eastern face.

He asked Julia if she thought Berliners were used to it yet, that absence through the heart of their city, or if they still noticed its ghost when out walking as a tongue always finds where a tooth used to stand. He asked if she thought they might miss it sometimes, for its firm edges if nothing else, the clarity of only one route to get from here to there. Julia said she didn't know. And Oscar said sometimes he did but by then it was late and neither of them had the energy to understand.

And now, in that small, stuffy departure lounge he looked at those young German faces in their sweaters and scarves and he wondered what had become of them. All the directions in which they had gone, all the lives that had likely crossed and recrossed a border that no longer mattered in the years since that photo was printed on the magazine's cover, now faded from sunlight though the room had no windows, on paper made brittle by time.

He stood to inspect the vending machine and was able to use his credit card to buy a slim sandwich in a shrink-wrapped translucent triangle. Turkey perhaps, or some other filling as pale as the bread and, for that matter, as pale as the plastic container, but it seemed at least many years fresher than the magazines. He ate while looking up at TV, half-hearing the news cycle repeating itself, then behind it he heard the hum of the big room beyond, the rush of inventory and outfitting. Oscar turned, quickly enough to watch the door closing after someone had left it to swing but not to see who he'd missed.

He finished his sandwich then bought a soda and drank half of it and he was just nodding off after a long morning waiting, his head sinking into the duffel bag set on a chair, when that official from earlier returned and announced, "Okay there, time to go, get yourself up!" and Oscar was back on his feet. The official hoisted the bag and led him out through the door by the vending machine.

Behind the building was an airfield, that desert of blacktop Oscar had seen when arriving by boat, and a small prop plane idled before them, a pale cylinder of anonymous white dust-coated to gray. Its steps were down but no pilot or crew were in sight, nor any of the other passengers he'd arrived with and seen outfitted earlier. The official urged Oscar toward the plane with his arm, saying, "Let's get you on board, no time to waste."

They hustled across the tarmac and his guide flung the gear bag through the door first then gave Oscar a push. "Get yourself buckled in," he called into the cabin while raising the steps. The last thing Oscar heard before the door slammed shut and sealed with the official on the other side was, "Off you go!"

So he chose a seat from among an unoccupied eight—four on each side of the plane with an aisle between—and he strapped himself in. Ahead was a door he presumed opened into the cockpit where he also presumed was a pilot responsible for flying the plane, but Oscar saw no sign of a crew apart from the indirect evidence of the plane lifting away from the ground.

Pressure built against his chest and in his ears. The plane rattled around him as he closed his eyes and gripped the armrests hard with both hands but in time the craft leveled off and the pressure eased and Oscar exhaled.

The constant motion was wearing him out. Even last night's sleep and yesterday's nap had seemed to go by in the turn of a page, giving him hardly a rest, but how far had he traveled? From Maine up into Canada? So it must have been hours and miles besides and as the plane rose and the gray building shrunk into a small smudge against the darker tones of the tarmac Oscar felt not so much tired as completely at ease. In himself entirely, as if here he was, in the sky, with the whole world turning below while he stood still and waited for his destination—wherever it was—to come to him.

It reminded him of Alexi's story about the hot dogs, not the throwing up part but what had seemed to be his larger point, about not expecting… then again, Oscar realized, he hadn't quite grasped what Alexi's point was.

He was flying overland, away from the water, but with nothing much to speak of as scenery: flat, empty stretches, brown and yellow fields, the occasional murky green pond, and all of it so far below it looked no more real than the sketches he and Alexi made every workday on their big paper sheet. Well, almost every day, because there had been no prognostication yesterday or today either, with the two of them off to the Arctic. Was he into his vacation days yet?

But where was Alexi? What had happened to him back in Portland? Oscar pictured his fellow prognosticator sitting at a restaurant table, ordering meal after meal as he waited for his senior partner to come or to receive some instructions, and despite himself Oscar smiled. And why wouldn't he, on his way to the Arctic at last? Despite all the past two days' strangeness, most of which had already blurred into that haze between memory and dream because so much had happened at once, one thing after another, with his brain getting no time to make sense of one event—to be worried or to be afraid—before it was forced to half-process the next. Motion made a blur of it all and kept Oscar something near calm at its center.

And calm, now, in the air.

He recalled Nansen's journal for September 25, 1893, one of his favorite days from that account of the *Fram:* "Frozen in faster and faster! Beautiful, still weather; 13 degrees of frost last night. Winter is coming now. Had a visit from a bear, which was off again before any one got a shot at it."

How calmly that crew had faced down the winter, the threat. How warmly they'd welcome being frozen into the ice—it's what they'd set out for, yes, but how many men would have cowered when that moment came? When the ice closed in around the wooden hull of their ship, squeezing the timbers and every crack a reminder they could no longer leave unless they gave up the ghost and departed that way. The reserve with which those great men had faced down the ice bear, knowing all along that if they went—and they must have thought it was more likely *when*—they wouldn't be going by sea.

On a whim of curiosity without expectation, Oscar slid out his phone and to his surprise had a strong, steady signal in flight. He knew not to use his phone on a plane but he was alone in the cabin with no one to scold him and surely the problem wasn't one phone but many, large groups of passengers all at once using their large groups of phones, so he pulled up the Pole cam and all was again as he'd left it: the ice, the sunshine, the not-quite-footsteps, so on. He watched for a while as nothing happened, the plane bouncing and shaking around him, the tight, stuffy air of the cabin no match for the fresh northern wind in his mind, and a long time went by with Oscar in two non-places at once.

A shadow moved over the ice or moved over his eye but whichever it was that shadow suggested a profile, a person, and he realized he might call his wife as long as the signal held strong as it had for the whole flight so far. Oscar scraped a thumbnail across the miniature landscape of his phone's case, across the washboard of faux-woodgrain, back and forth like a chanted mantra.

He tapped the speed-dial icon programmed with Julia's number—the only speed-dial in his phone's memory, the only number he called very often and the only one he ever called because he wanted to—and waited with the phone set on speaker (no one to eavesdrop, after all) so he could still watch the Pole where that profile of shadow morphed into an amorphous cloud on the shimmering ice.

It rang. And rang. But not really ringing, more of a buzz, a chirp, the kind of sound phones had come to make over time, further divorced from their wooden-boxes-with-bells origins. As far as the long, snowbound trekking of Peary was from Oscar's own virtual paperwork filing. As far apart, perhaps, as being at the Pole was from watching it on the camera, something that bothered Oscar at times but not then, not that afternoon—was it still afternoon?—because he, too, was on his way north. He'd tried other ringtones, older sounds, but they always led him to daydream rather than answer the phone, they led him backwards and onto the ice instead of forward into the future of whatever news the call promised.

The phone continued its chirping, maybe more of an insectoid whir after all, but either way it wasn't his wife picking up. Her voicemail did but he hung up without speaking: she'd know it was him from the number, she'd know he had called and tried to talk and that would be enough between them. There wasn't any message other than that: I was calling, I was thinking of you, I'll be thinking of you again later.

He positioned the phone on the armrest, leaning it against the window so he could watch both panes of glass in one view: the stark white of the Pole and the brown nothing broken every few minutes by something yellow passing under the plane. And in a few minutes his head leaned against the glass, too, and he was asleep.

Then awake, though hours had passed because it was dark outside and dark on his phone, which had also fallen asleep. He had a hazy memory of dreaming they'd stopped, of brightly colored lights outside his window and men rushing about with long hoses, so maybe they actually had.

The tray table on the seat across the aisle had been extended and a covered plate waited upon it with a bottle of water. Oscar lowered his own table then moved the meal to his seat and ate; a sandwich with a few different textures, something that crunched and something that didn't, a tastelessness that always comes at altitude but still, it was food. His phone woke to show a text from his wife reading, "Sorry I missed you—had a meeting. Hope you had a good night. Talk later? Love you."

He hung his arm down into the aisle and recalled in his muscles a moment a few days earlier on the balcony with Julia, over their afterwork beers. She'd taken his hand out in space, their arms a long V between lawnless lawn chairs, and she'd squeezed and he'd squeezed hers back. The angle was awkward and Oscar's arm began to feel heavy then numb but he hadn't wanted to let go because he didn't want Julia to think he'd let go because he wanted to and didn't know how to let her know it was because he had to, not without speaking which would have broken the moment. He'd flexed the muscles in his forearm and wrist to stir them to life, wake them up, and tried to do so secretly but she must have felt it because she let go of his hand, thinking, perhaps, he'd been telling her to and he almost said something, almost told her that wasn't so, but… it was too much, and maybe she hadn't thought that at all and had simply wanted her hand to herself. And in the air above some part of what he'd taken for Canada, over places he'd never actually see, Oscar clenched his hand to itself in the aisle along which he was the sole passenger.

All those moments between them, all that experience no one else knew about—others may have been there, they may have seen the ducks chased off by a kite or the couple side by side in their chairs, but without all the other moments that led them to the one they were in at some given time, without the right combination, how much could it mean? All it took was a word, a reminder, a pluck at the web of their lives together and like a spider feeling a vibration on some far strand Oscar knew what he was being told and how it all fit together. It was easy to miss that at home where less romantic, more everyday memories piled up around the good ones and where the unpleasantness of a bad day at work could so easily get in the way. On the ground, in the flesh, he'd be distracted by Julia and her body, by trying to unlock her reticence of recent years, that filing cabinet he'd lost the key to. But now, here, in the air and the dark, the web of their marriage could be plucked by an incoming phone call or text, there were only the best memories of their years together. They could be more selective in which moments they paid attention to and which they ignored and in how they queried the database of their marriage; they had better tools for the job across all that distance and space. The ducks and the kites and the lawn chairs three stories up off the street that meant nothing to anyone else but were the precise keywords to access their private archive.

At BIP Oscar could type only "school" or "factory" or something as minor as "red" into his terminal and the database would pull out every file tagged with or containing that word. And it didn't stop there, because he could mine deeper when "school" led him to an arts academy he'd discovered on King William Island and he might get distracted from there by the name of a particular student or teacher and follow them home, to the neighborhoods and houses BIP had discovered, until a whole life was revealed from a single, well-chosen word. And his own life, his own marriage and memories and apartment walls of magazines, didn't seem so very different from up where he was in the near-Arctic air.

He ate, and he flew, and apart from a blinking light at the tip of the wing there was nothing outside so far as he could tell. He imagined a view of the plane, his own brightly lit window alone in the sky, and despite himself pictured a rocket: an astronaut the only person in space gazing out a porthole into black as vast as the white of the north, and something in that made sense to him in a way nothing else about space travel had.

13

Oscar watched the ice for a while but soon let his phone sleep. His mind's eye fell upon his magazines back at home, by that hour catching moonlight in his apartment. He roamed their spines from one red dot to the next, from Peary's announcement of reaching the Pole to the excitement of Flaherty returning with the footage of *Nanook of the North*, that original blockbuster ready to bring the Arctic into every American home, to spread polar fever as fast as influenza once every boy, every girl—every mom and dad, for that matter—was captured by daydreams of the north. Sure, they'd read about it before but this, Flaherty's film, the seal hunt… it was faked, of course it was, but they didn't know then and they didn't know for so long afterward that it didn't matter because that scene of the Inuit battling something under the ice, tugging their line, tumbling and tightening their bodies, struggling for something to eat: those images were burned into every American mind. That's what it was to be alive, Oscar thought. That's what he dreamt of when he dreamt of the north, to have every decision be life or death, to have every moment matter as much as the next; it was a daydream and that's all it was, and it was better that way. It wasn't a desire to give up airplanes and electricity, it wasn't wishing he lived on the ice, but to be part of something that real, that powerful. To be pulled into something bigger than himself was why he had joined BIP at all, knowing he'd never go north (though there he was, somehow, with his envelope) but would be part of that legacy all the same, his own decisions secondary or tertiary relations at best of those others that mattered so much but at least they'd be in the family.

Seal hunting by association, as he'd described it on Alexi's first day in the basement, though his partner hadn't been listening.

In time light pooled on the horizon's rim and spilled onto land. Oscar knew for certain he was flying north—which he'd already suspected, of course—because sunrise came dead to the east and he had a perfect, perpendicular view from his window. But not for long because when the sun showed as only the thinnest cuticle curve taking its time behind the avant garde of first light, the plane leaned hard to one side, to the left so away from Oscar, shifting his view upward. Then it turned and his view was westward and the plane was descending; smoothly, under control, but fast enough to push him back in his seat.

No one had come to collect his dishes. There had been no announcement about returning his tray table to its upright and locked position, but he did so all the same and put the plate and utensils and empty water bottle under the opposite seat. It seemed safer than having them up off the floor. Then he sat back as the plane fell and while the world was still dark on the far side of his western view he had a vast panorama of dawn to inspect if he gazed out the east-facing window across the slim aisle.

The approaching ground grew details of boulders and bushes then some of those bushes became sparse, stunted trees. The plane bumped and rolled on a stripe of runway almost the same drab shade as the ground on either side of it and when it came to a stop the tail-tip of that fuselage raised on its landing gear was the tallest point in the landscape.

Oscar waited, then after the plane had gone a few minutes without moving he unbuckled his belt but stayed in the chair. Another minute or two after that he heard the thunk of the cabin door unsealing and opening behind him and a pilot's cap was followed by a pilot's head and shoulders into the space.

"Okay," that head announced, "this is you." Then the pilot grabbed Oscar's duffel bag full of brand new cold weather gear and dragged it off the plane, so Oscar rose from his seat, gathered his phone and envelope, and followed his bag through the door. As soon as he'd stepped to the ground the pilot was closing the door behind him.

Here?" Oscar asked, turning his head to take in the nothing that spread outward in every direction, still shadowed as the sunlight he'd watched creeping across the landscape from above hadn't quite made its way there.

"Here's what I was paid for," said the pilot over a shoulder as he moved quickly back to the nose of the plane where the cockpit door stood open. He pulled himself up and in with a hand on either side of the hole, then an arm came back out to pull the door closed and almost right away the airplane was moving again, taxiing down the runway while Oscar's eyes watered in the dust cloud it kicked up.

He walked off the runway with a hand over his nose and mouth, hauling his duffel bag, and it was only a matter of seconds before the plane raced over the spot where he'd been standing. It lifted from the ground, pulled up its landing gear, and was gone— well, it rose for a while before banking sharply and turning away to the south, so he could still watch for a while but as far as it mattered to Oscar once the plane left the ground it was gone.

Or he was gone, to look at it that way: left alone by the faded, cracked tarmac with a bag full of cold weather gear though the weather here (where?) was warmer than it had been at the strange customs station. He took in what looked like a pale desert of gravel in every direction, the stunted trees and stubby bushes and a few barely-green bleached tufts of grass all bent to one side like they'd spent their whole lives in strong wind, though at that moment the air was still.

Oscar sat down on his bag, a firm seat with all those thick layers of insulation and fabric packed in it. He unzipped the duffel and—wondering why he hadn't thought of it sooner—slid the envelope into the bag between the folds of his new parka where it would stay safe and flat. Then he pulled out his phone to check the time which didn't tell him anything, really, except it was early. So he checked for location and it was somewhere beyond his phone's map, and the weather app was no help, either, because it couldn't find any information about his location, then he realized it wasn't that his phone couldn't find anything about where he was but rather it couldn't find a network to ask in that no man's land of modernity.

But there was an airstrip and there was Oscar so he must have been somewhere, at least.

He thought of the crew of the *Fram*, intentionally freezing themselves into the ice, feeling it squeeze their ship tighter each day but at least they knew it was coming. They'd planned for it, which was a far cry from the *Jeannette* frozen equally fast but without intention. He'd often imagined them, those men on *Jeannette* and Lieutenant Commander DeLong at the helm, gone north to look for the lost ship *Vega* only to get lost themselves. They would have seen the ice coming, creeping and grinding up to their hull as it did for Nansen and the crew of the *Fram*, but without preparation, without planning ahead, without laying in supplies for a long overwinter, without knowing Wend would revise their fates in his files years later. Unlike Nansen's men, the crew of the *Jeannette* had been dropped in the Arctic—as Oscar himself had been now—without expecting to stay and without knowing quite where or quite why or quite what to do with their time.

Alive, yes, but without knowing for how long or what purpose or what was lurking out of sight on the ice. How long could any man survive without inuring himself, without preparing his soul to receive so much nothing? That's what separated the professionals, the great men, from everyone else, the ranks of amateurs. The men of *Fram* had that advantage, their months of training for what must have seemed like a lifetime of stasis. That practice must have made all the difference.

It was no wonder Wend had taken up the *Jeannette* as his

secret endeavor. No wonder he'd worked so hard to bring home that lost ship, to reclaim those overwhelmed, lonely men from the ice. Oscar, at least, had his duffel of parka and goggles and boots. More than at least, though: at most. The most of the actual Arctic he'd ever beheld in his life.

But was it the Arctic, he wondered. Had he arrived, had he crossed 66°33' north?

No, he couldn't have; the airstrip must still be subarctic because it wasn't snow and it wasn't ice and it was more gray than white apart from a strip of the sky and some of the gravel that studded the ground, but it still wasn't even quite fall and maybe the snow hadn't come. Not this far south, however far south he was. The air was cool but not cold, without the winds he'd watched cut across the ice sheet of the Pole, and his forehead and armpits even felt sweaty, but how much of that was the air and how much the adjustment of his body from the cabin's pressure to the outside world, to the pressure of sitting alone in the middle of nowhere with only a bag full of gear he hadn't paid for and hadn't asked for and didn't need for the time being... who could say about any of that.

He remembered an afternoon in Puerto Rico on his honeymoon with Julia, when they'd taken a launch from their resort out to an island not so far offshore, too far to swim but not too far to see from the beach. They'd had lunch and a nap then walked a lap around as much of the island's mangrove tangle as they could circumnavigate before opting to drift in the strong current of a channel that ran through a branch-canopied tunnel at the core of the island, where flying fish leapt over and around and against their sunscreen-slick bodies, and that channel deposited them right back at the dock where the launch was due to retrieve them any time.

Any time came and any time went but the two of them didn't, they sat at the end of the dock with their empty containers from lunches packed by the resort's restaurant, with their masks and snorkels and towels, their useless room key around Julia's wrist on a springy rubber coil like phone cords used to be. Time went and went again and still they sat, the sky getting darker, their twenty toes raking the same furrowed fields of water under the lip of the dock, and they didn't talk about being stuck. They talked about other things—the *mofongo* they'd eaten for dinner the previous night, a horse mysteriously tied by the side of a road and the arkloads of chickens and dogs they'd spotted wandering free all over the island while driving around, and how far south they were (farther than Oscar had ever been) and that he was managing the heat fairly well. About who had done what at their wedding, already sticking in place the shared memories that would make up their own private album.

Hours passed without the boat being mentioned and then it arrived. They heard its tiny diesel engine churning somewhere out on the dark water, in the direction of the flickering lights of the resort and the shadowed forest around it. Then its two weak running lights came into view, one the captain's elastic-strapped headlamp and the other a flashlight duct-taped to the bow. They climbed aboard as soon as the boat bumped against the slim pier and though neither Oscar nor Julia spoke very much Spanish the captain was obviously apologizing with vigor, pointing at the engine with grease- and oil-stained arms, waving a wrench, so they nodded and smiled and assured him it was okay. Then they took seats on one of the two single plank benches that ran along the gunwales of the low open boat and held hands as they steamed back to shore and a dinner that turned out to be on the house because of the inconvenience they hadn't much suffered from that broken boat.

Though there still wasn't a signal and he didn't expect to find one for a while, Oscar texted his wife, "That afternoon on the dock in PR." He sent it and the phone reminded him it couldn't be sent but he trusted his words to head off into the world when they could; the phone would scan for and find a network on its own however long it might take. Then he went back to his current wait, by himself and without a resort across the water, without flying fish or a packed lunch, without Julia's hand in his own, only nothing across the nothing with nothing beyond it so far as he knew. He pictured himself as a pin stuck in the wall map in his own office far away back at BIP: stabbed into the smudges where something had been erased and redrawn and erased again several times.

Bored, he went through the bag, trying on the parka, the goggles, the boots, and he passed for an Arctic explorer in the ghostly reflection of his phone's screen. And that cheered him up for a while. As he repacked the gear he started to slide the envelope back into the folds of the parka then opened it instead, sliding the smaller inner envelope of strange paper out, the one to be read by Northern Branch only. Oscar slid a fingernail under its flap but he paused, took a breath, reminded himself what Peary or Nansen or Franklin would do: the mission was all. Honor was everything and the great men would do nothing in his circumstance so neither did he, returning one envelope to the other then both of them to the bag.

And he went back to the nothing, trying his hands in his pockets and his hands in his lap and his hands hanging limp at his sides, eyes open then closed. Left foot extended and right foot tucked in and bent at the knee followed by the reverse. He counted rocks and he counted bushes and he tried counting seconds to add up to minutes but when he added all of those up to an hour it felt a bit bleak so he stopped. After so much motion for the past couple of days Oscar's mind was still going and his body seemed to think it was, too, despite being stuck.

Far away to the north a dark spot shifted on the gray ground. Oscar rubbed his eyes then looked again and there it still was. A moment later the spot had grown larger and a moment or two after that he could see it was a man, or a person, at least: he couldn't be clear about gender at such a distance, he wouldn't want to assume.

He watched the body approaching in silhouette and the shape of a large pack on his (or her) shoulders took shape and so did the long barrel of a gun extending up and over one side. Oscar wasn't concerned by that, though: it was recommended to always carry a gun in the Arctic, to scare off the bears if you had to, and to feed yourself if things came to that, and once he recalled that advice he was more concerned that he *hadn't* been issued a gun, sitting by the airstrip alone as he was.

He watched the walker step toward him and raised an arm for a wave that wasn't returned. Then there was a sound from the west and he turned his head to see an ATV racing across the gray ground, bouncing over rocks and low hummocks, its beehive engine getting louder the closer it came until it swung to a stop beside Oscar and his duffel bag, just at the edge of the airstrip's worn paving.

There were no words on the vehicle for identification but the logo on the gas tank was one of BIP's, one of the stamps Oscar had seen on form after form after folder.

The driver grinned from deep within a rust-colored beard and corona of hair above the floral explosion on his Hawaiian shirt, the brightest splash on the landscape by far. He lifted old-fashioned flying goggles to his forehead, blinked a couple of times, and said, "Sorry I'm late. I saw the plane come in but had to get a machine working before I took off. Anyway, let's get you back to the branch."

He climbed off the ATV, revealing cut off jean shorts and old leather sandals, then shook Oscar's hand hard and tight but not in that macho competitive way, more like someone who hadn't shaken many hands for a while.

"I'm Clark," he said, lifting Oscar's bag onto a luggage rack that extended from the rear of the bike then strapping it down with hooked elastic cords.

"Oscar," said Oscar, climbing aboard at the back of the seat. He looked north again, where he'd seen the walker, intending to tell Clark about it, but the silhouette was gone. He wondered if he'd seen someone coming at all and said nothing in case the answer was no, then again maybe that was a body-shaped smudge lying down among those far away rocks?

But there wasn't time enough to be sure because already Clark was revving the engine and swinging the ATV's wheels to hum away to the west once again and Oscar was wedged between his new BIP colleague's bulky body and the bulk of his own gear at his back as they bounced toward something or somewhere he could only assume was out beyond his sight, out there somewhere in the nothing.

That man with a camera, as strange as the last group of southerners to pass over the ice—the ridiculous trinkets they offered for sealskins and furs, baubles and gewgaws that wouldn't get a man through a cool day in summer never mind cold winter depths. They thrust their shiny toys with wide-eyes, worked up as children finding their first clutch of edible eggs, as eager for a pat on the head.

Look what we have! Look how shiny, how new!

And that one, the camera-man, interrupting each act of the day with the stab of his lens, the rattling whir of his machine on its three wooden legs—a mechanical creature that couldn't walk let alone run, as impotent on the ice as its owner if Allakariallak and his family lost interest in humoring him. If hospitality wasn't their way.

Now, here, in that trading post where he had exchanged skins for tools many times—for his rifle, for bullets, for steel fishing hooks, a scarf for his wife so brightly colored it seared their eyes and had to be trailed from their sledge frame to wash out in the sun—here the camera-man mimed ridiculous things. Play with the phonograph, he suggested with wild gestures from behind the lens; crank its arm and marvel at its weak southern music. He urged his leading man—the movie star who wasn't an actor, whose name was unspeakable on southern tongues so would be shortened and changed for the sake of marquees, sparking an outbreak of Polar Fever in the form of picture albums and toys and ice cream bars, a blockbuster before anyone realized there was such a thing—to gawk pop-eyed as those earlier white men had done, to gawk with the void gaze of a seal fallen under the club. Then he took up a phonograph record behind the camera and pretended to bite it, to make a meal of its wax, of the sad songs contained in its grooves. He bounced from one foot to the other like a monkey Allakariallak had seen once in a book in that same trading post and despite himself the northerner couldn't keep from laughing inside his furs, he couldn't help taking up a phonograph disk of his own and testing it with his teeth to mock the man-child's routine. Around the room and just outside the camera's view, Allakariallak's family laughed as he popped out his eyes, played up the ruse of encountering music for the very first time, and asked without asking, "Who are these strange men from the south? Will they never grow into their bodies?"

The camera-man laughed along with him, set down his own disk and cranked grinding gears inside the machine until its brittle film ran through and pulled free. While the man rushed to prepare a new reel Allakariallak stood, inspected the shelves of the trading post's wares: the matches in boxes, the hats knitted with stripes, the rifles and whip-thin fishing rods. Amongst them all in a jumble of harpoon heads too old and worn out to be sharpened again he found a strip of sun-washed walrus bone on a strap of the same animal's hide, two oblong eye-shades bearing bleached umber marks he had not seen in years.

Those shades were his father's once, out on the ice where he had learned to hunt and to fish, to make a block home and a family. They were his father's when his father was lost with one of his uncles in a year so far back he hardly remembered it now, but he remembered those markings, those shades, and as one white man laughed by the cashbox and another laughed wrestling the mechanical beast with its insistent, intrusive glass eye, the hunter whose true name would soon be erased was no longer laughing. He saw his father's body out on the ice and saw pale fingers picking him free of his eye-shades and furs, releasing the last wisp of warmth from his long-frozen flesh. He saw southern boots leaving his father's whole story behind, trampling it with their own tales and bringing back no more than they could salvage for coins to be carried away. He saw his uncles a season ago in the same trading post, speaking into the horn of another man's phonograph, telling his family's stories in exchange for the convenience of foreign objects and he wondered—too little, too late—where those stories were taken and swallowed by what hungry ears.

In the corner of a forgotten warehouse, the corner most unmarked by years of rain through a high leaking roof and where the windows remained most intact, the hunter spread his blanket and tools. By daylight and then by the light of his elastic-strapped headlamp he worked, connecting wires to parts stripped from a digital clock. Packing and tamping powders and chemicals into sections of pipe. Capping and welding their ends.

He worked. Sometimes he slept. He crept out for food and for tools and for sections of wire when he needed them. He hardly spoke, the occasional thank you to some shop clerk or a sidewalk good morning returned when it had been offered first. It was more than he'd spoken on his way south to that city. More than he'd spoken since everyone he wanted to speak to was gunned down and buried and burned in his sight. In his scope. More than he'd spoken since watching those black helicopters depart, headed south, headed toward the same city where he now squatted or if not quite to this city then to a place with a direct line to its power brokers, to men who declared themselves great. Great enough to act on others' behalf.

Everything was tied to this city. Every command started here, every killing. Every drop of blood in the cold soil of what had been his village had been squeezed through the clean hands of this gleaming white town.

He'd brought that blood back to their doorstep.

He welded shut the last of his dark canisters, removed his head lamp and wiped his brow with a sleeve; the weather here had started to turn, finally. The air felt like fall, even like winter coming, but after years in the north it stung like high summer for him. The heat. The flames of the sun and the shimmer off acres of asphalt.

Car doors slammed outside. Something rattled in the industrial courtyard, someone coming, and the hunter moved animal-fast to stow his tools and his pipes and his sleeping bag, too, in the pile of beer cans and trash where they hid when he had to go out. He hid himself, too, under a green canvas tarp encrusted with mildew and mold, gnawed by rats but not so much it couldn't conceal him amongst old oil drums.

He waited. He listened and watched through a small hole in his filthy shawl.

Soldiers, official or not, one way or another; they wore uniforms, they held guns. They were men and women in pixelated gray camouflage who stirred piles of debris with their barrels and boots, pushed boxes aside and stood on their toes to look through the few glassblock windows that remained on the sills. They spoke into headsets to say they'd found nothing and other soldiers in other parts of the warehouse and its ruined grounds reported they'd found nothing, too.

So much nothing in the heart of that gleaming white city, he thought.

A phone rang and everything stopped. It rang again but not ringing, really, because instead of bells it played music his ears couldn't place. One soldier, a woman, apologized to her colleagues and reached into a pocket with the hand that wasn't holding her pistol. She pulled out a slim phone, looked at the screen, and laughed to herself before turning it off to slide it back under a flap, out of sight. The way her arm moved, the way her shoulder rolled, the hunter could tell she was injured—not a fresh wound but one still sore and healing on her shoulder or back, belied by her tentative motions as she made a point of ignoring the pain. He'd seen it before, in the caribou he hadn't shot cleanly and in other wounded animals, too.

The hunter waited out their invasion as he'd done before, from the ridge. He watched their anonymous mechanical work and assured himself this would be the last time he stood by. And the soldiers, those uniforms without insignia, made their sweep, made their notes and radioed in, before departing as empty-handed as they'd arrived. Leaving the hunter to pack his belongings, his sleeping bag and rifle and bombs, and creep through the evening toward one of the other locations he'd mapped for himself within a few blocks in case he had to leave this one behind in a hurry.

14

They weren't on the ATV very long but long enough to get where they were going. Long enough for Oscar's legs to be sore by the time they arrived; after hours of vibrations from train tracks and boat engines and airplane propellers preceding that bumpy ride, it's no wonder he felt it in thighs that quivered and knees that almost but not quite buckled when that final vehicle—he hoped, for a while, at least—stopped and he next stood up.

"Whoa," said Clark, catching Oscar's shoulder when he wobbled beside the parked but rattling vehicle. "Let's get you into a chair."

The bigger man hoisted the duffel bag onto one bare, hairy arm as he led Oscar away from the four-wheeler toward a squat cinderblock structure with a corrugated metal roof slanted away saltbox-style, and a long entryway that looked like a miniature version of the same building turned perpendicular and stuck to the front of itself, offering up a bright orange door. A Quonset hut stood nearby, twice as tall and twice as long as its boxy neighbor, its rounded roof bent and buckled in places and with some obvious, angular bulges along its walls as if something had tried once to smash a way out. A tall spire of antenna rose between the two buildings, surrounded by a chest-high cinderblock wall inset with a gate, and heavy black cables ran from connections at different heights on the mast to boxes on one wall of the hut while still others snaked down the sides of the tower and, it seemed, into the ground. Oscar couldn't be sure but thought he heard those cables humming though it may have been the ATV's engine still in his ears.

"Home sweet home!" announced Clark, knocking the door open with a sandaled foot. It swung inward, Oscar noticed, and he wondered how many misguided shelters had been built during the Arctic summer with an outward opening door only to be rendered useless by winter's first snow. How many dwellings became deathtraps instead, their inhabitants as stuck in the ice as the men of the *Jeannette*? He was able to pass through the door at his full height but Clark had to duck low behind him to enter the narrow space. Benches and boot racks stood along the floor on both sides and parkas and coveralls on hooks and pegs draped the walls and the narrow windows running the length of the tunnel.

"I've got an envelope for you," Oscar said in the tunnel, turning halfway around so he would be heard. "A delivery from BIP. That's why I'm here, I…"

"Later, later!" said Clark, dropping the duffel bag on the lefthand bench and pushing Oscar forward with a large hand.

Another door stood at the far end—dark green instead of the outer door's orange, a solid door without a window—and Oscar moved toward it then opened it without being asked. Even before he'd passed through that inner doorway into the hut proper he heard, "Oscar! You're here!"

There was Alexi, legs splayed under a table at one side of the room, eating forkfuls of corned beef from a can while three empty chairs looked on. He didn't get up but waved hello with his fork. "What happened to you?"

"What happened to you?" countered Oscar, dropping himself into a chair across from his no longer absentee partner. "How'd you get here? You went into that store… I thought you'd still be in Portland, or gone back to BIP."

"Oh, that store! What a nice little place. Look what I got…" Alexi set down the can—but not the fork—to fish in a pocket, his body writhing as he worked all its corners. "Never mind, it's in my other pocket. I'll show you later."

Something clattered behind Oscar and he turned to take in

the rest of the room, temporarily overlooked in the surprise of seeing Alexi. The far corner was devoted to a kitchenette where Clark was now filling an electric kettle from a big stainless steel sink set into a stainless steel counter that stretched around the whole corner. Open wirework shelves held plates and bowls and multiple layers of boxes and cans, bags of pasta and dried beans and soup, tea tins and coffee cans and sauces and dressings galore. Transparent plastic canisters held sugar and flour (Oscar assumed, what else could two white powders in those quantities be?) while a pair of massive deep freezes stood under the counter on tracks to let them slide forward for access, and beside all of that the runty avocado green refrigerator, with an old-fashioned latching handle and the kitchen appliance equivalent of tail fins gracing its sides, looked—despite being pristine—very much out of place. An island stood in the L of the counter, making a second L of its own pointed into the room, and it hosted the stove and a microwave and tiers of drawers.

At one end of that island and bearing a beer company's logo stood a bright yellow semi-transparent inflatable palm tree with a sand-filled base of the kind Oscar had seen at bars, years before, though not the sort of bars he preferred, and beside it a pair of pink plastic flamingoes. They didn't make sense in the setting but they did match the huge travel posters advertising Hawaii and Jamaica and other tropical destinations hanging on several stretches of wall, not to mention Clark's shirt, and they went with the posters of shirtless men in swimsuits, too, he supposed.

Another corner had its own L of bunk beds built into the walls with drawers nested in their wooden frames, two pairs so four beds, but only one of them was made up, more or less, with a thick sleeping bag spread across it; the others had only linens and pillows stacked atop bare mattresses. And the final corner of the multipurposeful room was filled with a hole—the opening of a stairwell, to be more precise—railed off on three sides. A large metal hatch apparently intended to cover the opening had been removed altogether, its brackets and buckles complemented by matching ones at the lip of the hole, and it leaned against a wall not quite out of the way.

Clark raised a hand with three white mugs dangling from it, the thick-walled slightly concave kind you might get in any restaurant that served coffee. He asked, "Yes?"

Alexi nodded with a mouthful of corned beef and Oscar, confused for a moment then deciding whatever it was would be in a mug so probably coffee or tea both of which sounded good at the moment, and how long ago it seemed that he hadn't gotten to brew those grounds in their plastic tub confiscated or purloined or just plain forgotten by that Canadian(?) customs official, if that's what he had been, said, "Yes, please."

He turned back to Alexi amidst the sounds of Clark scooping and mixing coffee and whistling to himself at the counter. "Really, how did you get here?" he asked. "I got on a boat, then another, and…" He paused, expecting his partner to react, but Alexi went on eating and humming around the tines of tinned meat—and it sounded like the same wandering tune Clark was whistling—so Oscar went on. "I mean, there was an airplane, this building where they gave me cold weather gear, this woman with nachos…"

And it was that detail, of course, the food, at which Alexi raised his eyebrows: his mouth still too full to speak but his one track mind, his all-consuming appetite, suddenly took an interest in Oscar's story. A sound with only a passing similarity to the word "nachos" bubbled up through the mud of his mouth but Oscar, already well versed in his new partner's limitations, knew what it was; he would have known what Alexi was saying had he not bothered speaking at all once the nachos were in conversational play.

"Yes, but that's not the important part of the story," he said and though his partner's attention drifted back to the fork Oscar kept talking. "She knew about BIP. At least, I think she did. I couldn't quite tell what she knew or who she was or… but there was a gun, a man holding a gun, back in Portland and that's why I ran away while you were in the store. He was chasing me. With a gun! Chasing me! I'm pretty sure it was the same man we saw back in Boston, remember? Following you in the station, and I think I'd seen him before, on…"

But no one was listening so Oscar gave up. He closed his eyes for a few seconds, imagining the dark behind them to be the dark of the Pole on his screen. Then he came south again to that room perhaps in the Arctic or perhaps not, a precise location as hard to determine so far as it had been through centuries of seafaring risk. Alexi scraped the bottom of the can with his fork, making an awful noise Oscar felt in his teeth. Clark had moved from whistling to singing though the words were unclear; at first Oscar thought the lyrics weren't English, then decided Clark didn't know the real words so was just making sounds.

There was no point telling himself any more of a story he already knew so instead he pulled out his phone. It was impulse, he'd forgotten for a moment there was no longer a signal, and now somehow there was: the dead zone of the airstrip wasn't all that far away but here, in the hut, his phone was rearing to go. Champing at the bytes until it chirped, desperately, as it must have been doing for some time unnoticed, because while its signal was strong its battery was weak and isn't that always the way. Then it died altogether leaving only a glossy black window in its wake. Which seemed predictable, really: a signal regained, a battery lost… Oscar was having that kind of day. And he'd had that sort the day before, too.

He shook it as if that might help. He pushed the power button a few times, trying both short jabs and long depressions to no avail. So he turned toward the kitchenette where his host had hoisted three mugs in two hands—favoring, to Oscar's surprise, a pyramid method including a jug of cream and bowl of sugar on top rather than the more typical side by side triangular service—

and holding his phone up asked, "Clark, do you have a charger?"

"Hm... let's see what you've got there..." From deep in his beard he squinted at the dormant phone while approaching the table, then after setting down the mugs, cream, and sugar with a surprising degree of grace lifted the device from Oscar's still outstretched hand. "Hey, I like this case," he said, but the exaggerated creases of plastic woodgrain were no match for the dark seams in Clark's calloused hand. Oscar quelled his impulse to grab the phone back as Clark eyed it, rolling the device over one way then the other, inspecting each button and port. "I'm sure I can bang something up."

"Do you have it? The right one?"

Clark waved the phone back and forth—a bit precariously for Oscar's liking—and said, "Right ones, wrong ones, it's all relative up here, Oscar. We can't run out to the store so if you don't have the parts you're after, well..." He rotated the phone close to his face to peer into the metallic groove of its charging socket and pulled at the case to improve his view. "You make it work with what you do have. I've got a couple of plugs I can squeeze in here. No worries."

But Oscar was worried, to see his phone—his steady link to Julia, to home, to the Pole, the one thing he had left of himself after these two (or three?) whirlwind days—handled so roughly and promised such casual insertions (and had he just heard something snap?). "If it's not the right one," he said, "I can wait."

Clark laughed a deep Santa laugh, or the laugh of the deep drunken sailor Santa had always struck Oscar as: a jolly old drunk who distracts from what matters about the North Pole. "You can wait... that's a good one, O. You sure would wait." And he went on muttering and chuckling to himself as he picked at the phone's charging port with a long but clean thumbnail.

"Let's get you knocked up," he told the phone before clanging away down the stairs. The clanging seemed to come from all over, for a second, echoing oddly, before Oscar realized it was both Clark's feet on the stairs and nearer at hand Alexi's last efforts to fork the can clean. At last, corned beef accomplished, he dropped the spent can to the table with a loud, hollow thunk.

"So," said Alexi as he pushed his chair back and stood up. "Let's get to work."

"Right. It's in my bag, I'll just..." Oscar got up and moved toward the door and his duffel bag out in the tunnel.

"What's in your bag?"

"The envelope. Did you think I'd lost it? That was the whole point of our coming. Of putting ourselves through all this."

"What envel... oh, right. That envelope. Wow, you still have it?"

"Of course I do. I wouldn't come all this way not to do my job, Alexi. Would you?" and as soon as the question was out of his mouth Oscar wondered why he'd bothered to ask. "What else did you mean by 'get to work'?"

"That's just a thing people say, isn't it? I was done with my beef, I was getting up, so you know... 'to work!' So, let's get to work." He clomped down the stairs without holding the railing, into the hole, leaving Oscar no choice but to follow. No choice in the world but to descend.

15

Oscar had to pause at the bottom of the stairs to take it all in: what had seemed a small shack from outside and even from the upper room was revealed as something much larger, a wide open space with corridors and doorways branching this way and that, a hub offering portals for movement in many directions, an overwhelming number of possible paths. He clutched a dark newel post while looking around and said, "It's bigger than I thought it would be."

"It always is," answered Clark and Alexi nodded, so either he'd been to the basement already or he wasn't surprised. "Mostly I just use a couple of rooms, though, so I suppose I've cut the place down to my size. That's how we do, right? If something's too big or too complicated we ignore the parts we don't need. Out of sight, out of mind. Otherwise… Jesus, I suppose I'd go crazy up here thinking about all the distance and me sharing my home with more empty space than anything else. Tough to get your head around the size of the Arctic without ignoring the things that don't fit."

Clark had approached the door to a big, square cage of black metal that filled the center of the room, but after speaking he paused with his fingertip frozen on the keypad upon which he'd tapped out part of an entry code. Like he'd given himself something to think about. Oscar almost asked if he was alright but Clark said, "Damn," before shaking his head and punching the last of the digits. "Gave myself a moment there."

Inside the cage a cluster of servers hummed and hundreds

of tiny lights blinked in many colors. The whir of fans filled the space with a wind that seemed not so much to move as just hang in the air. The towers and racks were different sizes and heights, mostly black or close to it but with varying details and trims, and the whole display looked to Oscar like a miniature city behind a fence. The door to the cage stood open now, and inside sat a small desk bearing a computer terminal flanked by a stained coffee cup and a tiny red figurine of the Buddha on a minuscule dais.

"What is all this?" Oscar asked.

"This is the Northern Branch," Clark told him. "This is the permanent record. Well… 'permanent.' You know. You work here, too."

"So it's true. We always thought…"

"You didn't know?" asked Alexi, poking at some of the buttons and lights on a server through the mesh of the cage.

"You did? How would you know anything after two weeks? What… No, I mean… we've always said the database was kept at Northern Branch but I thought it was a joke about how slow the computers are. That they take so long to load something—anything—it must be coming from here."

Clark laughed. "It's not quite that simple but you aren't far off. All of this is a backup of what's in DC. Or that's a backup of this. To tell you the truth, I don't know which comes first in the chain." He picked up the dirty mug, gave it a sniff, and set it down again on the desk, all while holding the fresh, steaming cup from upstairs in his other hand. "Everything's in there, everything you folks down south have come up with and filed away. All the originals, too—if you change something, the version you replace is still kept up here. The data, I mean. I don't have any paper, though Wend told me…"

"You knew Wend?"

"Oh, sure. He was my trainer, rest his soul."

"I didn't know that. I took his place at BIP. I didn't know he was dead. I mean, I assumed, but…"

Clark nodded, unsurprised.

He moved from the entry to the cage, but held the door open with his foot, and Oscar leaned in to look at the servers. "Go ahead," Clark told him. "Poke around. You won't break anything. Probably. Well, you could, but not by looking. So maybe don't touch anything."

Oscar stepped in and the heat of the towers rose to greet him. Some of the machines were as tall as he was or close to it, and he thought he felt waves of electricity rippling back and forth between the dark boxes. He thought he felt its tingle across the hairs on his arms and the back of his neck but it might have been the wind of all those cooling fans or just the heat.

Then he wondered if "machines" was even the word: did a machine need to have moving parts all amounting to something? Weren't they defined by motion to make something happen? So what to call this, these... devices in which nothing moved (not counting fans, which weren't the point of the server) except pulses and streams of data and current, a vast database of parts waiting to be put in something that wasn't quite motion. Nothing moving but somehow producing heat all the same; he was almost ashamed by how little knew of electricity and how the world works, of what his phone was actually doing when he called his wife thousands of miles away.

He remembered Robert Flaherty's camera and movie making equipment, always frozen and its genuine moving parts crippled by cold while he tried to shoot *Nanook of the North* so he could carry those images home to show curious eyes in the south. The elements he'd had to endure and get his canned reels of film through so the moviegoing public could see those iconic moments of seal hunting and Nanook's introduction to phonograph music in the trading post. Oscar wondered if these servers, these maybe-machines, would also suffer from cold or thrive in it like those room-sized computers he'd seen in old photographs and TV clips that always made a point of saying how cold the rooms housing them had to be kept and how much bigger computers would be in the future.

He laid a hand on the metal case around one of the towers and the heat was strong but not painful. The whole unit vibrated and Oscar thought of the colleges and spoonworks and bauxite mines he'd created from his basement office at BIP, he thought of Slotkin's unlikely Ellesmere Island beachfront resort and of Symmes' Hole and the new settlement the hunters there had just discovered before he and Alexi came north. All of those, his years of work and he assumed all the work done before his own time by Slotkin and Dimchas and Rudnik and Wend—who had somehow found his way here!—all of it humming inside these machines. Or whatever they were. None of it with any form, any shape, just… what, he wondered, numbers? Was it binary code? Something else? It wasn't iron filings lined up in order or the celluloid frames of Flaherty's film, and it wasn't grooves like the phonograph records Peary brought north on his ship.

It was the work of Oscar's life reduced to the vibrations and heat of a tower roughly the size of himself and buzzing away in some other basement than the one where he worked. He pictured the journals left behind by Peary and Byrd and Amundsen, leather-bound volumes stained and wrinkled by voyages, ripped and stitched and ripped again then copied and typeset and published and read, and here was his own contribution: a buzzing that made hairs stand up on his arms. Less tangible, less visible, than the glow of the lightbulb he'd left behind in his office but perhaps, if these servers had the longevity BIP seemed to inspire in its equipment, just as fast.

Efficient, and persevering.

His work had traveled even when he stayed still. While he slept, while his fingers crept across the yellow spines of his *National Geographic* magazines and he chose an old volume to read and reread, while he rode the Metro and sat on his porch and stood at half-attention in Director Lenz' office. While he failed and gave up on crossing the white tundra of bedsheets between his own body and Julia's in the dark… through all that his work had zipped back and forth between home and away, between north and south, between the fingers he typed it all with and whatever was done with it here.

Oscar couldn't quite tell if his life had taken on more or less weight with this discovery but he could tell its mass had somehow changed, like Frankenstein's monster—another man driven north, you might even say dragged, like Oscar himself—moved from one side of things to another by an electrical current without quite knowing which side was which.

"Not a bad set up, eh?" Clark asked from the other side of the cage, pulling Oscar out of the stream and reminding him he wasn't alone.

"Yes, really impressive."

Beyond Clark, off in a corner of the large room, Alexi dug through a bin of spare parts. He held a donut-sized gear to his eye and peered through the center then rotated it to squint along the line of its teeth. Oscar watched his partner turn the gear toward himself, as if it was rolling, his grin getting larger and more beatific the longer it turned.

"But," he asked Clark, "what do you actually do with it all? I mean, what's your job in all this, that you have to be here? I've known there was a Northern Branch for years but I've never heard anything about what you do."

Clark dug a hand into his mane and rocked from one flip-flopped foot to the other. "What do I do… mostly I make sure the servers keep running. I've got this little fella"—he reached in to pat the terminal on his desk the way someone else might a dog—"and he tells me when there's a problem. Something's not backing up, a file's corrupt, hardware failures. The usual things but a bit trickier without an office supply store around." He pulled three fingertips through the snarls of his beard and looked at the ceiling. "That's about it."

"Doesn't it get, I don't know… boring, maybe? No offense."

Clark gave him a clap on the back. "None taken! But no, never boring. Some days I get an email from Director Lenz…"

"You know Director Lenz, too?"

"Oh, well, sure. We both work for him, don't we?" Clark wove a thick hand through the mesh of the cage door and swung it a bit while he talked.

"I hadn't thought about it. He's never said."

"He wouldn't though, would he? Doesn't say much but the usual Tuesday afternoon pep talk."

"Ours are Monday mornings," Oscar said through the door as it moved toward his face, then away.

"Right. So sometimes he gives me an order, above and beyond. To erase something, mostly."

"The data?"

"I'm the only one who can. I can't change anything, and I can't read it, but this is the only terminal able to delete any files. Yours can only put data in and mine can only take data out. I could crash the whole thing if I felt like it." He laughed. "Not that I would! I'm not supposed to know but poking around in the database a few months ago I accidentally figured out how. There's a bug in there that could wipe the whole map. Someone should probably fix it. It can't be done from up here, the fixing I mean, but if the wrong people found out… you know."

Clark got quiet and Oscar pictured the map taking up a whole wall of his office back in DC, and how much of it was marred and blurred by old erasures.

"Sometimes I envy you guys down south, roaming all over the Arctic while I'm stuck here in this cage." Clark let go of the door a bit to scratch his beard and it swung closed on its own, latching into place with first a loud thunk then a buzz from the keypad and lock. "Whoops, locked you in there. Hang on."

"Why?"

"Hm?" Clark punched a few numbers and the door buzzed

again when a light on the lock changed from red to green.

Oscar pushed the door open and held it that way with a foot. "Why? Why such a system?"

Clark laughed. "Ours is not to wonder why..." Then he looked toward the corner where Alexi was tapping the gear he'd found against a canister of some sort. "Whoa, buddy...," Clark said, rushing over. He took the canister from Alexi's hands and told him, "You don't want to do that. Or BOOM!"

"Ah," said Alexi, and he went right back to digging in the big bin of parts.

Oscar had come out of the cage and walked over to the others. "What's all this?" he asked Clark, nodding toward the bin.

"Some of it's a truck. A couple of snowmobiles in there. A windmill, I think, unless I've used all of that."

"Used it for what?"

His grin went supernova within its own whiskered corona. "I'll show you!" Before Oscar or Alexi could say anything else Clark was charging away toward one of the corridors branching off from the server room, so they followed because what else could they do?

They found him in a small room to the right of the hallway, a room ringed with shelves and bins and buckets of parts, wood and metal and leather and cardboard, sprockets and pipes and planks. Two massive workbenches stood back to back in the center, piled with tools and scraps, and in the middle of it all a dented silver orb sprouted a headful of stripped copper wires.

"My workshop," Clark announced, standing by the workbenches with his arms wide, a bishop welcoming the flock to his cathedral. Oscar and Alexi turned to take it all in, looking up toward the ceiling where a glider made from old nylon tents and their aluminum poles hung beside a dogsled framed partly in metal and partly in wood. "What do you think?"

"Wow," said Alexi.

"What do you make?" Oscar asked.

"Oh, whatever I can. Whatever I feel like, I guess. Mostly I find the parts, pile 'em up, rearrange 'em sometimes, and eventually they look like something so I put it together. Sometimes it's something I need...," he rooted around in a pile at the end of one bench before pulling out a cobbled together device with a pie plate flat at one end of a long handle and a small circular speaker up top, "like this metal detector I came up with after dropping the snowmobile keys outside. And sometimes it's just because I have the parts." He nodded toward the wire-coiffed sphere, which perhaps wasn't a bomb after all, so that's a relief.

"It's a hobby," Clark said, "but it's important, too. Like I said about your phone, I can't run out to the store. And no one delivers even if I could get online. So I have to make most things myself. Fortunately, the parts have piled up through the years." He laughed. "As you can probably tell. But... oh, you'll like this one, Oscar." He dove into an apothecary cabinet with dozens of drawers, half-mumbling, half-singing to himself as he searched.

"About my phone...," Oscar asked, an eye to the rectangular lump in Clark's back pocket. "We were going to charge it?"

"Here we are!" Clark turned, holding a green brass buckle attached to a withered, cracked strap of leather. "This," he said, extending the offering in the wide cradle of his grease-stained, callused palms, "is from Nansen's pack."

The air left Oscar's lungs. "For real?"

Clark nodded.

"May I...," Oscar asked, raising his own clean, soft hand, and his host laid the artifact in it. It was light, barely there after the ravages of time and weather, but Oscar felt its heft throughout his whole body—as electric as his hand on the server had been, the closest he'd come to one of the greats.

"But Nansen was never here. I mean, I don't think so, wherever we are."

"No, he wasn't. But things have a way of moving up north, don't they? Think about his ship. *Fram*, right? Frozen in place on purpose so it could drift around the Pole without sailing and without fighting the ice. Without wasting energy to chart its own course. Everything's that way up here. Everything moves by sitting still: old tools, lost gloves, bits of native sculpture, whatever gets dropped won't stay where it falls. Or where it falls won't stay where it was, because places move, too. Even the Pole does a dance. It's the best way to get around sometimes, I'd say. Wait for whatever you're after to come to you. Hold fast and go slow."

"Fast as a lightbulb," Alexi said from the workbench where he had his back to the others and was clattering around in a box.

"What the hell does that mean, anyway?" Clark asked. "Director Lenz says it pretty much every Tuesday."

But Oscar was too rapt to answer as he fingered the sliver of brass tongue in the buckle, worn away by the years but he imagined he could still see the fingerprints of Fritjof Nansen, adjusting his pack to ride high on his shoulders as he set out for another day's skiing. He pictured that buckle pulled free by the claws of a polar bear narrowly missed, a swipe at the explorer's shoulder and a bloody end staved off by quick thinking and— more so—fast action, whatever that action had been. The action of a great man among the great men.

"Pretty cool, huh?"

Oscar nodded, in thrall.

"I thought you'd like that. And think of it, here we are, a century later—more than that—and the bits and bobs of those old expeditions are still floating around all over up here. Little scraps of old equipment to pick up and make part of our own. It's like whole big damn place is our database, right? Like in there." He nodded toward the other room. "And all we have to do is run the right query and put together the parts we need for whatever we're trying to do. Think about that, Oscar."

He laid a hand on the smaller man's shoulder and added, "Of course, half the fun's finding whatever you're after, and the other half's finding what you didn't know you were after along the way, the more exciting left behind bit of junk sitting on top of the junk you thought you were looking for. *Ikiaqqivik*, you know?"

"Hm?"

"*Ikiaqqivik*, moving through layers? Like shaman track down ancestors or lost spirits of vanished animals when the hunt is bad across, you know, time or dimensions or whatever you want to call it? Digging through the past and the present and the future too, maybe, through everything there ever was to find what you're after or maybe what you didn't know you were after. And when the Inuit needed a word for the internet—I love this—when it arrived in the north, they called it *ikiaqqivik*, too, like this invention, this cutting edge of the future, wasn't a new thing at all but just what they'd always been doing."

"Wow."

"Right? It bugs me about the BIP database sometimes, you know? That I can get straight to what I'm after, no stumbling along the way, no surprises… it's faster that way, I suppose, but no happy accidents either."

"Are you going to use it?" asked Oscar, but Clark had drifted off the way he had earlier, so Oscar had to ask him again.

"I hope so. Some day. But it's hard." The buckle and its strap lay in Oscar's palm between them as he went on. "I need to make it part of just the right thing. I don't want to waste it on something dumb so I'm saving it." He lifted the canvas strap end between two fingers, leaving the weight of the buckle still in Oscar's hand. "I'm afraid when I use it once I may not be able to change my mind. There are parts here I've recombined dozens of time, putting them on something and taking them off, mixing them around and seeing what works. But this one… it's special, you know?"

"I know. Believe me, I know."

They stood for a moment, each holding an end of the artifact, while Alexi went on rummaging. When he laughed, the other men looked up to see him wearing a pair of Inuit snow goggles, a thin strip of bone with two slits to cut down on glare off the ice and prevent snow blindness.

"Oh, geez, I forgot about that old thing," said Clark. "Popped up out of the ice one day, too. Not much use now, though, is it? Sunglasses have come a long way." Alexi flipped the visor or goggles or glasses or whatever they deserve to be called on his face, so left became right and right left.

"Okay," Clark said, "let's see about that phone. Then he moved beside Alexi at the bench, pulled up a cardboard carton from a shelf underneath, and began hauling out cords and plugs and connectors. Alexi looked around the room through the goggles, tilting his head this way and that to get different views, and Oscar held Nansen's strap and buckle a few seconds longer then returned them to the drawer Clark had left open in the chaos of the apothecary cabinet, laying it flat on the clean wood inside with both of his hands, an offering up of some kind, then he slid the drawer closed with a whisper and hush.

Behind him, he heard a clack as Alexi tossed the bone eyeshades down and asked if there was any more coffee upstairs.

His eyes had never quite been the same and the world never again quite so clear, not after the snowblindness he'd squinted through all the way home from the Pole, all the way back to New York where he was dismissed without so much as a glass of champagne. All that white, all of that glaring whiteness, left its mark on his eyes and now sometimes they watered and sometimes they dried but the result of each was the same. He'd blinked his way through these last years as if everything he encountered took him by surprise at an age by which he'd seen so much nothing could.

He still felt the absence of touch where the Commander dropped fifty parting dollars into his hand. He still sees the man's famous fingers, even more pale after months on the ice, dancing over his own dark palm like the money between them was no more than change tossed to some monkey grinder. The Commander hadn't addressed him for a long time by then, not since he'd dared to point out that by sending him ahead as a scout the Commander had ceded his claim to be first at the Pole. That he, the sidekick, the help, had been first to stand on the top of the world.

And he'd watched the newspaper arguments rage over which expedition leader had reached the Pole first, Peary to some minds and Cook to others, but while both men built careers on their failure he was invited to build nothing on his success.

There in the Explorer's Club, ensconced in its rich wooden walls still scented with the jungles and forests that gave up the lumber—Borneo, Alaska, the Amazon basin—he stood before rows of white faces, heavy with mustaches and serious eyes. Portrait after portrait, scowl after scowl, an overgrown jury with its gaze on him in the box of life back in the south. Back at home, so to speak, or so had been spoken but rarely by him.

A rare benefactor, a member of the club who recognized at least quietly that wrong had been done, had delivered him into those exclusive chambers on his coattails that day before rushing off to lunch with more suited companions, leaving the man who was first at the Pole on his own once again. Leaving him to these portraits, these peers if only they'd know it. Leaving him to blink at the space between two ornate frames where his own face belonged, between one white face and another, beside the Commander and before him, perhaps. And all those other spaces between other frames, whose portraits, too, deserved an insertion? How many Iroquois, Navajo, Cree...how many Maasai and Pygmy, and how many Eskimaux like those guides who set foot at the Pole when he did, their outcast pack topping the world in tandem to await the arrival of their trailblazing leader.

Those empty margins could go on forever, filling with faces whose portraits had never been painted or photographed once, and he was tempted if only for one passing moment to draw a pencil from his vest pocket and sketch his own face on that wall in light marks, easy enough for other eyes to overlook but dark enough he would know it was there. He was tempted and temptation may have given over to action the way it does and it must in great men had he not been interrupted by a porter's footsteps at his side, by the face of a younger man his own hue, asking, "Sir, are you meant to be here?"

16

Later on and back at the table, Oscar and Clark drank another cup of coffee and ate some brownies Clark had baked the evening before, during the hours Oscar spent adrift in the plane if he'd pieced the timing together correctly. Alexi was downstairs again, puttering with those buckets of parts he'd been so taken by, unaware food was being eaten above.

Nearby, on the kitchen island, Oscar's phone charged through a tangle of loose wires pulled from another phone's charger, stripped at the ends, and connected one at a time to the tiny pins and leads in the phone's socket. Oscar couldn't help sneaking a glance every so often as he and Clark talked but the hack seemed to be working: the charging icon on his phone was alight, the outline of a battery filling and refilling with bars of energy and the assurance of future connection.

"Think of it," Clark said, "all that data. The whole Arctic, everything we've learned over the last, what, one hundred years? Longer? And all of it humming away downstairs. Wild."

"Seems like a lot of pressure, keeping that safe."

"Like I said, there's a backup. I think. Or this is the backup. But yeah, sometimes it is. Crash that, wipe it all out, and it's the whole world. Well, not the whole world, but the world up here. The world I've spent my life thinking about, anyway."

"Me, too," Oscar said. "It's always been the Arctic for me. I've always looked north."

"God, yes. How could anyone not, right? It's the best thing about this job, maybe, not having to be reminded how little other folks know. How little they care. Even my…well, it's hard to find someone who gets it, you know?"

"I do," Oscar said. "I really do."

"Up here I've got nothing but north. Nothing to remind me the world has moved on, or thinks it has. You and I know they'll be back, am I right?"

Oscar nodded. "Sure they will. Once they really get desperate for oil, unfortunately. Or figure out a good way to get it from under the ice."

"Or, for fuck, climate change and what it would…do you think about that? If there's enough of a melt for everyone to start moving north, to make it the same as the south? What that would mean for guys like us?"

"Don't get me started."

"You and me both, O. You and me both." Clark took a sip of his coffee and sighed. "I was reading the other night about the Soviets, right? About Stalin and his five year plans. I'm no fan of Uncle Joe, don't the wrong idea, but man. What he did in Siberia. Not the gulags and that shit but the scale of it all. And just by deciding he would. That the country would, I mean. He made up the outcome and everyone else had to make it come true. He said we'll reach the North Pole and someone had to come up with an icebreaker or a plane that could do it. He knew they could, he trusted his people, and again, O., don't think I like Stalin, he was a bastard, of course, but he said, 'Russia's a big fucking place and somebody here is going to know how to do what I want.' Like the database, right? It's all in there, the whole story, you just have to figure out the way to ask a question to make the right parts fit together. Stalin, at least, knew what questions to ask to make all the parts come together." He watched his coffee steam, both broad hands wrapped around the white mug. "Man."

"That's what we do," Oscar said. "That's what BIP's all about."

"But we don't make it *happen*. We make it true, sure. We make it the map. But we don't make it happen, O. I'm not saying we should. We couldn't. Who'd pay for that now? But you can't help wondering, right?"

"No. You can't help wondering. I can't."

"Making something out of nothing. That's something."

The two of them sipped coffee at the same time, bringing their mugs back to the table together.

"Hey," Clark said, "you want something stronger in that?" He was already rising from his chair before Oscar had time to answer.

"But it's work hours."

"In which time zone?" Clark laughed. He pulled a bottle of Scotch from a shelf of various whiskeys and rums above the kitchen counter and brought it back to the table. "You're in the north now," he said, pouring a generous dram into first Oscar's mug then his own before setting the bottle between them, uncorked. "Cheers!"

"Cheers," Oscar said, clinking his mug against Clark's and, what the hell, having a drink. Clark was right: he was in the north. He was sure Nansen and Peary and even Franklin snuck a warming drop or two of their own. No atheists in foxholes or teetotalers at the North Pole, not that it was so cold outside.

"I thought there'd be snow here by now," Oscar said.

"There should be. There usually is. But like I said: climate change. Everything's fucked one way or another. Summer's too hot, winter's too hot. Nothing knows when to grow. Look at me, still wearing flip flops and shorts in September, fuck's sake." He laughed, but weakly. "You all should get on that. Rewrite global warming down there at BIP, fix it in our files and make it come true."

"Right." Oscar drank then again, what the hell, grabbed the bottle and splashed a bit more into his mug.

"Now you get it," Clark said. "Make up your own hours. It's wild, though, right? To make the world what you want it to be? It's a pretty powerful job."

"I haven't really thought about it like that."

"That's the Arctic all over. The whole thing's blank paper and everyone comes up here—or doesn't—to fill it in however they like. I mean, not the locals. Everybody else, though. All the way back to the Vikings settling Greenland and their lost colonies and carving runes into stones—we ought to put them in the database, right? Make things turn out better for those settlements. Hell, even Peary got to the Pole on blank paper. What marketing for Crane's paper company that was, sponsoring a search for the biggest blank page of them all."

"It wasn't all blank, though, was it? Crane made their money on money, the paper for the US mint."

"Hell, money's only blank paper until it gets some stains on it."

"Fair enough."

The two of them drank, each man in his own thoughts but both of them in the same landscape, the same hemisphere, something Oscar hadn't felt in a while: another mind knowing his own. The way things had been with Julia for so long, the way things had been between them, before "PF, Oscar" became more than a joke.

Through the back window of the hut—though he couldn't think of it as a hut any longer, knowing how many rooms were below—he watched one of the thick black cables he'd seen attached to the tower sway in the wind and pass across the top panes of the window every few seconds. It was hard to say how windy it was because there was nothing else in view to be shifted, only that single segment of power cable and for all Oscar knew it always moved, independent of weather, because of the tension between building and tower or the force of the current running through the wires within. A flashing glare on the glass made him think of his phone (so a glance to the kitchen) and he worried Julia would be growing worried: he hadn't been in touch for a while, though perhaps she'd been busy with her inspections of new tire tread designs with no time to realize how long he'd been quiet.

The two of them, working, miles apart at their respective professional tasks. In a way it almost felt like they were together, connected at least by the shared purpose of their separate lives. He thought of her for some reason in a white lab coat and hard hat wearing protective glasses, holding a clipboard and pencil with an array of new tires spread out before her, probing their treads with the eraser and point of her pencil. He had no idea, really, what she did at work. He knew what her job was, her title, but the daily ins and outs of it? The minute to minute routine? He knew as much about any of that as Julia knew about his own days at BIP, he supposed. For all he knew Julia's job was as secret as his, the tire treads a cover like color codes and filing systems were a mask between between one version of BIP and the other. What were the odds of that, though: both of them having jobs they couldn't tell the other about, two secret lives in one marriage? That's the kind of thing that only happens in stories.

"It's good to have you here, man," Clark said. "I mean it. It's been quiet since Slotkin took off."

Oscar choked on his whiskey and Clark had to reach over and thump his back. Recovered, he asked, "Slotkin was here? When?"

"Not long. He was only here a few days ago before heading north, up to the ice station."

"Why was he here? I thought he retired. And what's the ice station?"

"I don't know, really. Most of you prognosticators make it up here at some point, I think. Pass through, anyway, on your way there. And now here you are. Like I said, it's good to have someone to talk to. Someone who knows what's what and who knows the north."

"But what was he doing?"

"Slotkin? Nothing, mostly. Talked about volleyball a lot. Made sketches. I'd show you but he brought them along. He was okay. I liked him."

Oscar poured another big drink, the excuse of coffee long gone from his cup. He looked back to the window and thought about Slotkin, and Wend, and he wondered who else had come through Northern Branch. And most of all why. But Clark didn't seem to be saying and there was too much whiskey in Oscar's head now for him to wonder too hard.

Clark stood up and even watching someone else move that quickly made Oscar's Scotch-soaked eyes swim so he closed them for a few seconds, calming himself in the black of the North Pole at night. Then the twin thumps of Clark's palms on the table pulled Oscar back.

"Okay," his host said. "Let's see what that partner of yours is up to," and he was away down the loud, clanging stairs before his sentence was over so what could Oscar do except follow, again.

They arrived to find Alexi in the server cage, its black door blocked open by the canister he'd been knocking on earlier. He leaned over the terminal with fingers on keys but not typing, though whether he'd stopped or was yet to begin who could tell.

"What are you doing in there?" asked Clark with an edge to his voice, looking down past Alexi's shoulder at the screen. He had to lean and crane to get a view around the smaller man's body.

Alexi jerked upright and turned. "Oh, just curious. Having a look." He stepped away from the terminal and through the door, leaving Clark to hit a few keys of his own then put the terminal to sleep before stepping out of the cage. He lifted the canister and the door swung closed with the same thunk and buzz as before, then he returned the canister to the bin in the corner where it belonged. Or where it had taken up residence, anyway: with so many junk piles and workbenches and cabinets to choose from down there, there were any number of places it might have belonged. Any number of ways it could go.

Clark gave Alexi a look from behind, equal parts suspicion and confusion and what looked to Oscar like anger, too, and enough of it to make him nervous for his partner's wellbeing. "So," Oscar asked, "should we go back upstairs and have a look at that envelope?"

"Envelope?" the other men asked together.

Outside that building, that jumble of cold glass and steel, that great hollow space full of people coming and going and more emptiness than presence all told, outside that building he waited. He sat on the edge of a concrete planter, invisible in plain sight, a bear overlooked in the landscape.

Suits and ties, heels and skirts came and went. They revolved through doors and stood smoking outside or argued and laughed into phones while urging the last drops and dregs of their coffee to slide from paper cups before vanishing into their next day of work.

And the hunter sat still. Sat in silence. The hunter hunted without lifting a finger or gun.

Then his moment came, a herd of anonymous suits the same shade as his own stolen clothes, and as they moved toward the doors he moved among them, within them, and was inside without being stopped, without swiping a card or a thumb and without drawing any more scrutiny than the others.

He wasn't new to that world; he hadn't walked within it for a very long time and had never intended to again but he had walked within it before so he knew its ways.

The hunter scanned the board of suite numbers and agency names and found the one he was after, or its pseudonym, really, and he moved toward a windowless door and into a descending stairway. Into the basement, into the emptiness that held the rest of that building's emptiness up in the air, so much nothing to be held aloft, and the bag on his shoulder— the bomb on his back—was heavy and light all at once, earth- bound and ethereal at the same time as the hunter moved down those stairs to the offices where, once and for all, he would make his unmissable mark. Where he would speak for his family, his neighbors, his friends, whose bodies lay lost now so far to the north. Whose spirits swirled now round the Pole.

17

"The envelope's still in my bag," Oscar said. "In the entryway." He moved toward the door but Clark stopped him with a big hand on his shoulder, said he'd get the bag, and urged Oscar to sit at the table where Alexi already sprawled as if he hadn't been downstairs at all.

Oscar was just settling himself in the chair when Clark roared from the other side of the open door, a sound followed by the slam of the outer door against the wall. Oscar jumped up and rushed outside and Alexi moseyed behind. Clark was stomping the ground, cursing a blue cloud in the air, and it only took Oscar a second to figure out why: the ATV they'd arrived on and left outside the door was gone; tracks led away from the hut back in the direction of the airfield, crossing and recrossing the tread-marks of Oscar's own arrival.

Clark punched the side of the Quonset hut, hard enough to leave a deep dent and send reverberations through the ground so Oscar felt them, he thought, coming up through his shoes. All those bulges and dents he'd spotted earlier made more sense now as he watched Clark hit the thin metal walls again and again, cursing and shouting what weren't always words.

"Clark… calm down. We'll find it," Oscar said, not even convincing himself, and his host went on punching, hairy and huge, Bigfoot on a rampage in a Hawaiian shirt.

"What's he all worked up about?" Alexi asked.

"The ATV. Look, it's gone. We parked it right here."

Alexi nodded. "Even so," he said. "That's pretty worked up

over an old ATV, right?"

Oscar stared at him, wondering if his new partner—though Alexi hardly felt new any longer after the odyssey of the past couple days had given their partnership its own patina—was really that dumb. "Alexi, we're in the middle of nowhere. How's he going to get anywhere? How are we?"

"Where do we need to go?"

Oscar gave up and shook his head as Clark hit the quonset hut so hard it seemed the whole metal arch might topple. Still muttering and growling Clark stomped to a pile of junk heaped against the wall around the base of the antenna, pulled out a section of rusted rebar, and stomped away from the buildings, away from Oscar and Alexi and the tracks from the ATV. For a few seconds Oscar could still hear him swearing but the wind had picked up so it wasn't long before Clark was reduced to a bright rainbow smudge moving silently into the distance.

Oscar watched for so long his vision grew blurry, then he rubbed his eyes and realized the blurriness was snow beginning to fall. Flakes settled on his hair, his shoulders, the toes of his shoes, and he couldn't resist catching a few on his tongue after noticing Alexi doing it first. Clark had vanished into the snowfall and gloaming.

Alexi yawned, then again a bit louder and a bit more drawn out, then he went back inside. Oscar watched his partner move into the entryway but stayed waiting outside for ten minutes, fifteen, then twenty. The gray of the sky had deepened and darkened and the air had cooled with the snow. When another twenty minutes or so had passed he started to worry Clark was not coming back, that something had happened, and that it was getting too cold to stay outside without a coat or a hat so he followed Alexi into the entryway then into the room at its end.

"He's not back yet," Oscar said, and Alexi, rummaging in the refrigerator, nodded. "Should we look for him?"

"He'll be found when he wants to be found." Alexi had

discovered what looked to Oscar like leftover chili and the end of a loaf of brown bread, and he was scooping one onto the other still in the cold pocket of the open fridge.

"Unless something happened to him. Unless he's hurt. Or unless he's not coming back, Alexi. I'm not kidding around here, he's actually gone."

"He'll be back. Or not. Nothing we can do about it right now."

"What are you... we can go look for him right now. We can find him right now and make sure he's alright, that he..."

"Or we can wander around out there and get lost ourselves, because we don't even know where we are." Alexi took a big bite of his chili on bread, considered it, then nodded and closed the green door of the fridge which made a loud clunk as the old-fashioned latch fell into place. "Clark's the only one of us who does, Oscar. We've got more chance of getting lost than he does."

Which was true, of course, Oscar had to admit. So as much as he didn't like it he agreed they should wait for Clark to come back and if he didn't... that was something they'd figure out later but for now they would wait. So he checked his phone on the kitchen island and finding it charged tried to unplug Clark's jury-rigged wires but worried he'd damage the port so in the end left them attached when he turned the phone on.

The faux-wooden case had split somewhere along the line— the "snap" he'd heard earlier, Oscar supposed—and a thin wedge of plastic extended over the bottom of the screen now. He had to push it aside and hold it away with the fingers of one hand so he could access the whole touchscreen with the other, and the edge where it had broken was sharp.

No messages, which was a surprise, and he wondered what Julia had been doing while his phone was off, what she'd been so busy with that she neither called just to call or because she was worried after not hearing from him for so long. He'd forgotten to feel out of touch while his phone was charging but now that being in touch was an option again, now that he was back on the web with all its vibrations, the absence of those messages was a lump in the throat of his thoughts.

He weighed the phone in his hand and considered calling but Alexi was only a few feet away and the room felt very exposed. So Oscar summoned the Pole cam instead, where the the ice sheet and swift swirls of snow fogged in the view within the narrow space of the camera's lamp. He was closer now, in that building at Northern Branch, than he'd ever been. Closer than he'd ever expected to be. The last trace of sunset outside the hut's window was the same light he'd seen a few minutes before on his screen, the two places almost in sync, and he wondered how much farther north the Pole was, how far he'd have to travel until the world faded fully to white from the gray and brown mud and gravel outside. It seemed a shame now, to have come all this way, so far north, only to end up so near to but so far from the Pole. To leave the envelope with Clark as he'd been assigned and go home.

"Nice to get away," said Alexi, swinging his sneakers up onto the table. Oscar wasn't certain but he didn't think they were the same shoes his partner had been wearing when they'd boarded the train back in DC such a long time ago. Still, the sneakers were scuffed and stained so couldn't have been purchased along the way or during his sojourn in Portland.

"We're still working," said Oscar. "Even if it's taking a while. And we're probably on vacation days now. You heard what Director Lenz said."

"So? We'll make a vacation of it."

Oscar just shook his head. "How'd you get here, anyway? After Portland, I mean? I rode a lobster boat out to a ferry, and that brought me to an airport and a plane brought me here. But what about you?"

"I ran into some guys."

Oscar waited for more but it didn't come. "What guys?"

"You know, I don't remember their names. Nice, though."

And before Oscar could dig any deeper—if there was any deeper to dig—he heard the bang of the outer door and a few seconds later Clark entered the room, no worse for wear though he looked a bit chilled and no wonder in just his Hawaiian shirt, shorts, sandals, and skull-splitting grin. His round beard was frosted and white not unlike that more famous denizen of the north.

"Okay!" he boomed, clapping his hands in a way Oscar first thought was shaking the cold off but no, turned out to be only excitement.

"Aha!" said Alexi.

Oscar asked, "Where have you been?"

"Nowhere. I took a walk." After Oscar had stared for a moment, Clark said, "Walked off my anger. It's an Inuit thing I picked up somewhere. If you get mad, upset, out of sorts somehow so not thinking straight, you've got to get rid of that. It's a danger up here, you need to keep a clear head. Right?"

His listeners nodded.

"Right. So you take a stick and you walk. Doesn't matter, any direction, you walk until all that anger or frustration has dissipated. Like you're trailing it out behind you or something for the wind to scatter away. I don't know. But once it's gone, when you realize you're no longer angry, you stop. And you plant that stick in the ground, turn around, and walk back the way you came. Back home or wherever you are."

"And it works?" Oscar asked.

"Always," Clark said. "Always. See, it's the motion. Just moving, not to go anywhere, not toward a point, just to go and to honor that unintended arrival by planting the stick. It's accepting you can go only one way at a time and being okay with closing off all other directions once you've made that choice. Because look, when I was angry, you saw me hit the shed, right?"

Oscar nodded.

"Right. Sorry about that, by the way. You didn't need to see that. But that was me trying go in every direction at once. I wanted the ATV back, I wanted to go after who took it, I wanted to know where they'd gone and why and what they're going to do, and was wondering how I could have done something different so it wouldn't be taken. Too many directions. Too many stories. Too much frustration. Trying to account for everything all at once would drive anyone crazy—you'd never get far enough in any direction to make it worth going at all. So I picked one. Only one. And I walked. Get it?"

Another nod.

"Whichever direction you're feeling that day, no particular endpoint in mind, no particular query, just… I don't know, turning your frustration into momentum." He laughed and looked down for a second. "It's like sex, right? All pent up, won't let you focus on anything else, and you just need to release it somehow. Either you do it yourself"—Alexi snickered—"or you've got to find someone to help. But you're gonna be useless until you've got your head clear and that's no good in a life-or-death place like this."

Oscar saw his nights at home spent with magazines, his wife's disinterest driving him from the room to calm down.

"Hell," Clark said, "isn't that what explorers are doing, sometimes? Going as far from home as they can stand until they find a place where things make sense? Half of them are guys who weren't much use at home, guys who never quite found their footing in normal life, setting sail until they came into their own way up here."

Alexi was back at the fridge and Clark raised an eyebrow as he watched his guest rifle what must have been limited stores.

"Anyhow, we were going to look at your envelope, weren't we? Even if it took us a while to get there, and I'm sorry for that."

"Yes!" Oscar said. "Let me get it." And he was out to the entryway before Clark could beat him there, in case some other surprise might be waiting to drag it all out; it's likely everyone had reached their limit of patience with that envelope and its delays. He brought in the whole bag, dropped it on the floor, and pulled out the brown envelope then extracted the smaller, lighter brown one from inside and handed it over to its addressee.

Clark stuck a thick finger under the flap and more or less exploded the end of the envelope with what hardly even looked like a pull. He slid out a tri-folded sheet of cream stationary— again, a paper unfamiliar to Oscar—with two or three stamps at the bottom under a jagged signature.

"What does it say?"

"Hm?" Alexi called with his head in the fridge.

Clark took his time and he took Oscar's, too, and even Alexi's who didn't seem to realize his time had been taken. At last the bigger man said, "You two are still headed north. You're meant to get yourselves to the ice station. No surprise there, all you prognosticators get sent up there sooner or later, but you two are doing it quick."

"But Director Lenz said we should rush back from here. He never said anything about an ice station. And you never told us what the ice station is when I asked you before. And..."

"Whoa!" Clark laughed, facing his palms toward Oscar the way a doctor faces charged paddles at a crashed heart attack patient. "The ice station's just another BIP branch. You can call it the Far Northern Branch if you like."

"Have you been there?"

"Me? Well, no, I've.... I've never been sent. But Slotkin went just recently, and Wend a while ago when I'd finished my training. I've seen it in Lunden's notes—he was here before me— that what's his name, Rundy, went that way, too."

"Rudnik? But why another branch? What do they do? Why do we... why are we..." Oscar trailed off, out of questions or perhaps overwhelmed by how many he had, getting out of his depth of inquiry.

"Do you have any more bread, Clark?" Alexi asked from the

kitchen. "Just another loaf or so, maybe?"

Their host sighed, exasperated by his guest's appetite, we can suppose, and no wonder; perhaps we can sympathize after spending so long with Alexi ourselves. "Tomorrow's my baking day but I guess I can get started early." And a few minutes later Clark stood at the counter mixing ingredients for a new loaf with Alexi beside him putting away the thick heel of the last. Oscar watched them at work then asked Clark how he could unplug his phone from the makeshift charger, but rather than the delicate operation he anticipated Clark grabbed the phone in one floury hand and the wires in the other and pulled them apart without looking. He tossed the phone across the room to Oscar, trailing a white cloud in its wake, and smudged flour fingerprints on the dark screen were so much like swirls of snow at the Pole via camera that he began to relax before even turning it on.

"So I guess we'll go up to the ice station then," Oscar said. "Should we call for a plane to pick us up there, or back here, or what? To bring us home to DC. Do you know how that works?"

Clark had become much more interested in the large bin of flour he was scooping from, leaning in so far his head and ears were out of view, so perhaps he hadn't head Oscar and that's why he didn't reply.

Leaving the others to their recursion of production and consumption, their circle of bread, Oscar went downstairs with his phone in search of a quiet place to call his wife.

There was a statue of the Buddha on a high shelf, a round body carved or perhaps molded from light gray stone or something like stone, and beside him—a sidekick, an echo—a second Buddha perched tiny and red in ceramic, cross-legged, laughing in the shadow of his larger, more serious self. A mirror leaned behind them and a second mirror hung on the opposite wall, creating an infinite recursion of Buddhas or Buddha or both, all in one, all at once.

Also in that far mirror a polar bear crept on the ice, filling the frame of a postcard tucked into the mirror's own frame, head down, paws spread, her weight distributed until she had nearly no weight at all and walked her great bulk across ice too thin for men to follow. And between those mirrors, between those two walls, the polar bear forever stalked her enlightened companions.

And, too, between those reflections and reflected themselves a man and another man stood arm's length apart but not reaching out for each other. The smaller of the two said, "You're erasing our story. Our future. You're giving it up and for what, a field trip? A little boy's daydream of playing explorer?"

"Don't be dramatic," the larger man said, the man with a face that looked born for a beard but on that particular morning was freshly shaven and raw. "I'm not 'erasing' anything, anyone's story. It's just a job for a while. It's something I have to do. I've always wanted to, you don't know…" He turned to stare down his own face in a dormant TV, triangulated in the room's corner so his partner, himself, the Buddha, the bear, all converged in that dark space.

"I do know. I do. Clark, Jesus, you've talked about it forever, but—"

"Since I was a boy. I have to do it, Sven, you—"

"And now I have to do it, too! You've chosen for both of us. You've decided what my future is going to be for the sake of your own and you didn't even ask me about it." Their antique windows rattled, old glass in old frames, and they knew from living there long enough a train was passing on the elevated tracks a full block away; they could not hear the train, it was too far for that, but somehow close enough to shake the rippling panes in that house they'd renovated together.

"What could I ask you?" the bigger man said, rubbing a broad hand on his unwhiskered cheek. "I knew I was going as soon as they offered the job."

"Then why did we bother with this? All of this? Three years, Clark! Three years! I thought we were building something here and now it's burning. Everything's burning."

"So you're the Buddha now?" He nodded not toward the shelf but its reflection on the far wall. "I thought he—they—were the Buddha."

"Oh, shut up. Don't intellectualize this, I—"

"Who's intellectualizing? Is that a word? Calm down, Sven, you... we—"

"Fuck you! Just, fuck you, Clark!" spat the smaller man, Sven, his face red, his eyes dark, shoulders tight; he got that way, he carried his disappointment and anger always in his back and Clark often warmed his hands on the cast iron coils of the radiator before rubbing that laden back and its muscles, soothing their anger and ache. If it were any other day but that day, if they were having another conversation, he would.

"This is not about your abstract fucking desires, your unfulfuckingfilled dreams. This is real, us, the two of us, right here. Now. Me. You're throwing that away, for what? For some stupid goddamn job in the middle of nowhere? Well fuck you then. I guess none of this ever mattered to you the way it mattered to me. I guess I've been wrong all this time, that I'm some fucking chump."

"Sven, it's not like that, I—"

"I don't care what you think it's like. It's not 'like' anything, it *is* something. It fucking *is*: it's you leaving me for no reason. You call it whatever you want in your head. You take it apart and put it back together like your damn radios or machines or whatever those pieces of crap are I'm always tripping over. You do that but you won't change anything. Whatever parts you take this down to just add up to different versions of you and your selfish decision. What am I, then? The dutiful husband left waiting at home, watching the horizon for the return of his big, brave explorer? How romantic. How quaint. Something right from the pages of those bad goddamn novels your mother read. Wait, wait, let me loosen my bodice and stand in the billowing wind of the shore."

"Sven, don't..." Clark stepped forward, arms out, and he tried to embrace his partner but Sven moved away, turned a shoulder so each side of his face hung in a different mirror, cast to opposite sides of the room. "I'll be back, I promise you. It's for now, it's... the house is paid for, that money from my parents' estate will cover most of the bills, just use it, and..."

Sven's body softened, pulled itself together at the center of the room and he moved closer to Clark but not all the way and he laughed in a last resort way. "So I'm your kept man now, is that it? The explorer's houseboy? Oh, Clark, you need to think sometimes before you open your mouth, you really do." Their reflections fell into each other but their bodies still stood apart.

"I understand, Bear. I do," and Sven reached to lay a hand on his partner's arm but upon that big wrist his fingers were the faintest of lines. "But like this? Why like this? We could have talked, we could have gone somewhere together, the two of us. Wouldn't that have been better? Better than going yourself? Somewhere warm, even. Somewhere not so far north, not that you'll even tell me where, exactly, it is. Did you think I was going to just follow you to the North Pole?"

"Sven," Clark said and he eyed the polar bear in its frame in a frame, that stilled ursine image forever crossing the same sheet of ice while its reflection reflected ad infinitum, bear after bear after Buddha, long after men had all run out of words.

Six hundred fifty five thousand hands of cards dealt, give or take, and the same pile of spent matchsticks and extra brass buttons, odd stones, and battered, bent feathers won back and forth countless times.

Every volume on board read cover to cover and read again until sentences became clusters of meaningless words then words fell apart into jumbles of empty letters then letters melted into meaningless smudges of ink, all too familiar to eyes that could not stand to see them once more.

Every timber and lapstrake and peg and nail counted to pass the time. Each inch of canvas and rope, every stave in every barrel and each one of their hoops catalogued and re-catalogued by minds desperate for something to occupy them. The whole ship and its contents ground down into data, long chains of counting, moments separated from moments because to see them together, to watch how one second led into others and minutes to hours and hours to days into weeks into months on that ice was too much for even the minds of such strong men to take.

So they stripped it all down, every scrap of the ship, every scrap of themselves: their memories told and retold, memorized, carbonized, until one man couldn't remember where his own memories ended and his crewmate's began, until a man couldn't tell you his own story without telling everyone else's, no longer able to pull them apart. They swapped stories the way they'd swapped brands of tobacco when they still had a choice months before, tasting each other's flavors, the tang of another man's life for a while if only as a change from their own.

And the ice, too, they broke down in the long dark of months and the half-light of strange seasons: its colors, its shapes, how "ice" isn't ice, it's not just one thing but myriad variations it takes time to notice and those men had nothing but time and everything but variation. They could tell, by the end, by the time it broke up, what sort was grinding the walls of their hull by its sound, if it scraped or it rang, if it scarred with a slim claw or rammed with a fist. They knew one ice from another sometimes by its smell or they swore they did and those are the same thing when there's no one within weeks' or months' traveling distance to possibly tell you you're wrong.

Those men, those great men, took the Arctic apart and themselves apart, too, as they swung slowly around the Pole's orbit without ever raising a paddle or sail. They gave up their time and what they were given, what they were shown...

Of six hundred and thirty one polar bears spotted on the horizon (the same ones recurring or different creatures, no matter), two hundred and eleven of those had crept close, their translucent fur storing old sunlight to cast its white shadow still in the dark. Ninety-six showed the men steaming breath, close enough for the crew to make out the rings in their eyes, and seven of those scaled the sides of the ship to investigate what the deck offered. Those seven insisted on making a place among men.

18

Oscar wanted to sit, to make himself at home in the Northern Branch basement, but there was only the wheeled office chair in the cage and however Alexi had gotten inside it before, that cage was firmly locked now. He considered some of the mysterious vehicle parts and barrels and bins littering the corners of the large main chamber as resting places but none looked comfortable so he wandered the warren of underground rooms in search of a seat.

In Clark's workshop was only the uncomfortable-looking upholsteryless metal frame of a bench from the back of a car, and though tempted to stop and hold Nansen's buckle again as long as he was back in that room Oscar decided to wait until after he tried calling home. Through another door he found a garage with half-assembled snowmobiles and ATVs and sleds of various sizes, some that seemed a century old and others so shiny and sleek they might be brand new and never used. Then at the end of a corridor he hadn't seen earlier, past a filthy bathroom that took Oscar's mind back to his college dorm days, he found what he was after: a reading room, shelves from floor to ceiling and deep leather chairs arranged with their backs to each other so facing all sides of the room. A side table stood with a chess game atop it already in progress, and an antique phonograph dominated one corner with its dark wooden cabinet and heavy black arm. Beside it, almost lost in the phonograph's shadow, a modern stereo minuscule by comparison lurked black and boxy, a single red standby light the only indication it might be more than a purposeless shape. And, most of all, magnificently casting their warm yellow gaze, hundreds of issues of *National Geographic* lined the four walls, shelf after shelf after shelf, rivaling Oscar's own incomplete collection. He dropped into a chair facing those rows of sunshine and the leather exhaled a welcome as if waiting a long time for him to come home. He sank into the seat and his body slid forward and down, legs stretching out, shoulders slipping below the chair back, and he basked in the glow.

With his eyes closed the room smelled familiar, the brittle, browning old paper and sweet but almost sharp tang of the ink in those decades of exploration and reflection and explanation. Ink printed when Peary was alive to enjoy it, when names now lost to history could confirm their own exploits by turning to pages between those ubiquitous yellow covers, when a great man could walk in off the street to any ordinary house in America with a decent chance of finding a copy on a bookshelf, an account of his own achievements—bright strands of a web reaching into each family and home and library and school; whatever else all those citizens and their lives may or may not have in common they had those magazines and a partnership, however unequal, in every great man's great endeavors.

He pulled up the Pole cam and it was dark, as dark as the world outside Northern Branch, but in the narrow range of the camera's light snow fell heavily. The flakes and their myriad paths wove a screen to reflect the light and lens back at itself, back at Oscar on the other side. He watched, tracking the almost but not quite straight lines of descent, wavering back and forth in the wind and drawn by a shaky hand.

In college, on an afternoon in December the week of final exams, he'd been sitting in the campus library studying for something—the history of science, maybe, or the biology of aging, or something else altogether—and looked up to discover the year's first snow had begun. He'd watched that other snow curtain weaving itself on the far side of the glass, a few threads at first then a gauze then a thick sheet of fabric waving beyond the window and hiding the city beyond.

Oscar's mind had gone blank, a fresh sheet of paper awaiting a map; he lost track of time and of studying and of the world. A long time had passed when at last he came back to himself, came in from the snow, and realized the woman studying in an identical chair to his own with one empty seat between them had just come back, too, after getting lost in the snowfall herself.

They caught each other's eye and smiled, then laughed and eventually talked until they were eating together, a late supper in their dorm's dining hall. He and Julia had eaten together most nights ever since, until lately. They'd been drawn together by snow though these days it more often drew them apart.

His phone's broken case was hurting his fingers and getting on his nerves, too. If the break had been cleaner, if he could have bent the broken strip back into place where it wasn't so noticeable; Oscar could have lived with the crack. But it wouldn't go back, the broken edge wouldn't fit as if the plastic had somehow contracted—he pictured the ice around Nansen's ship, and around *Jeannette*, too, filling in every space as soon as it opened and sometimes not waiting for that, sometimes forging its own path into the wood. He couldn't focus on the Pole cam like that, with that crack in his housing, so he pulled the case off and set it out of sight on a shelf. He'd need to replace that when he got home, when he got back to the south; he might even replace the phone altogether, between the cracked case and whatever internal damage had come from Clark's jury-rigged charger.

Oscar hit the memory key for Julia's number then waited through a few rings, and after she answered but before she spoke he heard a loud thumping.

"Hello?" he asked.

"Oscar?" She seemed to be yelling.

"Why's it so loud? Where are you? It sounds like... it sounds like a helicopter or something."

She laughed, he thought, or something like it. "No, just construction outside. Still that same work under the street."

"So late?"

"There must have been an emergency. You know how it is in this city." He could hardly hear her as it was and had to hold the phone away from his ear because of the noise, which made her shouts even more faint. "Where are you?" she asked.

He looked around the room, at the magazines, the chairs, the phonograph…he thought of the cage full of servers a few steps down the hall and the machine parts everywhere and the buckle and strap from Nansen's pack in the apothecary drawers with who knew what else. He pictured the stick Clark had marched away with and planted, and the distance from wherever he was to wherever she was, the nowhere between them where their voices met and there was no lie long enough to reach across all of that so he said, "Fine. How are you?" as if he'd misheard.

"Fine," she said. "I'm fine, too. Do you know when you'll be home?" The thumping seemed to get louder. Behind her, in the background of what she'd called nothing, Oscar heard voices and banging and other strange sounds then a voice closer up to the phone he thought he heard calling his wife by name.

"Who is that?"

"Oh, it… just TV. It's up loud. For the construction."

"I was thinking," he said. "I was remembering how we met, in the library…"

She laughed. "The two of us lost in the snow. A couple of Eskimos." Oscar was sure he heard more shouting behind her, not from TV, but she said, "Eskimo kiss!" like it was nothing.

He laughed too, despite himself, remembering that old standby between them. He'd said many times that it wasn't true, it wasn't the way Eskimo really kissed and that "Eskimo" wasn't even the name they should use, no more than French people had no other toast, but she didn't care and he'd let that bit of misinformation slip into their database of private jokes, an error they'd agreed to without ever saying. Another Arctic lie he'd learned to live with because of the truth it had grown into the more times she said it, the more it had grown into a ritual of their bodies, a culturally inaccurate, perhaps even racist ritual but their own private gesture, innocuous in the envelope of their marriage though they'd never want it to get out. It wasn't the rubbing of noses that mattered, it wasn't the unfortunate words to describe it, but the privacy and fragility of it: a gesture that in the wrong situation, overheard by the wrong ears, would at best be humiliating, a risk to credibility and social respect—not that Oscar worried much about those kinds of things—but a risk they took together like marriage itself, the potential for shameful implosion and awkward discovery so that almost olfactory inaccuracy became an embodiment of their commitment and history together.

An embodiment now disembodied over how many miles, the ghost of a gesture performed by voices alone somewhere out in space where two signals met.

"Where did you say you were?" she asked.

"Just… a different office," he replied, not even convincing himself and he heard in her sighed response he wasn't alone. "And you're at home?"

"Right," she shouted, leaving doubts so thick on the ground their conversation had nowhere to go. A siren exploded behind her and multiple voices yelled over it. "Oscar," she said, frantic now, "I have to go. I… I'll see you at home, okay? Are you coming home?"

It took him by surprise, the question, the sudden panic of how—or was it why?—she had asked, how much thicker her own doubts might be than his own, but he said, "Of course. Of course I'll be home. Where else would I be?" and he didn't ask if she would be, too.

"That didn't sound like I meant…," Julia started to say but a shrieking, grinding, metallic sound overtook her and the call was cut off and Oscar was alone in the Arctic again. Or subarctic, maybe, because he still wasn't quite sure; his phone's GPS didn't seem to be working any better than compasses had worked for men of the past at these latitudes. He was somewhere north, anyway, somewhere far from wherever she was.

He slipped the phone back into his pocket and pictured Julia at home in her white tank top and plaid boxer shorts on the couch; he saw again that shadowed patch of blood on her shoulder the morning long ago but not really so long when he'd left. He almost felt the curve of her side under his palm—his hand curled on its own, as far as it was from her body, muscle memory in tune with his fantasy—and the slight (slighter now, after so much karate) dome of her belly his hand used to cup when they slept as two spoons, two curves that fit together as if by design. They'd never called it spoons, though; the first time they shared a bed and he fit himself behind her she'd said in the dark she felt like Tetris shapes and it stuck. Sometimes, years later but not in years lately, she'd softly sung that game's Russian folk music when he fitted his body against her in the dark and they'd laughed, pressed against each other and completed the level.

For a moment, for a few precious seconds, he was with her on that couch but the banging and shrieking of late-night construction forced its way in from outside and he couldn't help wondering what work was so urgent, so loud after dark when people were trying to relax or to sleep, or if Julia had been somewhere else altogether, but where? He pushed that away, seeing moonlight instead on the spines of his magazines, the glow they cast on her face in that room and he watched a few minutes: her watching TV, alone in their home, her legs, her hair up off her neck, the press of her breasts against that tank top worn thin by washings and time, a bandage protruding from under the strap, the yellow glow cast on all of that like a warm, watchful eye…

The clang of swift feet on the stairs snapped him back. The magazines filling the wall before him in that basement room glared under fluorescent tubes, not moonlight, not even the warmth of the lightbulb at BIP those footsteps were coming fast as.

Clark rushed in, already talking and holding Oscar's bag of cold weather gear. "You've got to go. They're outside and coming in." Alexi strolled into the room behind him, gnawing a large hunk of steaming bread and holding a large bag of his own in the other hand.

"Who's outside?" Oscar asked as Clark pulled him out of the chair and onto his feet, then into the corridor. "Who's coming in?"

"No time. Follow me."

He led the prognosticators down the rest of the hallway to the foot of more stairs. "Suit up. Fast." He'd already unzipped Oscar's bag and dumped its contents on the ground—parka, goggles, boots, socks and liners, all in a heap. Alexi, bread hanging from his face, calmly picked through similar gear of his own, putting on a sock and thinking about it, then a shirt or a glove, but somehow he was making progress: when Oscar looked up from his own methodical dressing, his partner was almost encased in cold weather gear. He almost looked like an Arctic explorer, and when Oscar caught his own reflection in Alexi's blue-black goggle lenses he realized he looked like one, too.

"Up," Clark said. "Hurry." He led the way up the stairs to a small landing and a door split in two by a horizontal seam at waist height. When Clark cranked a handle the halves separated, the top sliding into the ceiling and the bottom into the floor. Outside was black, but Clark pulled a large electric lantern from a mount on the wall and shoved it into Oscar's hands. "Go," he said. "Go and keep going. I'll find you if I can but I've got to wipe the database first. They'll get through the door soon."

"The database? Why? What's going on?"

The sound of a drill or a power saw or some kind of tool whined in the dark, interspersed with metallic banging. "No time, "Clark said. "They're coming." He took the stairs in two leaps and ran back down the hall toward the cage full of servers.

"To work!" said Alexi, stepping into the night, leaving nothing for Oscar to do but follow. The temperature had plunged since they'd last been outside and snow fell now in big flakes as it had on the Pole cam a few minutes before. A snowmobile stood outside the hatch, a key in the ignition, but although the ground was already white Oscar didn't know it was enough for the tracks and skis to work yet. But the door slammed closed behind them—had it been on a timer? Would he have been crushed had he lingered?—leaving the snowmobile their only choice.

"Do you know how to drive one of these?"

"Nope," said Alexi, climbing on. "But we'll figure it out."

"What about Clark, though? Is he okay?"

"He said we should go. I'm sure he knows what he's doing."

Oscar couldn't or at least didn't argue with that so he got on the vehicle behind his partner, the best option considering there weren't any others, and the machine rumbled and rattled beneath him for a few seconds before the engine turned over and the snowmobile shot forward across the ground.

"Just like flying a plane!" Alexi shouted.

Oscar asked if he'd flown a plane but by then they were moving fast enough for the wind to throw his question away.

Only then, once he was back in motion, almost flying through the subarctic evening one conical splash of headlight at a time, did it occur to him to wonder where the hell they were going, and why, and if Alexi—who seemed to know what he was doing at the controls after all—had any direction or destination in mind.

19

In his cold weather gear Oscar felt far from the snowmobile beneath him and from the air and from everything else. Far from his phone, though he felt its shape and weight in his pocket several layers deep, close to his body but far from his hand as he sped through the dark and held onto his partner. Even that felt distant, his gloved hands gripping the tail of Alexi's red parka. Oscar knew what his hands were doing, he could see them, but felt nothing beyond the ambiguous interior of the gloves. His fingers could have been anywhere, doing anything, so far as they knew.

There he was, in the Arctic or at least near the line between latitudinal zones, dressed like an explorer, racing through a snowy night on the modern equivalent of a dogsled (apart from the actual dog sleds still in use, but those were probably the equivalent of something else by this point, something less often used and more of an anachronistic novelty brought out for tourists and visiting enthusiasts of native craft and Iditarod fans) but it all seemed so... vague. So abstract and unreal. Maybe because their exit from Northern Branch had happened so quickly and in such confusion, amidst Clark's panic and rush to get rid of them. Oscar entertained for a few seconds—before those, too, were whipped away on the wind—the possibility all of this was somehow fake, as artificial as BIP's whole database, the mapping, the blueprints, the lies they filed in a folder marked Truth. That Clark was playing an elaborate prank for unspoken reasons of his own.

He'd imagined, sometimes, while drawing up documents for the settlement at Symmes' Hole, that a similar settlement had arisen from the disappearance of the *Jeannette*. That DeLong and his crew hadn't been lost, at least not all of them, that they'd stayed together and crossed the ice until finding a place they could live. Or that the ship hadn't sunk and had instead been the center of their settlement, a town hall of sorts with other tents and skin huts and igloos spreading from it, becoming more permanent structures over time as the residents had accepted their destiny. Ridiculous, of course, he knew that, but Wend had no doubt known that, too, yet had needed to pretend otherwise. He had needed to bring those men home, to keep them alive with a different destiny in their paperwork, and on that snowmobile in the dark Oscar saw why.

The tragedy of the *Jeannette* wasn't that she got stuck, because *Fram* got stuck, too, frozen fast in the ice. What was different about the *Jeannette* was they made nothing of it, took that ice as a trap, while Nansen turned stillness into the point. He made action of stasis in a way anyone could admire, anyone who grew up with a John Franklin lunchbox and dreams of the Pole and who found himself working in a basement department few people in the world knew existed and fewer still cared what they did. Anyone in a marriage with a tundra of bedsheets between bodies, wondering if there was a safe way across the frozen terrain; *Fram* was a reminder there was no failure in just staying put. That stillness was its own kind of motion, sometimes preferable to the real thing.

Right then on that snowmobile, snow falling harder and beginning to stick to his goggles, the night getting darker outside their bright headlight cone, the real thing was too much. Too real to be real and too perfect an Arctic experience for Oscar to admit it was happening. If he had seen it on PBS or photographed in a magazine—two explorers in the appropriate gear riding the appropriate vehicle across the appropriate landscape—he wouldn't have doubted at all. But it was him, he was there, and Alexi's piloting of the snowmobile seemed so expert, so adept, that Oscar could almost tell himself they knew what they were doing and were meant to be doing it. Which was too much to believe. He knew his own life and this wasn't it. He worked in an office. He rode the subway. He had a wife and an apartment and a collection of old magazines. He wasn't a man who rode snowmobiles and got chased out of buildings in the far north by... what had Clark said? "They're coming in," whatever that meant and whoever they were.

The night had become very real, etched in more permanent ink than the faded lines of the *Erebus* on a child's lunchbox thermos. Every so often an upright stick flashed through their lights, sticks of varying thickness and angles and heights, dozens of them stretching away from the buildings of Northern Branch. If they were all Clark's he got angry a lot, but perhaps it was a tradition that reached back before him. In a landscape absent of trees, those limbless sticks blurring by were all that reached above the occasional larger than average stone and they were frequent enough to easily be mistaken for trail markers actually leading somewhere by someone who didn't know the trailblazers planting those totems always turned around and went home when their anger had been walked off.

He knew how cold the air was but could hardly feel it: beneath balaclava and goggles and gloves he felt only its weight, the rush of it rustling the many fabrics encasing his body, decades of chemistry and engineering and patents instead of the wool and leather and fur of old photos. He felt the push of wind as light pressure—or at least the push of the snowmobile's speed—but only as pressure, not cold. As if he was watching a film in 3D, some senses stirred but others left out.

"Hold on," Alexi yelled, and because he was in front the sound carried back to Oscar's ear as if from a distance, overheard rather than heard. He gripped harder on his partner's coattail as Alexi leaned hard to one side, tilting Oscar along with him, and the whole vehicle swerved sharply onto a new course. A few seconds later it shifted again, then again, and Oscar asked why they were moving so much, why not keep going straight, but as loud as he yelled his questions were borne away off the back of the seat and Alexi carried on with designs of his own, whatever they were.

Seeking out the nearest pizza, perhaps, or the closest at hand pile of hot dogs.

They swerved again and in their new direction the moon was visible for the first time, dull behind clouds and snow but still there, a low sliver. Then Alexi zigged one more time and it was lost, but now Oscar thought he saw the glistening of water off to their left; it was hard to tell what was what, what was where, because moonlight and headlight alike bounced off the snow in the air and on the ground so everything reflected but almost nothing was actually lit. Oscar became so disoriented he closed his eyes and pictured the Pole cam instead, the calm of it, the stillness, the comfort of being limited to only one sense so he could focus more fully on being in the north than was possible here on the back of a snowmobile on a subarctic tear.

He stayed in his head for a while, at the Pole, while Alexi steered the machine and Oscar lost track of their course. He suspected they'd gone in circles at least a couple of times but perhaps not all at once, perhaps those wide loops kept them moving away from Northern Branch. Or perhaps Alexi had no route in mind and really was circling in unending motion for its own sake, or waiting for something to happen.

None of this made any sense. He'd realized that hours or days ago as anyone would whether it happened to them or they just heard about it. The trains, the cars, the boats, the plane... the bunker and servers and now snowmobile... none of it. The first thing that had felt right to Oscar was the room full of *National Geographic* in the basement at Northern Branch because it was almost like home, but everything else that had happened to him since being dragged from his coffee—or maybe as far back as being called into the director's office—was unlikely to the point of being absurd. So absurd, in fact, it could only be true because what purpose could all of this possibly serve except just being life, nothing more, nothing less? How could it add up to anything more than the nonsense of being alive?

He was glad to be moving again, glad to be on that snowmobile wherever Alexi was taking them even if he was taking them nowhere. Oscar settled into the motion, into the snow he could see but not feel, the distant weight of wind on his cocooned body and the whispering rush across all that fabric he couldn't hear in his layers of balaclava and hood and the engine's drone coming up through his legs.

He'd stayed still for so long but after only a few nonstop days it was movement that made the most sense. Standing still only opened up doors to doubt, left spaces for second-guessing and glances back over a shoulder. Alexi, he noticed, hadn't turned around once since they'd left Northern Branch. He'd put his head down and leaned over the grips of the snowmobile and every so often, every few miles, hummed a bit of song that drifted back to Oscar's ear and he only realized much later it had been the opening theme from *To The Moon!*.

They marveled sometimes and they more often cursed, his brother and sister-in-law on the other side of his walls and any neighbors who found their way into his half of the house, eyes wide and jaws dropped at the chaos in heaps, the decades and acres of objects piled up and stored. How did he find anything ever they asked, always that same absurd query, because they saw only what made one item the same as another—one book like all books, one boot like all boots—and he saw only what set them apart. His was a world composed of the unlike.

Their chaos was his catalog, a deliberate life fully provisioned, and he could lay knotty hands marked with old patches of frostbite on his cameras and plates, his tripod and gaiters and microscope, as quickly as snow started falling outside; his windows were always kept clean so he would know right away if snow started to fall but more often than not he knew in his bones it was coming before the ground or sky did. He could lay hands on one book or another, on just the right line from just the right page, as soon as he remembered he'd read something once. No two objects in his side of the house were remotely the same and it couldn't be helped if the small eyes around him could never see that.

"The Snowflake Man," they dismissed him as if it would hurt. As if that name wasn't his and he hadn't spent every storm in the wind, out catching crystals and preserving their shapes and their stories—from how high they'd fallen through what kind of sky, from which direction they'd blown and in what month they had come to earth. He knew them, those snowflakes, as closely as he knew the inside of his house and his mind and someday the others might see it if he kept his photographs clear and his logbooks of weather updated. If he kept his camera steady and sure and if the racking coughs that had lately plagued him paused long enough for each portrait.

Other men had gone north and he'd followed their exploits for years between the yellow covers of his magazines, their triumphant returns and sometimes their loss on the ice. Other men had gone north to find the source of the snows and why not, while he waited for those same snows to come south to him. While he made expeditions into the deep known and the familiar acres of his Vermont farm. His greatness, however much there might be, would come close to home where he inscribed those fleeting hieroglyphics—already melted before their image had set—onto paper and glass plates and time.

Rarely he was asked what he saw in the snow, more often asked what was wrong with his head, but the nearest he'd come to an answer was explaining each storm as a library's wing, a collection of disparate complementary volumes he would never read the whole of but, if he did his work well, might leave behind some useful key for other readers he had yet to meet. They might read in his steady hand, *Cold north wind afternoon, Snow flying*, and see his snowflakes photographed and blown up to fit in an eye, and they might discover a world both larger and smaller than they'd ever known and might set out to see it themselves.

20

It's possible he fell asleep, and why not: the thrum of the snowmobile as steady as quiet, the fresh air through his balaclava… or perhaps Oscar stayed awake and daydreamed at night for a mile or three. Either way Alexi brought him back to the near edge of nowhere with an elbow to the ribs which may or may not have been accidental. It was still dark. The snowfall had thickened and a white wake spewed to either side of their vehicle's skis and tracks, spraying higher and farther than it had earlier. More snow slid up the nose and broke in waves on Alexi before splashing around him to pile between their bodies, in the basket of Oscar's extended arms.

And though he couldn't feel the wind any more than he had earlier, he felt the cold now in a new way. It burrowed through all his layers, becoming both an ache and a sting, a tight cramp in his muscles; he tried shaking it off, one leg then one arm at a time, extending his limbs to the sides, but no good. All he accomplished was contradictory turn signals to no one, suggesting every possible direction his course might take, never mind he wasn't the one setting direction and the vehicle never changed course and there wasn't a driver behind him to care which direction he went.

Beyond the snow, far off but closing, Oscar saw red: a cluster of lights. He tapped Alexi's shoulder then pointed over it, and his partner nodded then shifted direction to take them toward the beacons. It took longer than Oscar expected; those lights seemed to grow a bit closer then stay where they were for hours and miles, then get a little bit closer again. It took long enough for him to realize they'd gone blindly into the night, into the snow and the north, and by dumb luck alone they'd actually gotten somewhere and just as easily—easier, even—could have gotten nowhere instead and frozen to death in the dark. Yet now he saw not only the red lights but pools of yellow light, too, from tall spotlights on posts. And in those pools buildings, four he could already see—three boxy, one domed—and he wondered if like BIP's own Northern Branch a whole complex lurked underground.

As they drew nearer he saw the boxes weren't three buildings but different wings of the same one, the ends of which had seemed separate against the white screen of snow from afar but were in fact all connected.

A door loomed in one pool of light and Oscar pointed toward it. Alexi killed the engine so it dropped to a soft rattle as the snowmobile slid for a few seconds longer, turning slightly as he leaned into the steering handles, and the vehicle drew parallel then stopped inches from the wall, by coincidence or because Alexi really did know what he was doing—he'd gotten them that far through the dark, after all. Perhaps he was a natural at snowmobiles. Or perhaps, though it seemed unlikely, he'd spent time training at a secret facility where all variety of clandestine emergency skills are taught and learned and it hadn't come up between them yet in conversation.

When the rattle of the engine had died altogether, they found the quiet of snow falling behind it. As windy as it had felt while they rode, that current was gone. Thick, tufted flakes came down straight, piled high, and only strange snuffles and snorts, the occasional grunt, growl, or bark, gave the night any soundtrack at all.

Or perhaps it was morning by then; Oscar had lost sense of time along with his sense of touch.

"That was fun," said Alexi, muffled by his balaclava but audible.

"It was something," said Oscar. Beside the door, the bas-relief of letters showed through snow that had stuck to the wall. He dusted them with a gloved hand and found a sign declaring this building to be a research station, a joint endeavor of Arctic nations, without indicating which ones or what kind of research was conducted inside. For all Oscar knew it was another outcropping of BIP. Was this the ice station that second envelope and its contents had directed them to—and it only occurred to Oscar now he hadn't read that interior document himself but had only Clark's word to go on—or was this somewhere else, a second station not belonging to BIP? There were still people who worked and lived in the Arctic, after all, as easy as it was to forget that in the south, in their office, or even in the north when you weren't paying attention.

He knocked despite the late hour and despite his suspicion that had anyone seen their approach the door would already be open. Then he waited before knocking again, one-two-(pause)-but his partner pulled the door open first.

"Unlocked," said Alexi, stepping inside. Oscar followed.

They found themselves in the small cube of a room with another door on the far side, like an airlock in space on TV. The other door was also unlocked so they passed through to a bright corridor reminiscent of hospitals in so far as anyone reminisces about being in those. Signs with arrows indicated directions toward sleeping quarters and laboratories and a dining hall, and emergency instructions hung in a frame on one wall with a map of the building's layout indicating various escape routes and priorities with key-coded colors.

Fluorescent tubes buzzed overhead, loud after the quiet of snow and snowmobiles, and when Oscar pulled the tinted goggles off his eyes the glare forced them shut. He tested opening one then the other in slits and it took a few seconds for him to see more than well-lit patches of blurry color.

Despite the warmth in the room and now on his face, Oscar's body still felt that cold ache from outside and he stamped his feet a few times to get his blood moving again. His boots sent dull echoes across the room before he remembered the hour and the scientists who were all apparently sleeping, amidst dreams of ice cores and climate change models and perfectly photographed snowflakes.

"What do we do?" he asked Alexi. "Should we wait until morning? Should we wake someone up? Maybe they could send help for Clark or at least radio to make sure he's okay."

"Could be," said Alexi but what could be what was lost on Oscar. Before he could ask, his partner had moved down the hallway and turned right into an office so Oscar rushed after. Alexi was already at a computer and sitting down, goggles on his forehead and gloves on the desk as he typed.

"What are you doing? What if you get caught?"

"By who?" Alexi asked without looking up.

"Whoever's office this is. Whoever is here, I don't know. The scientists."

"We'll tell them we're BIP, right? We're here to update their filing systems. Something like that. Isn't that what we do?"

It made sense, Oscar had to admit, so he did. "But still, Alexi, should you be doing that? Maybe we should find someone to help us. Someone who knows what they're doing." The computer pinged then beeped from whatever his partner had done and a few seconds later Alexi announced, "And... send!" as he pushed Return with three fingers at once.

"What was that? What did you send?"

"Just an email. Work stuff."

"What work stuff? We work together. This is work right now, isn't it? We're working?"

"Hm," said Alexi, strolling past Oscar and out of the room. In the hallway, he called out, "Hellooooo! Anyone home? Time for a filing upgrade!" before Oscar could shush him.

Alexi called a couple more times and Oscar let him because by that point whatever damage he might do was done.

Oscar rushed down the hallway after his partner, turning

a corner into some kind of lounge with a TV and a pool table and shelves of books and a familiar face he nearly ran into, or its familiar body at least, the body of the redheaded woman from the train and the boat and the other train, too, standing now in this research station. She wore a full-length snow suit of glossy white fabric, lined in the hood with that same high-end plaid he'd noticed before, days ago, and trimmed with silvery fur. It looked as functional but far more expensive than the snowsuits of the two men with pistols standing to either side of her, whose outfits were more or less like Oscar's own though their guns were nothing like the phone in his pocket.

Around them lay overturned tables and spilled fans of paper across tiles and carpet, and bodies collapsed backward in chairs so their feet stuck up in ways that would have been comical if those bodies hadn't been real. A man sprawled on the pool table and a dark stain crept across the green felt from under his chest, and everything looked to be damaged or smashed or hurt in some way save for the TV which, though its volume was off or down low, was still showing—of course, what else could it be—scenes from *To The Moon!*. Whether the episode itself or a recap of it after the fact or some other show reporting as if it was news, who could say; perhaps Alexi who stood behind the armed men and below the wall-mounted screen gazing up, already rapt, but Oscar had no chance to ask.

"This isn't how we wanted it, Oscar," the redheaded woman said sounding earnestly sad, disappointed at least, but he didn't get much time to dwell on her emotional shadings because something struck him hard in the back of the head and he blacked out.

And then he came to in the dark, on his side in the cold—still in his snowsuit though his balaclava and goggles and gloves had not been replaced—and the whole world was throbbing and thrumming until he lifted his head so it throbbed and thrummed slightly less.

"Hello?" he called but could hardly hear himself over the

noise. His head ached where he'd been struck but it was hard to tell how much of that was from the blow and how much was a headache brought on by the rattle and hum of the floor and the ceiling and walls, which, he'd now realized, weren't parts of a room but parts of a trunk, albeit a large one, and that he had been tossed with his hands and feet tied into the dark compartment of some vehicle now in motion.

The bindings made reaching his pockets impossible so Oscar rolled sideways a couple of times, back and forth, to feel for the bump of his phone in a pocket. First with his legs and then, when he felt nothing, with his torso and at last he detected the shifting weight as his phone slid from one side to the other of an inner pocket below his snowsuit. He wasn't able to touch it, of course, he couldn't make or receive any calls, but the link was still there—unreachable as he was, as far off the radar and out of sight, he was still tethered to his wife and his work and the world outside that dark trunk. He couldn't do anything about it but at least he still had the reassuring possibility of perhaps being able to later, if whoever had struck his head and was driving this transport hadn't killed him by then (the likelihood of which Oscar was trying not to consider at that very moment, so let's not dwell on it).

Oscar imagined what he might say and how Julia might reply if he could call to tell her, "Oh, fine, just locked in a trunk somewhere in the Arctic after being run off into the night on a snowmobile. You?"

"Well, apart from you waking me up, I'm okay," she might tell him, assuming it was still the small hours of morning and still dark outside, as it would be in the southern latitudes, too. "Tired, of course," and she might yawn.

"Julia," he might ask her, "do you remember the blackout a few summers ago?" because he was thinking about darkness for obvious reasons. "That night the whole city was dark and the AC stopped working and we sat all night on the balcony watching people navigate the streets by the glow of their phones until all the batteries died?"

And she would remember, of course, because it had been one of their best nights in a long time: how they'd raced to finish not only the beer getting warm in the fridge but also the ice cream from the freezer. How it gave them stomachaches of a kind that were almost funny, not nauseous, not sick, but aware of their bodies because the strange combination of foods gave a corresponding sensation to the strangeness of the overall night, a physical imprint of the memory and Oscar felt it in his guts even now remembering that conversation they'd never had.

Who would have seen them from below on the street? Sitting next to each other in their lawnless chairs, the clink of bottles every so often when they reached toward the table between them at the same time or a shifting foot kicked one of the empties they had set down as the hours went on. Who knew how many other marriages, how many other husbands and girlfriends and boyfriends and wives had watched the dark from their own balconies or rooftops or windows, talking or not, laughing or not, eating together whatever they didn't want wasted if the blackout went on for a while, a darkness as far reaching as night in the Arctic and as wide open to expectation and dreams. As vast and optimistic as the most unbounded visions of scientists sleeping.

"Remember the guys on their bikes with headlamps?" she'd ask, and he'd laugh and say yes. "The hydrant," she'd say, "how they…," and together they'd rebuild the moment, finishing each other's sentences and leaving some phrases not finished at all because they both gave in to laughing instead, no need to say what both already knew, the sharing the thing, the secret shared memory no one else in the world could call up.

"And the morning," he'd say. "How many people fell asleep on their stoops and balconies like we did and all of us waking up face to face across the street when the sun rose? Oh, and the guy asleep on the roof of a car? The pizza delivery car? Remember him? Do you remember?"

"I do, Oscar. I do."

And they'd laugh about it together, across all those miles from their apartment where she was waking up to the north wherever he was, perhaps past the edge of nowhere by now, in a trunk, in his head, closer than the two of them had been in a very long time, closer than they'd been on the plane or from the basement room of Northern Branch. Closer than they'd been in their own bed that pre-dawn morning a few days before when he didn't wake her before departing the city.

The vehicle ground to a stop, metal quaking around him, so Oscar ended his call that had never begun and waited for what would come next. There was no muffled slam of a door, no voices made distant by walls, just the same dark and the same Oscar stuck in it as there had been a moment before but now, his call over, that same Oscar was much more alone.

The hunter stood outside an office in which two men worked with their backs to his eye. They stood before a wide sheet of paper, the outline of a map—the same shape he'd seen on that pink sheet left behind, the map that delivered him there—and they marked its white spaces in pencil and talk. One man was so tall he could reach to the top of the map without straining and his partner was shorter so stood on a stool. A single bare lightbulb swung from the ceiling, its filament strands looped into a fine, glowing noose at the end of a cord.

An intercom buzzed and spoke, the voice coming only in crackles to the hunter's ear still unused to such indoor, echoing spaces and to words reduced to weak currents for crossing distances greater than speech does in the north. It's not that he'd never known those things, of course, but it had been a long time and his trip south not quite long enough to inure him again, not that he wanted it to. And whatever that crackling voice had announced or demanded or said, the workers at the map seemed to know what it was because they turned around, they rushed for the door, and gave the hunter only a second—the crack of a shot—to duck out of sight in a coffin-sized alcove from which he could watch the backs of those men move away down that sterile green corridor.

After they'd knocked at and entered a room farther down, and when that room's door had been closed, he moved into the office. His shadow rippled, a trick of the lightbulb at sway from the hasty exit of those two cartographers—if that's what they were, with their map—but that kind of unsteady light the hunter was used to: the blurred edges of everything up on the ice, the way nothing quite holds its shape. Something a few yards away can look miles off and the more deadly reverse occurs, too. A ship or a bear might sit on the horizon for days without seeming to shift until suddenly it falls in your path and will not be denied.

The way the hunter moved unnoticed off the horizon and into that room.

The way he would not be denied.

The way he slid the laden bag from his dark-suited shoulder, tucked his stolen tie between buttons and out of the way, lifted the bomb from its padding of bath towels and bedsheets found in a laundromat's driers, and settled it onto the floor in front of that map, nearly blank, too blank for the hunter in places.

21

Several identical arms belonging to several more or less identical bodies (owing to their identical parkas and sleeves) pulled Oscar up and out of the vehicle and dropped him other than gently into the snow. Once his eyes left the dark of the trunk he was blinded by sunlight and glare, brightness in all directions, bouncing off vehicle and snowpack and sky, the whole world erased in a bright flash of light; bomb-like, perhaps, but let's not overdo it. When he hit the ground the impact made him exhale and his next breath filled ears, nose, and mouth with fresh, powdery snow, cutting his senses off from the world once again but only for a sliver of second before he reentered it coughing. He lay blinking in the powder, sputtering and sneezing, but not long before he was hoisted to his feet and a dark bag was pulled over his head. His eyes, into and out of the light, were by then as confused as his brain.

He was marched or dragged more like across crunching snow with other boots crunching and whooshing around him and at least five firm hands gripping his arms and one more dragging him by the scruff of his snowsuit's hood and the other hood pulled on outside it. Each hand seemed to have its own speed in mind so Oscar stumbled with every step, hardly walking in any real sense of the word, and it was all he could do not to topple but he stayed balanced, he supposed, because some hands pulled forward while others pulled back and a couple of others worked as lateral guys and the whole assemblage of counter-grips kept him upright.

Wind swirled snow up and under the hood, up his nose, across his face as soft, wet grit in that dark fabric chamber where his own breath was as loud and all-consuming as the vehicle's engine had been a moment before.

The hands dragged him onward then upward, the surface beneath his feet changing as he ascended a clanging ramp ridged with rungs. He could smell the sea now, not the fishy, briny sea back in Portland but something colder, more raw. The hands shifted position, the voices muttering above them moved too, and Oscar felt the narrow space at his sides as he rose and his elbows brushed railings and bars. Overhead but hard to judge where from under the hood a helicopter rumbled and stuttered and seemed to draw close.

Then the ramp leveled off and he stepped onto flat ground, or not ground exactly but the echo of his steps was replaced with flat, solid thunks. One arm pulled him hard left while the others went right and he pitched over onto an elbow so stars flashed and swirled as voltage ran up his arm and throughout his body.

Yet none of those hands' voices spoke, really spoke, just a couple of grunts, one seeming to acknowledge it had gone the wrong way, no apologies to Oscar or his electrified elbow, and he was dragged right—in unison this time—then out of the wind so, he guessed, into a room and finally pushed into a chair. His hands were tied behind it and his legs to its own then several pairs of feet stamped away and he was alone, in his hood, in a room, and he could tell for certain he was on a ship, its roll undeniable now that Oscar himself had gone still.

And he sat.

And the dark in that hood came and went as his mind wandered in waiting, sometimes as bright in his mind's eye as the phone when first activated and a few minutes later as dark as its dormant screen.

He may have slept or merely daydreamed but either way his mind wandered across the ice, toward the Pole, back out into the snow through which he'd been traveling since some time last night; the movement felt real, more real than that chair in that ship in those ropes and that hood. Motion—momentum—made more sense to him now than sitting still as he'd been doing for most of his life and he saw himself crossing the Pole, rounding the curve of the Earth, and instead of turning around to go home he saw himself carrying on and moving south along its far side through Siberia, Russia, across the equator and all the way to Antarctica and that other Pole, the one he'd never paid very much mind to but now wondered if he should have. Oscar saw himself never stopping but he saw Julia meeting him on the way, the two of them skiing and mushing and sailing together, forever circling his dream world at each other's side.

Then he was stopped, pulled back from his wandering when the hood was jerked from his face.

His was a room with gray walls dotted with rivets the way gray rooms in ships always are or at least always were in scenes set in ships that Oscar had watched on TV and in films. Two men in white parkas and dark watch caps stood by the door, machine guns in hand.

"Hello?" Oscar asked for lack of anything better to ask but he got no reply. "Where am I?" he tried and then, "Who are you?" with equally useless results. So he went back to waiting though now without the hood, and he tried not to stare at the men who were staring at him, both of them, and more than that tried not to stare at their guns. He shifted his weight in the chair just to feel the click and shift of his phone but the movement was too much for his guards who without really moving shifted their stances in a way that made clear to Oscar he should sit still. So he did.

There were no windows in that gray room, no portholes through which he could see the ocean or feel the breeze coming in. But the rumble of engines somewhere below carried up through the ship, vibrating the floor and his feet upon it, carrying up Oscar's legs and rattling his teeth and making him have to pee with increasing urgency the longer he sat.

About which he said nothing.

He doubted his captors would care.

He heard voices outside, beyond the door and its guards: a woman, smoky and serious, talking to… was that Alexi? Wasn't it? He couldn't tell what they were talking about but maybe his partner was tied up as he was, a prisoner in his own right in the next room. But no, Alexi didn't sound captive because now he was laughing and the woman was, too, while no one in his room—not Oscar nor the men in white parkas—was even smiling at one another. So if Alexi was indeed imprisoned his confinement was somehow more fun.

He heard Alexi ask about breakfast then more specifically pancakes as the voices got closer and easier to make out in detail. The woman said something about the galley, about not long now, and Oscar heard his partner groan. Then the redheaded woman—her again!—stepped into the room and Alexi entered behind her, dressed in a black commando-style sweater, patches on the shoulders and elbows and all, a black pistol hanging at the end of his arm and so matte it seemed to suck in all light, more shadow than object to Oscar's eye.

"Alexi?!" he asked. "What are you… why… you have a gun."

"Oh, well, you know. It's for work."

"Oscar," said the redheaded woman, shaking her head, sounding genuinely sad on his behalf. Or perhaps disappointed in him. "I hoped it wouldn't come to all this. I really did."

"To all what?" he asked, trying to stay calm, to represent BIP in the steady way he'd been trained. Then to Alexi, who was standing beside him now, the gun hanging unnervingly close to Oscar's side, "But we work together! What are you talking about?"

"Oh, Oscar," she said, laying a warm hand on his cheek then dragging those rose petal nails down the side of his neck, stirring a downward shiver to rival the one rising up from the floor, his whole body ablaze, and now Oscar really needed that piss. Alexi yawned then smacked his lips.

"I—"

"Shhh," she said, laying a finger across his lips. "Let me offer you this one more time." She leaned forward and a cloud of her scent—new-fallen snow, the Arctic's fresh air, not being tied up with a gun in your face—filled his nose. The warmth of her body radiated across his own but Oscar was a trained professional and he persevered, neither wetting himself nor giving in to her charms. And they were, let's be frank, very charming.

"Just tell us," she said. "Just tell us, Oscar. How did you know? How did you find it? And, most of all, if nothing else, can you find it again, somewhere else? Can you teach us how? That's all we want. That's all we're after and you can go home, go back to your wife, to your magazines and all of that. You can go back to your life. I'll take you myself and I'll make you rich, too." She laid a hand on each of his shoulders, pulling their faces so close they could kiss. "It's really not very much we're asking of you. No one's harmed. Nothing's lost. We all win. You. Me. The people I represent. BIP, naturally. Your Director Lenz."

"I don't know what you're talking about! I'm in filing. Re-cords. It's pretty dull stuff! I don't even know what's in the files, I don't even know where they are, just how to keep track of them as hypothetical objects in some other department." He turned to his partner as far as his binds would allow. "Tell her Alexi, tell her what we do. Tell her the truth about BIP, tell her it's pretty dull stuff!"

"To be honest, Oscar," Alexi said, "I still don't entirely understand what BIP does. I haven't been there very long, you know."

A lesser man, a less professional man, might have lost control at his partner's amnesiac betrayal. But it was easy as second nature for Oscar to focus, to reassess the situation and summon his training and respond as if he had no idea what she was talking about because he had, in fact, no idea what she was talking about. No idea what she was after.

"I'm not sure why you're so interested in filing systems," he said, "but I'd be happy to take a look at your archives and help you bring them to order, if that's what you're after. Off the books, of course. Unofficially. I—"

Her face wrenched itself into a snarl, her eyes darkening as she snapped, "Damn it, Oscar. Goddamnit. Why are you making this harder than it needs to be? Stop dicking around. Do you hear me? Do you see this man?" She stood up, away from him, an arm gesturing toward the man in the sweater.

"Alexi? Of course, he's my partner, he—"

"This man is going to shoot you in the kneecap if you don't tell me once and for all what I want to know."

"Shoot me?!" He turned again to his partner and strained against the ropes and the chair which had started to wobble and rock with his anxious contortions. "Why would you do that? Why are you helping her? What is this, Alexi?"

"Eh, work, what can you do? I promise to be fast."

"We can do it that way, Oscar. We really can. I don't want to but I will. So why are you holding out? Think of the villages, the people who live there, of what this might mean for them. We can all get rich, Oscar. They can get rich. There are enough mining rights to go around. All of us."

"Fast as a lightbulb," chuckled Alexi.

Oscar swallowed, all instinct now, nothing but training, able even to ignore Alexi's misuse—again—of that treasured maxim. His palms were sweating and soaking the ropes on his wrists and beads ran down his face. His crotch felt like he had a wet washcloth down there and he felt a steady drip down his back and into his shorts, layers deep under his snowsuit and fleeces and shirt. But he kept steady, he kept all Slotkin's lessons in mind and replied, "As I said, I'd be glad to take a look at your filing system if—"

"Son of a bitch. Fucking shoot him," the redheaded woman

growled, stepping back, and Alexi crooked his elbow, raising the gun as his other hand slid back the chamber. He was lowering it again, back toward Oscar, who was concentrating on running through a complicated filing code in his head to stay calm, when something hit the ship hard, shaking the room and everyone it. That impact was almost enough for Oscar to miss the fact that the gun, the gun aimed at him, had been fired and, in fact, fired before being lowered again all the way to his knee (if that had indeed been the target) and instead he'd been shot in the head.

Hence the screaming he started to do, and the bleeding, which no one else was paying much attention to at this point because they were rushing out of the room, their guns leading the way, and yelling at each other about what that impact and noise might have been, what had been big enough to shake the whole ship.

In other words, they—not just "they," some anonymous "they," but Alexi, his very own partner—had shot Oscar in the head then left him behind, fallen over now whether because of the force of the gunshot or the impact on the ship or his own failed attempt to jump out of the way while tied to chair. Whatever the reason he was on his side though still bound with blood spilling over his face and onto the floor.

He was still screaming, of course.

There really was a lot of blood, after all—headwounds, you know—but not so much damage to Oscar's eventual relief when he'd later had time to look back on it all. At the time, though, before he'd had time, he was sideways and screaming and for a moment believed his head had been hole-blown straight through (which would have made screaming unlikely, if we stop to consider, but Oscar was in no mood for logic just then). So he screamed. And he bled. And he made too much noise of his own to notice at first the noises outside and above and below, the shooting and yelling and frequent explosions, the clanging and thumping and sometimes a splash. And the many, many gunshots that echoed and ricocheted and, frankly, did not hit him in the head—the vast, vast majority of all the shots fired that day, the sheerest number of sheer possibilities and likeliest outcomes considering all those moving lead parts set in motion, those projectiles intent on projecting until something got in their way, the greater part of the space of that ship filled with bullets and shrapnel going one way or another and often in several directions at once—so all in all he'd been pretty lucky to only get shot in his head the one time.

22

Oscar bled for a while. A pretty long while but not so long he died or anything like it. As it turned out the bullet had grazed to the left of his scalp and just barely so it was bloody and sure, it would sting, but no harm really done in the end. Which was good luck for him and for us, too, because that wouldn't be much of an ending.

His ears rang, his eyes swam, everything throbbed that was capable of throbbing and the parts of him that weren't capable throbbed anyway because of the enormous diesel engines still thundering away in the bowels of the ship. Beyond that ringing and those engines, too, the ship had gone very quiet. No more gunshots or bootsteps, no more shouting or clanking or bangs. Not even the echo of somebody whistling.

"Hello?" Oscar called, not entirely sure it was a good idea considering he was tied up and bloody, knocked over now, while everyone else on the ship had arrived with a gun. But what else could he do so again he called out, "Hello? I'm in here! I'm tied up!"

And again no one came so he went on bleeding and ringing and being alone.

He also struggled against his bindings, because that's what you do when you're tied to a chair, and whether it was falling over that lessened their pressure or the slipperiness of his spilt blood, those ropes weren't so fast as they'd been before. It wasn't pleasant, it burned, stung, and strained and the exertion pumped blood faster from the wound on his head and made his ears ring even louder but in time—which he had plenty of for the moment—Oscar was able to wriggle out one of his hands. From there it was easy enough to untie the other, then his hands could team up at freeing his legs, and all four of those appendages helped him stand with the extra aid of the chair because his head was swimming quite badly by now, he'd been shot, and had stars and black squiggles at the edge of his vision so it took a few minutes upright to come back to himself.

And to come back to that room on that ship where, from the sound of it or lack thereof, he was alone.

He wiped as much blood from his face as he could with the sleeve of his snowsuit but the waterproof fabric wasn't much for absorbance so mostly he smeared it around. Supporting himself with a hand on the wall Oscar crept from the room, stepping over the lower rim of the elliptical door and into a long corridor the same shade of gray. Behind ringing ears his footsteps echoed but no others did and as he turned a corner Oscar learned why: bodies lay heaped in the hallway, sprawled on the floor and collapsed against walls and one draped over a threshold half inside and half out on the deck; three were jumbled together in the hatch between rooms but if they'd been killed while charging or fleeing he couldn't work out. Their blood had already cooled on the floor, not quite frozen but jelly-thick and a dropped cigarette stood in the gel as if planted. Cold wind blew through that open door but the chill took the bite from Oscar's head wound so that was okay.

There were guns all over, too, and more blood, and though he was tempted to pick up a pistol if not something larger from the many weapons laid out to choose from Oscar decided against it: he wasn't a gunman, he wasn't a soldier, he was an Arctic explorer and database specialist. He was a prognosticator and all that entailed. Guns had no part in that.

He found a towel in the ship's galley and wiped his face, washing it more or less clean at a sink piled with pots, then made his way up to the bridge. There were bodies all over the ship;

not dozens of them—this wasn't that big a ship—but a couple large handfuls, at least, so more than enough to unsettle. At the bridge he saw a man dead in a naval uniform without insignia, a dark blue sweater and blank admiral's hat, a captain without a flag. At that highest point on the ship (Oscar wasn't about to climb an antenna) he unzipped several layers and dug out his phone, fingers crossed, but no, there was nothing, and he was disappointed but not surprised. At least it was charged, though, at least it was ready if a signal appeared or if he got a call. He had the hope of a battery ready for use.

Passing from the bridge into the next room and the next, stepping through one egg-shaped hatch after another, Oscar heard voices. He rushed, barking his shin on a doorway, so slowed himself down. "Hello?" he called, "Hell…," then remembered the gunfight, the blood, the dead bodies all over the ship and regretted he'd opened his mouth.

Still the voices grew louder, into laughter and screaming, and he stepped at last into an entertainment room of some sort not so unlike the room back at the research station where the redheaded woman and her men had been waiting and not so different, either, from the lounge at that strange Canadian airport and again, as in those rooms, as in every room it by now seemed to Oscar, that show that damn show played on a TV mounted high on the wall. Those would-be astronauts for whom the stars weren't so much the point as the stardom, the inane challenges they put themselves through, manipulated pawns in some producer's cruel machinations, incessantly steering them this way and that, week after week to earn the privilege of being flown by computer and ground crew without so much as a button to push on their own and…

After all he'd been through, all those days on the road and the air and sea and the run, Oscar couldn't bring himself to be indignant. He couldn't care what those smiling heads did and he almost turned off that TV and that show but he couldn't even be bothered to make that much effort as he turned around and went back as he'd come through the galley and finally outside.

After wandering above and below decks, in and out of the wind, Oscar was certain no one else had survived and was equally certain all the dead had been from the ship: there was no sign of their killers, whoever had saved Oscar's skin, whether they'd meant to or not. And there was also no way off the boat. Its engines were running but idle, its anchors weighed with their chains wound round the capstans on deck, but the vessel stood still. The shore was, he supposed, within swimming distance if it hadn't been far too cold for a swim. Not that Oscar was much of a swimmer, certainly not up to the demands of those Arctic seas.

He went back to the bridge, wondering if he might sail ashore, but beyond his bafflement at the buttons and knobs and displays of the helm he couldn't imagine such a large ship was meant to touch land, not after it had been launched. Once adrift, always adrift is what Oscar knew about boats whether he was right or not.

So he sat in the bridge, watching the windows, watching the sun sail low on the horizon. Head in hands, fingers stuck in his blood-matted hair, Oscar forced himself to think about Nansen, the *Fram*, about how they'd fared so much better than the men of *Jeannette*. Be ready, he told himself. Be prepared to sit still, to freeze in. Be prepared, always, for wintering over. Be prepared even when you aren't prepared: always be expecting the doldrums and ice.

Fast as a lightbulb, he thought and then said it aloud. "Fast as a lightbulb," he chanted again and again, a mantra now, echoing in the steel hull, the slow, steady electricity of those ancient filaments rippling through his body as their warmth calmed his mind. And he was ready once more to stand up and try. His battery charged, his signal strong. His keen bureaucrat's instinct restored.

He returned to the deck and this time found a life raft stowed under a hatch, a bit big to row very far on his own considering he'd never rowed anything but surely manageable as far as the shore, and if not then like his Arctic heroes who had so often abandoned ships of their own he would drift. The raft was already stocked with a lifejacket and a bright orange survival suit, and of course paddles, a flare gun, the usual tools. From the galley he collected a seabag of food and even remembered to take a can opener. He packed matches and knives in two sizes, and blankets and sweaters and other dry clothes, all in a second watertight bag. He reached into his pockets for the BIP envelopes, hands with a mind of their own by now and ready to pack those papers safely away, only to remember he no longer had them, they'd been left with Clark back at Northern Branch, and he hoped Clark was okay after whatever it was that had happened. He hoped he might someday find out.

And Alexi, too, whoever he was, whatever he was really doing. Oscar was certain now (maybe not as soon as the rest of us were but he'd gotten there in his time) his partner was somehow suspicious, perhaps not a real prognosticator at all; the shot in his head had been a strong clue. Now his erstwhile partner was nowhere to be seen, his body not among the dead on the ship for which Oscar was grateful despite Alexi's frustrations. The redheaded woman wasn't on the ship, either, though he'd spotted the armed men in white pitched headfirst and dead at the foot of some stairs, their lifeless arms fallen around each other, for which Oscar didn't feel bad though he felt a bit cruel about not feeling worse.

When his lifeboat was loaded with everything he expected to need, the best selection of gear he could make by picturing all those provision lists he'd pored over from expeditions real and imagined, all that unexpectedly practical knowledge he'd gained through years of socially awkward obsession, Oscar couldn't figure out how to get the boat down to the water. There wasn't a pulley system the way he'd seen in sinking ship movies, and there wasn't a ramp or a stairway down to a waterline door. Was he meant to just throw it and jump? To leap with the boat held beneath him the way he'd done with an inner tube sled as a child?

Then he spotted a ladder down the outside of the hull, easy to miss because it was the same color as every other gray shape apart from the rust spots that gave it away. He could tie the boat to that ladder then drop it so it stayed alongside, and climb down with his gear even if it took a few trips. So he found a strong rope, then a second and third just in case, and tied them all to the ladder. He brought down one seabag then the other and went back up for a final check of the ship intending to untie the ropes, which he'd hold on his last climb down, because he might need them again later, ashore. But as he was about to release those lines he looked off toward land and creeping across the horizon saw a pale silhouette, a droopy, loping wedge of white body and a too-tiny head supported on massive legs, lumbering along in a breeze that rippled its fur. He watched that polar bear in the distance until it was gone, until Oscar shivered from standing still. Almost too late he remembered his hat and gloves taken from him back at the research station but found them now—mercifully, to avoid stealing clothes from a dead body—in a heap of Alexi's own left behind gear.

And at the last moment, because of the bear or because he remembered what every explorer suggested in every account and even the government's own guidelines for Arctic science, he stopped and picked up a handgun from the open hand of a corpse (and thank goodness for that cold air to keep the smell down and flies off), heavier than he expected but somehow lighter, too. He dropped it into a pocket of his parka but didn't like how it shifted as he climbed down the ladder so in the boat, before setting off, he shifted that pistol into a seabag and put his phone in that pocket instead. Then Oscar gathered his lines, had a last look up the ladder at the now-lifeless ship, and pushed off with a clacking paddle blade against the hull, shifting himself toward land, setting sail alone into the Arctic as so many great men had done and now he had, too.

Her nostrils caught something new on the wind, a new warmth, a new flavor. She snorted. Swung her head one way then the other, shook her senses clean to confirm the scent on a clear palate and yes, there it was still.

She couldn't see it yet but might as well when the scent was so strong. And she moved over the ice, legs widespread, neck and belly low, sliding her paws with hardly a lift so her weight dispersed enough to hold down the world. To keep the ice and the land beneath both in place, to hold them attached to the sky and the water, to fix them in time. Make them fast.

Hers was big work, as big as her body, and she did it well and had done it for years and for ages untold.

That smell now, she knew, was just over a rise where the water met land. That smell was moving over the water to her. A warm body, all bodies, are moving to her in due time, often so slowly they don't feel the motion and don't feel her breath but always they are moving to her. Always they are on her wind and her weight is always already spread over their ice.

"Lenz. Listen. Lenz. No…no…no…not…

"There's enough for all of us. For us all to get rich, you, me, the generals, everyone. What your man found…yes, 'found,' obviously, but…

"And how's he working out, the new one? Fitting in?

"Good… no… no, I wasn't concerned about him getting the job, more about how he would do it.

"Good. Good. No, I'm sorry, too, he's a good man, I'm sure, but it has to be… he has to… let me finish, for fuck…he…

"No, he has to, he knows too much. Much too much.

"The usual people. The same ones we always have take care of things… do you… no, right, I don't think you want to know who they are.

"Right. So you'll put it in the records yourself? No one else?

"Excellent. Good. Yes, we've created the shell, it…

"No, not a mining firm, too obvious. Petroleum, it… no, it's… under the umbrella of an umbrella of something we already own, that's where. One of our others.

"Because no one trusts them already, because the worst is already assumed. Yes… exactly… yes, easier to get away with something in shades of gray if everyone thinks all you're doing is black. They won't see the iffy if their eye's out for evil…

"Oh, yeah, I'm a poet all right.

"At your door now? So you're sending them?

"Good. Excellent. Lenz. Listen. Lenz. Tell your man…no, the new one…tell him to keep an eye. I think there are others. Lurkers. I think our project is on the radar and he'll have to watch out. Others thinking the Arctic's in play, again, after so many years.

"That's what I'm saying, that… because the settlement, that's why. No, bunch of fucking shacks, but… exactly: who?

"Okay, call them in. Send them off."

23

Oscar pulled the lifeboat ashore on a gray strip of beach unhidden by snow. He could see snow elsewhere, across the water at a far off spit of land to the north and on another longer spit stretching to sea from the south. But here, where he'd put in, the ground was bare. A treeless plain stretched flat toward a jagged sneer of mountains and rocky hills with tangled scrub caught in their teeth. Those visible rocks and plants stood out against the rest of the landscape, against the ice he'd just crossed, against the mud and the gray, and Oscar couldn't help wondering why.

When he'd hauled the boat as far up the beach as his arms sore from rowing were able, he dropped it and sat. The ground beneath him was warm, not hot but warm enough, warmer than anything else and he pulled off his sea-wet gloves to lay chilled hands on soft clay. Resting, scanning that plain, Oscar spotted puffs and plumes of steam jetting out of the ground, one every few seconds but not in the same places.

When his legs had stopped aching, when his fingers could again curl and grip without pain, he stood up and left his seabags and gear where they were in the boat while he walked a bit of that plain. It was familiar, not familiar as if he'd been there before but not the vagueness of déjà vu either: he knew this land in some genuine way whatever and wherever it was.

As he walked, turning every minute or so to look back to the boat where he'd left his supplies and the gun—his phone safe in his pocket, of course—he warmed up enough to put down the hood of his snowsuit and tuck his balaclava, already rolled up as a cap, into a pocket. He unzipped the front of his suit but left the fleece layer beneath sealed to his neck. He nearly stepped on one of those steam spouts as it erupted but pulled his foot back in time; its hot spray on his face and hands wasn't quite scalding—it cooled in the air before reaching his skin—but it was hot enough to sting and would have been worse, he realized, had he been blocking the hole.

At about the midpoint of the plain, equidistant from mountains and ocean alike, a strange blackened area lay dead and charred. The ground there was heaped as if recently turned but no softer than anywhere else. Oscar paced its edge and found that burnt area to be almost round, a slight oval, the size of a small city block, maybe, the size of his block at home where so much groundwork and road work were always undone, but why? Why was it there, or why wasn't it if something had been but was burnt?

From the farthest point of that charred patch he spotted the worn rut of a trail, heading north and west toward a gap in the hills. It seemed to offer the way he should go; there was no one here on this plain but someone had followed that trail, many feet had worn its route into the ground, and perhaps he would find them at its other end.

Running on fumes intermittent as the geysers around him Oscar dragged himself back to where his gear waited. He checked his seabags, opening each cylinder of bright blue vinyl to make sure its contents were dry and unharmed after his lifeboat crossing. He rolled the first one re-closed, snapping its heavy plastic buckle to form a handle, then set to the second but stopped, unrolled it again, and withdrew the gun. He dropped the pistol into a pocket opposite his phone—an impulse, professional instinct, perhaps—then closed the bag and set off.

With a bag slung on each shoulder—one hand holding an energy bar scrounged from the ship, requiring a twist of his body and a shift of those bags each time he wanted a bite—he walked back to the trail and set out away from that patch of scorched earth. But just before entering the cut between hills where that path led away he stopped to adjust the weight of his baggage and turned to look back. In the half-light of afternoon in the Arctic, the sun nearly gone over the rim of the mountains, he realized why the place seemed familiar.

He'd hadn't been there, not really, but he'd made that place up: the steam vents and potential for geothermal reliance, the clay-rich ground stocked—in his version—with minerals and ores, the clear space the right size for a village, all of it. If Symmes' Hole existed, if it were real, this was the place it would be. This nondescript stretch of land between mountains and sea, this empty space blank as the map on the wall back at BIP, had made Oscar's name. Or he had made a name for that place, a name left unprinted but implied on his award plaque. It was one or the other or both but so hard to say now quite what his southern speculations were worth as ground down as he was by the reality of a landscape—that cut in the hills and the dark seeping in—ready to swallow him whole.

But he pictured his map, the land as he'd drawn it, and yes, this was it. Or could be if someone arrived and went to the trouble of raising a whole village here. If they found a reason to do it or if they discovered the reasons he, Oscar, had already given in his prognostications; someone might read his reports and arrive here expecting a village then set about building what they didn't find. Stranger things, he supposed, had happened. Men on foot ever finding, of all things, the North Pole, shifting and shapeless as it was, seemed fartherfetched in its way than building a village in this most unlikely of places.

It was too much for him now, though, too tired and worn out and weak. Too far from what was familiar he thought for a moment before realizing this was familiar in its own odd way, so too far, then, from something familiar in a familiar way. The known unknowns, so to speak.

He re-slung his seabags and set back to the trail, passing between the high rocks of the cut and leaving Symmes' Hole or this
coincidence of it to be wrapped up in evening at his back as he
moved—if his prognostications and the map back at BIP were
right about more than this plain—toward the settlement found
on his last day in the office before going north, that settlement
he'd speculated the hunters of Symmes' Hole discovered, and
why not? If one unlikely thing could be true, why not another, at
least? Why not a whole groundless continent made up of unlikely
things?

24

But unfortunately for Oscar it wasn't and a few steps into that cut the warmth of the geothermal pockets and the ease of crossing clear ground had been lost. Snow lay thick and each step meant hoisting his knees past his waist and he was glad for his snowsuit. He'd sealed it back up, restored his balaclava and gloves, but in that snowbound pass balls of ice on his eyebrows bobbed in time to his awkward steps.

The weight of the gun, small as it was, threw him off. He walked self-consciously, too aware of it being there, too aware it was loaded and too unfamiliar with that tool and its ilk, afraid despite knowing how unlikely it was the weapon might somehow fire in his pocket. So he favored that side, tried to move gently despite the high steps and the snow, despite the wind pushing him back and his need to lean forward to walk. The seabags were awkward, requiring his hands be held at his shoulders, because if he carried them low those blue anchors dragged in the powder and pulled him down.

But Oscar pushed on with the weak beam of a headlamp before him, something else he'd found on the ship. He recited, first in his head and then right out loud though lost to the wind, provision lists from old expeditions, from Peary and Nansen and even *Jeannette*. He ran through every item he remembered of Greeley's fitting out of his ill-fated airship and the meticulous records of Charles Francis Hall on his quest to confirm Franklin's fate, yellowed lists and accounts he'd pored over time and again through his life for until now no practical purpose yet here they were perhaps saving his life. He recited passages from Franklin's own preparations and from the pages of *National Geographic* two centuries later and he let his mind's eye trace every line of each side of his John Franklin lunchbox and its illustrations. He felt those great men at his back, supporting him against the chill wind even as it burned his eyes and his cheeks and he heard, soft on the wind but certainly there, he would swear it, Julia urging him onward, calling, "PF, Oscar! PF!" He heard his wife reminding him from far away but as clear to him now as if she had called on the phone that his whole life, his whole devotion, had prepared him—had prepared both of them—for this frozen trek, his early polar fever endured from afar an inoculation against mishap on the ice if anything was. If anything could be.

He pictured the phone at his hip, the electronic archive of his magazines, and in his head flipped through favorite pages behind squinting, scorched eyes. The snow thickened, its flakes heavier and beating now against his skin layers deep and audibly pelting the heavy fabrics of snowsuit and bags. He saw his fingers, glove-less and warm, on the touchscreen and speed-dialing his wife, he almost heard the rings in his ear as he waited for Julia's answer.

He remembered for no reason why except perhaps every reason that mattered right then a suitcase they'd had in their early years; where had it come from, a gift from one of their parents? Her mother? His? How it came to them didn't matter but one of its wheels had been broken, it spun, and in an airport while flying somewhere (What trip was that? What destination? Oscar's mind was thickening to mud, then to lead in the cold.) that broken wheel spun the suitcase in the opposite direction of wherever they wanted to go. Somehow, by some strange mechanism, it overrode the other three wheels, it took charge, and however they pushed or pulled the big gray hardshell of that bag it avoided their course. It was determined to drift, to make its own way, and they laughed—Oscar and Julia, not the bag, which was quite serious, and he laughed now behind his balaclava, a puff of breath bursting through its polypropylene skin to freeze in midair—and they shrugged and they smiled at each other. Without either one of them asking, without needing a pause to inquire or agree, they decided to follow the bag, let it lead them, why not? They went where that insistent bag rolled, took a long route through two terminals then awkwardly down a stairway instead of riding an escalator designed for large bags and it took both of them to haul it down, laughing together, impervious to the angry and baffled and worried looks they earned from all eyes but that bag led them straight to their subway station at the airport's far edge, took them right where they needed to go when they gave it a chance, and by the time they got there Oscar and Julia were holding warm hands and had another story for their private shelf.

They'd told it once and it hadn't gone over, hadn't made sense to someone not them, and they agreed again without asking that the story was better that way, better without being ruined by trimming and shaping and carving down to a husk so it might make sense to somebody else. It made sense to them, after all.

He'd tell her, when she picked up her own phone, where he was. He'd tell Julia about the snow in his face and the bags on his shoulders and he'd tell her the truth of his trip. He'd make it a story between them if it wasn't too late. As soon as he again reached someplace with a signal, as soon as the path he hoped was still under his feet and under the snow delivered him to a place where he could rest.

The cut had widened around Oscar since he had entered and the cliffs at its edges grown taller, high purple shadows in dusk, and he found himself traversing a deep, narrow valley, a perfect wind-tunnel for that storm and a bullhorn for its awful howling. He struggled to stay on his feet, never mind keep moving forward, and it may have been only the pull of the snow piled now to his thighs that anchored him against the gale, strong enough in that rocky funnel to make the cloth of his snowsuit crack sharp as whips; he would not be surprised to find bruises later even through his other layers.

Something moved to his left, not the snow but something beyond, a shape hard to make out behind the white curtain. Then he realized the shape, too, was white, a long, laden body on thick legs and a torso angling into the wedge of a head. A polar bear only a few dozen yards from where Oscar walked though higher up on the snowpack than he could stand despite its much larger body, and turning its head toward him now. Oscar's hand went to his pocket but the wrong one, grabbing his phone through the fabric of the snowsuit and the glove and the fleece it was zipped within layers down and had the bear charged he would have been much too late for the gun. But with his thick glove and inexperience it would have been no more useful than the phone, anyhow, and he took a strange comfort in that: knowing he wasn't a person who grabbed for a gun even when doing so might make sense.

And besides, the bear didn't charge, it sniffed the air and perhaps Oscar smelled rancid or did not smell at all in that snow but the bear swung its body and moved toward a the foot of a cliff. Some shape was there in the half-light, perhaps some body more appetizing than his, for which Oscar was grateful without creeping closer to find out what it was. Hurrying as much as he could, lifting his legs with adrenaline traces, Oscar moved away from the bear and its fortunate meal, toward the far end of that valley and into the dark and the snow.

In time—who knew how much, or how far, traveling in those conditions, the usual measures of distance and time rendered moot—that valley opened onto a plain more vast than the earlier one or maybe just seeming that way in the dark to Oscar with only the reflected moonlight on the snow and an eager but almost ineffective headlamp as his guide. He kept moving, not knowing what else to do, every part of him numb, his eyes watering and freezing at once, burning cold, every part of him moving only because it had been set in motion and hadn't been stopped, then something shimmered ahead.

A light. Not his own headlamp reflected but a new light, another, and Oscar found a last burst of willpower and urged himself on, stepped a bit higher for those last yards, and found a small hut in the snow. The door stuck when he first tried the handle and he almost panicked but years of training kept his mind calm and he pulled himself up in the doorframe to stand on that frozen steel arm until his weight brought it down and the portal swung open. He rushed in, dropped his bags, and slammed that door shut and already he felt the room's warmth.

That light, he discovered, was the orange glow of a space heater's coils, a long metal box on four stubby feet, standing to one side of the room. He dropped his gloves and with steam rising from between blue-tinged fingers knelt in something near benediction, likely the closest he'd ever come, a space heater found in the middle of some frozen nowhere at just the right moment, and do any of us ever come closer than that?

First the port side sagged, pitching the first mate and spilling his tea which by that time, after more than a year, wasn't quite "tea" at all but a foul brew of whatever could be scraped from canisters that had once held food.

The ship rolled to starboard then port again, over hours, of course, not at once, then it did shift at once with an exhale that echoed across the whole world. As much as the men could take in, anyway, from their high vantage point which was quite a lot: the curve of the earth, the far reach of space, so much to be seen from that patch of nowhere they'd long occupied.

The ice exhaled, the sea finally sighed, and the ship dropped with the kiss of a splash and after so long aloft, so long as an aerie instead of a craft set for sailing, the vessel was returned to the sea. The captain stood on the ice for a last time and saw his ship reach the water. Its force pushed the pack at his feet, widened cracks that had been forming slowly for days, floes rising and falling independently of one another for the first time in a year, no longer a monolithic horizon. The world once again was made of moving parts and neither he, the captain, nor they his men nor their ship would have a unified, predictable gaze on that white world again.

Everything had its own motion. Everything had its own course whether set for itself or by some other on its behalf, and these men, these explorers, destined for greater fame than they already knew once they'd steered their still-solid ship back to the south with a full crew intact, when they'd told tales of their exploits on the ice—of ice bears and ribbons of color across a night sky that lasted for months without lightening—they would never again take in the world the same way nor would anyone else. Too much was in motion, too much was in play, for one panorama to capture it all. The men of the future would come on skis and snowmobiles and great massive ships with bows that mauled ice from their paths, they would chart a strange course to the Pole, perhaps crossing only what fell before them by weather or chance without attending to all of the rest. Without finding time for surprise.

And the captain, leaning back and forth to keep his own chunk of ice balanced as in a game he'd seen once at a fair, knew his own age was passing even as he reached its peak. But the ship began shifting more swiftly, began sliding away and pushing his ice block away from its hull leaving the captain no more time for reflection. He rushed on slipping seaboots to its ladder and over its gunwale before his own ship could sail home without him.

In his rush he tore a strap from his parka, a strip of leather with a buckle-end on it, left behind on the ice to freeze, in time, between layers and make its own slow way around the Pole, north and south, east and west, across time, inert and insensible but in its long voyage the envy of men.

How little she had to bring home after so many years in that office. After so long at that desk and, earlier, at a different desk in a different building but at the same job, mediating land claims and disputes over mining, making sure clinics and community centers were constructed and corporate promises kept. A nondescript office in a nondescript building set on an anonymous block in a grand city but she was headed into retirement knowing she had made a difference, had done work that mattered—the reservation school she'd gotten replaced at the expense of the paper company upstream responsible for its contamination, and the permits she had made possible for a village determined to become self-sustaining, finding them money for turbines and streambed dynamos—and that her long route to get there was worth it.

The plaques and certificates, the files and trinkets from conferences and retreats, none of it would mean much in her new life. But she packed them all the same into a box so her colleagues wouldn't see how much she'd thrown away and, perhaps, be insulted. She would carry them down in the elevator or most likely some younger colleague would offer to hold the carton for her. Down to the glass and steel lobby that looked dated now even to her ancient eyes and had looked ugly even when it was new, and she would carry that box all the way home on the Metro to throw those artifacts out quietly or perhaps, in her home, change her mind about one or two that might later strike her as something worth keeping.

She had been in the south for decades, the vaster part of her life, but her tastes still ran to the starkly unornamented, the snowed spaces of childhood and the ice stretching for miles from her family's block home back north. She had only one picture of

those years because there was never a camera, and it had hung
for decades in her living room's pride of place over the mantel, a
not so large print in a not so large frame surrounded by the full-
ness of a white wall. It showed herself as a child, perhaps three
years old, holding hands with a snowman she'd made with her
father, most of the work done by his craftsman's fingers strong
with centuries of knowledge known deep in his bones. In the
south she'd seen stacks of two or three lumps with a scarf pass
for snowfolk but her father's were almost alive; in the photo the
edges of an anorak and hood were carved sharply into the snow,
sharper than the fur edges of her own coat made blurry as she
danced beside that man frozen twice. He wore the narrow eyes of
her people that outsiders had always mistaken for myopic views,
and his mouth—a joke of her father's—was so flat and unsmiling
in a way her people never had been even deep in their hungriest
winters. That was something the photographer who only passed
through her childhood at least understood, letting her grin and
dance instead of hold still as other men with other cameras had
done, once telling her father to pose like an Inuktitut—trying
to what, pass himself off as local?—and her father had been too
polite to laugh in that outsider's face, instead striking a serious
visage that wasn't his own and giving the family enough jokes to
last the whole of that year's long night.

And only that single outsider, that one photographer of all
the scholars and filmmakers and journalists who passed through
her village, ever bothered to send something back. The others had
kept their photographs and recordings and books to themselves,
had kept them from her until she came south and sought out the
ones she could find, making an effort to know of herself and her
home what those southern others had laid claim to upon their
return. But that one black and white image had arrived in their
box at the general store miles away from the house a year or two
later, the first piece of mail she had ever received, and though it
was a picture of herself and showed only familiar surroundings it

made the world wider than she'd ever known. That photograph in its own way was why she'd gone south, left her family and their blockhouse behind, but it was also so much of why she went back whenever she could, as much as her village—and it was a village no longer—had changed.

That old photograph as much as anything else was why she had spent nearly her whole working life in this office and a couple of others just like it, making what difference she could and hoping, sometimes actually knowing, she was impacting lives like her own. That was enough to take home from that last afternoon, after the cake had been cut and the speeches all made and the gift of a clock (as if she would have much more need for its kind of time) etched on the back with her name and her dates and an outline of her northern home far away.

Outside a helicopter approached and she looked away from her desk to the window, craning around her computer's monitor molded from plastic yellowed over time to the shade of a dog's urine traces in snow; an unsavory shade but one she'd known well at one time and so had been unable to avoid laughing during the years that plastic had darkened. She couldn't see the aircraft but the shadow of its rotors stirred over asphalt four stories below and a man in a dark suit walking fast on the sidewalk turned his head without stopping to look up at the sound. If she hadn't known the helicopter was there she might have thought he was looking at her.

25

It took some time for Oscar's eyes and his everything else to adjust. But as his blood got back to flowing and his mind calmed (after he'd checked that the door was closed tightly three times, that polar bear still looming large in his thoughts) the room began to take shape around him in the soft orange glow of the space heater. It was about the size of his office at BIP, not that he measured; it just came to him, the space felt familiar without even thinking about it. It had windows, though, that was something, even if at that moment all those windows showed him was murk.

At least they didn't show him the bear, or the guns, or the interior of a snowcat's trunk. Or being chased through the streets or across a train station or a door smashing into his nose or an elbow cracked on the deck of a ship or… there were any number of things Oscar was glad not be looking at in the dormant screens of those dark panes of glass. By then, in fact, he might have taken a nice, dumb episode of *To The Moon!* over the last few days of his life if he'd been offered the choice.

Instead he had a space heater. A space heater and a dark room.

The orange coils reflected in the pool of melted snow running down Oscar's sleeves and pant legs, and constant fresh drops kept that puddle in motion and those lights were a shimmering, shivering aurora borealis on the floor at his feet. And why not, the way his world had turned upside down?

In time Oscar spotted a switch on the wall and flipped on an overhead fluorescent light but visibility didn't change the room much: it was still mostly empty and still mostly gray. A desk stood against one wall with only a large, leather-bound ledger on it, spread open with a thick sheaf of pages laid to each side. A pile of books and magazines stood a bit chaotically for Oscar's comfort on the floor, leaning against the end of that desk, though he was buoyed to see a few bright yellow spines peeking out of the scrum. A stairway had been cut into the floor of one corner as at Northern Branch though narrower this time and without cover or railing; had Oscar wandered the room before finding the light he might have broken a leg or a neck.

A second switch on the wall lit that hole in the floor into life, a beckoning gleam underground, so he went. Downstairs, unlike Northern Branch's vast subterranean hive, was the same size as upstairs but more claustrophobic without the windows. One corner was boxed off on its own, a bathroom as Oscar discovered, and an Army-style cot piled with blankets stood by another wall with a bureau to serve as headboard. The rest of the room was given over to storage, of canned goods and boxes of freeze-dried and powdered foods, cereals and crackers and jerkies of meat. That room was as thick with Arctic objects as the archives of BIP, a database of northern necessity packed in tight around him, all those many choices offering a seemingly endless but finite supply; he could imagine them ticking away, those supplies, without replenishment until food and life were all gone. Each morsel and carton was carefully labeled with nutritional facts and energy stats. Each bore a uniform chart telling the consumer how long it would power them at what low temperatures. Those foods had been specifically packaged for the Arctic, then, but without any labels or logos to indicate to Oscar by whom.

And he didn't much care as he tore open a packet of un-specified jerky of meat, ate it as fast as he could without choking, washed it down with a bottle of water, and collapsed in a heap on the bed, still in his snowsuit and boots on top of its blankets.

Then he woke, looked around at that underground room full of boxes and bottles and bags long enough to recall where he was, how he'd gotten there, how completely he didn't know how to get anywhere else, and went back to sleep because he was tired and what else was he going to do?

Then he woke again, went through the same process of re-realization, but this time his body insisted on staying awake and outvoted his brain by enlisting his bladder to assert irresistible pressure. How long since he'd spoken Oscar couldn't figure exactly but his silence felt drawn out over years, and that self who had called for help on a ghost ship a few miles and millennia ago seemed like a whole other person entirely, not the same man who had passed through the gauntlet of that cut in the mountains, that snowy tunnel, and the clouded hot breath of a bear (he flattered himself with that last part but felt like he'd earned it by now). He'd walked, he'd slept, he'd eaten, he'd pissed. His life had been reduced over the course of days and hours into the basics, stripped down: the life of an Arctic explorer.

Appetite and action.

Necessity.

Essence.

Fast as a lightbulb, fixed as the north.

Efficiency and perseverance, anything but pretty dull stuff.

If only he had someone to tell but his phone, while still charged, couldn't connect to the world and he almost laughed at the cliché of not having a signal but the stakes were too high for humor by now. He wished more than anyone Julia could see where he was, what he was doing and what he had done. He wanted to see her face—and her dress!—from that awards banquet when he'd stepped up to receive his plaque, how proud she was, how she seemed to understand him again for that evening in a way she hadn't for years. In a way he hadn't gotten her either, and hadn't much tried. That plaque had been half a lie at the least but now, this, making his way through the snow and across the cold water and into this... hut? Shed? Outpost? Station, of course, the ice station. This was real, he was here, he wasn't in an office in a basement pretending to travel and discover the world. He wasn't faking his footsteps and he felt for the first time in years like the man she deserved. And more out of touch now than ever.

The great men rarely wrote about that in their memoirs and journals and scientific reports: the lonely distance, the rusty raw tang of home on your tongue and the bitterness of your greatest moments coming so far from everyone you wanted to know what you'd done. In that room surrounded by preserved foods Oscar skimmed the archives of his magazines and books, queried his mental database one way and another but no, nothing much; the great men hadn't been lonely, perhaps.

Gnawing another strip of that unspecified jerky Oscar climbed the stairs back to ground level.

He crossed the room to that desk with the ledger upon it and scanned pages yellowed by unceasing sunlight and time in concentration, a year's worth of wear in a few moonless months. Line after line all in the same handwriting and all of it Slotkin's. Until he flipped back a few pages and it was all Wend's, and if he had any doubts they were dispelled by each man's initials to the left of each line and a signature in the right margin. Paging back further he found remnants of Dimchas and Rudnick and other names he knew only from the archives of BIP but also names he did not know at all, all the men whose time under the lightbulb had come and gone and now Oscar stood in their footsteps in that new room. Poised over the ledger himself. Line after line, page after page, more or less the same thing had been written: initials, time and date, and some notation about the operation of that space heater followed by a signature, sometimes a notation that stuff, so to speak, had remained pretty dull. A database built up over years out of nothing. Busy work and vacant observation.

Sometimes there was a difference, some variation, the occasional worry one orange coil or another was about to burn out, followed inevitably a line or two later by reassurance to some future reader the heater still worked as well as always and there was nothing to fear. There were other exceptions, the odd annotation about something hunted or caught, the arrival of an unexpected visitor or scheduled drop of supplies, and the very last line left halfway down a page and not returned to, a note from Slotkin that read, "Visiting the settlement this morning; leaving station ship shape and fast as a lightbulb. Heater per normal."

Apparently he hadn't returned, but from where? If there was a settlement within walking distance—assuming Slotkin had walked and a snowmobile or sledge wasn't gone along with him—perhaps Oscar could get there, too.

He'd look for a map.

For snowshoes. For skis. For something in the cramped space downstairs that might help. No good to imagine how many of each must be ready and waiting in the serendipitous scrap piles of Clark's basement warren back at Northern Branch. No use to pine.

Oscar lifted his head from the ledger toward the window set over the desk, nearly bright now after his hours of sleep. The glass was smudged, dusty and hazed as memory, but familiar, too: he'd seen it before, the clean field of snow, the swirling clouds of windblown powder... he'd seen it. He knew it as well as he knew his own mind and pulling his gloves and balaclava back on in a rush Oscar moved to the door, out into the wind, and passed into that view himself.

The hunter settled his bomb where wall met floor, directly under the map, the white expanse of which he then craned to inspect. He searched the room's desks, one messy, one neat, until he found a sharp pencil, pausing his search for a moment at a plastic intercom yellowed as if by sunlight despite that basement room having no windows. It was out of sync with its surroundings, a tall dark cairn marking a death on the blank ice and visible from miles away. He reached toward the top of the map, toward the sketched outline where something had been erased, where a village had been and should be and still showed as a shadow of rubbed out impressions, and the hunter darkened its lines, traced them once, twice, a third time, until that village was as much a part of the map as the inked outline of the Arctic containing all those fainter decisions in pencil—no longer as transient as the gray marks and smudges and erasures all over, but permanent now as a bomb.

He stepped back. Checked his work and set down the pencil again where he'd found it, almost as if he hadn't been there apart from those few darkened lines, apart from that bomb on the floor.

He knelt before the device, adjusted a wire, pinched a connection tighter. A red switch loomed large, the kind you'd expect in a movie or show, the kind that screams, "Bomb!" and that no real bomb ever uses. They aren't so straightforward until they explode which is about as straightforward as something can be.

Satisfied, the hunter laid a finger upon that switch and he paused. He knew he could flip it. His finger was there and his mark had been made. He had planted his stick in the snow and was done. So he stood up and turned toward the door. The lightbulb swung with his motion as he passed beneath it, that bulb on its old-fashioned cloth cord. He lifted a heavy ruler from a desk and raised it as if to smash the bulb, to darken its filaments once and for all—the image of glass all over those desks when their occupants returned was appealing—but something in those burning coils prevented his swing. There was something admirably steadfast about that lightbulb, something Arctic about it and he left it be.

He set down the ruler and left the room, returned to the stairs and the lobby, remembering in the stairwell to untuck his tie, tighten the flap on his now-lightened bag of someone else's clean laundry, remembering to make himself blend, then he revolved through the door and out onto the sidewalk, back into the sun and the autumnal gleam in that city of marble and mirrors. He turned north and began walking in the direction from which he had come as overhead, behind the engines and voices and horns, a low helicopter chopped at the air and grew louder.

Whirling rotors flickered in shadow below and Julia leaned through the open helicopter door to watch that dark wheel cross the ground. She imagined those shadow blades to be real ones, a variation of a childhood game she'd often played in her parents' car on rainy days: she'd imagine the windshield wipers were longer and sharper and whatever they fell on was cut down to size. She'd watched those blades rise and fall in their sweep of the glass, slicing through forests and buildings and other cars in smooth diagonal lines, all the world's scenery cleanly bisected. It seemed a benign kind of destruction, harmless divisions as consistent and predictable as the metronome sweep of those whispering blades.

Was anything that reliable now?

Was anything safe?

It was hard to tell in a world where keeping things safe so often meant burning things down. Where keeping one person from being shot sometimes meant shooting somebody else. Clean lines had been lost. Smooth divisions no longer occurred and all the old concrete walls had come down. Everything spilled into everything else until even the best designed treads lost their grip on the surface of things, the closest Julia had ever come to telling Oscar the truth of her job in the guise of the false, passing that off one evening a few years ago as an attempt at a slogan for some new high-friction pattern when it was, really, her terrified sense of a fracturing world.

There wasn't much left so predictable as those wiper blades, nothing she knew of apart from her husband, wrapped up in his magazines and his dull biographies of famous explorers and a job of his own that hardly made sense when they talked about it, reassuring in the steadfast flimsiness of his lies. Her own body couldn't even be trusted, eager for his touch until it actually came and she closed against contact, pretended to sleep and sometimes actually managed before humiliation and guilt and confusion crept in to keep her awake as she knew they were keeping him, too, a few inches away.

If she could have told him about her job, her real job, that might have helped. If she could have told him what she'd learned of how the world works, the unpopular decisions made in anonymous offices like her own, weighing up options, seeing all sides, then carving clean lines through a too-complex era, taking actions that kept the most people safe for the cost of least harm, though sometimes those distinctions were fine. Sometimes the losses were great and the greater good hardly seemed greater, but someone always had to decide.

Or if he could have told her about his. But they were professionals, both of them, and they were better than that. They had trained. They had perfected their secrets for years, as anyone had to if they wanted to rise to those levels and wanted to last for as long as Julia and Oscar had. They were model government workers.

Someday she would tell him, she had long told herself. Someday she might be able instead of sputtering nonsense about tire tread patterns and depths of wear relative to the length of a road.

She'd tell him someday about her mother's funeral and what it had meant; he'd been there, of course, he was always there in the big ways, but she'd never spoken of the decision she arrived at that day. She'd pictured her mother as the priest spoke, the drawn out pain of her illness and failing body, the crabbed hands struggling in her final days to sip juice or direct tasteless broth through a straw, the loss of her ability even to swallow, and in the thick of the service Julia had promised herself. She'd put in for a transfer away from her desk, away from analytics and into the field; no longer content to pore over data and determine what others should do, she wanted to do it herself. She wanted know the world had been made even little bit safer by her own hand. Her supervisors hadn't believed it could last but humored her because they knew of her loss, and they let her suffer through all the training in hope, perhaps, she'd wash back to her office and get back to work. But she hadn't washed out, she had thrived, had shown younger women and men how to grind and what it meant to know why you were there. What it meant to be willing to do anything, to give up anything, to keep the world and its secrets safe. To truly know what was at risk.

Because Julia knew. She'd never been able to explain it to Oscar, and where could she start when she couldn't even tell him what her job really was? How could she make him understand that she needed to feel like a body again, not in the ways he missed her being one, not in their bed, but in her own right, in the world, exerting force and feeling pain. She needed to find the steadfast steadiness of those windshield wipers and their clean divisions even if that meant becoming the blade herself.

She hadn't even told him about her shoulder, the bullet and blood. There was no lie to cover how she might have been casually shot, no way it could require less than a crime and so newspapers, TV, a story he would surely have heard. Even then, still, in that helicopter its ache was a constant, the bleeding long over but the puckered scar on both sides of her body stood out in fresh purple and pink, such dainty colors for something so violent and raw. She'd have to explain that in time. She'd have to allow him to see her again.

Her phone buzzed in a pocket on her sleeve so she tore its closure open and slid out the device, the screensaver image of Oscar reading in front of his magazines, his back to her, his eyes to the Arctic in their apartment and no clue she was standing behind him and never mind taking his picture. Her thumb fell to the screen, to see what was coming, but the buzzing had stopped and the screen showed no sign of a message or call, nothing missed, nothing dropped, and once it had returned to its dormant dark state she returned the phone to its compartment.

In her headphones, in her helmet, the pilot said they were coming up on their objective and asked Julia for her command. She watched those rotors chewing the ground up below and behind their rapid path, she gave it a couple of seconds and noticed the difference in shade between the floor of the helicopter where it had faded in reach of the sun by the door but had stayed dark and unscuffed down the center strip of the craft between seats where no one could walk, not showing a sign of decay, a vivid division made by that bright stripe.

The pilot cleared his throat over the com. Nothing left now but to act on her training.

"We've let him run free long enough," she spoke into her helmet's microphone as the devouring shadow rolled toward the silhouette of a man down below. "It's time to finish all this. Bring us down so we can get him."

26

Outside, on the ice, squinting against gritty snow on the wind, Oscar rounded the building to the window he'd been looking through over the ledger. With his back to the glass he took in the view, the emptiness, the stark white as far as he could see. Behind him were mountains, large hills at least, and the sea wasn't far off he suspected—it had been near enough to that strange geothermal plain he'd crossed on his way to this hut. But looking this way, out onto the ice, none of that met his gaze. It could have been anywhere in the Arctic.

It could have been the North Pole.

It was the North Pole, in fact, though not actual fact: that view, that empty expanse, was what he had looked at so many times every day for so long, in his apartment and underground in the station, on the balcony and the bus and sometimes in the car. In airports and waiting in doctors' offices and pushing a grocery cart with one hand as his other dialed up the Pole cam.

The Pole cam that was not, it turned out, anywhere close to the Pole. It couldn't be, Oscar knew. He hadn't traveled anywear near farthest north. The air was too warm, his skin stung but wasn't frostbitten. He couldn't be there and he wasn't, and yet in some way he was.

There wasn't a pole anywhere holding the camera as he'd always imagined the arrangement must be, perhaps only due to the power of suggestion and association of words. But hanging under an eave of the hut a small gray dome glinted with a spotlight beneath it, the kind of camera you might see in a bank or a store, nothing special, nothing he hadn't encountered at home. Under that eave Oscar spotted a wire snaking into the building; there must be a server inside it somewhere, a transmitter, and yes, he saw a satellite dish on the roof though he hadn't seen any equipment inside.

He turned back to the view. Back to what had been the Pole until a few seconds ago.

He understood very little of what had happened to him during the past few days. So few things seemed to have been resolved in any way he could use: not who was following him or what they were after, not why he'd been sent north by Director Lenz in the first place and not what Alexi's story was, either. Not why the Pole cam was—which is to say wasn't—where it was or even why people watched *To The Moon!* apparently wherever he went. So much left unresolved and he feared he had gone too far now to resolve it.

He felt a bit more optimistic about his marriage, at least: the time away had cleared his head about that, so maybe that was enough, though it might never matter if he couldn't get home. He'd know it, and perhaps he could text Julia to say so. Maybe that was the whole story though it seemed a bit out of proportion to go through all this just for that because who else would care about Oscar's marriage, about his drifting apart from his wife? Julia, of course, obviously, but not the people who'd set all these moving parts into motion whoever they were. Getting a single strained marriage back on track couldn't be worth so much complication for anyone else. There had to be more, something else going on, some way of fitting all those parts together, but Oscar was at a loss to say what that something might be and he had no one to ask.

And he didn't mind either, not so very much, and wondered if that was *quinuituq*, the deep patience that arose from life in from this region.

He took out his phone, now missing its faux woodgrain case and scratched and dented and scarred and showing its age in so many ways. Oscar peeled off a glove and his fingers felt the bite immediately but it couldn't be helped, he had something to do. He tapped out the URL of the Pole cam website from memory and sent it in a text to Julia knowing she might never get it or not for a while but still he felt the comfort of having sent it, at least, of having gone through the motions. Then he stepped back, into the view of the camera with all the world's ice at his back. He peeled the balaclava up off his face then pulled the glove back onto his hand, and smiling, breath steaming, he waved. He waved to the camera and to his wife, hoping she'd see him, hoping despite himself she'd somehow gotten his message and was watching just then, seeing him on the ice of the Pole and knowing this was his way of telling her something: who he really was, what he did for a living, that he'd ended up by strange circumstance so far to the north. That he wanted her to know this one thing about him, whatever else might occur.

He waved with both arms, a big smile on his face, and he shouted to his wife that he loved her and he only looked away from the camera when the chop of a helicopter came into earshot and grew rapidly louder. He looked up, away over the hut toward the south, and anyone watching the website just then would have seen the shadow approaching, a wheel rolling over the ground; there was no microphone on the Pole cam so they wouldn't have heard the helicopter any more than they'd heard Oscar's voice telling Julia he loved her though he'd exaggerated his mouth shapes enough they might have easily made out what he'd said. But the helicopter would be a surprise.

He gave up waving to watch the craft come, not knowing yet if it was to save him or not and he wasn't willing to guess after all the turns of his last days. And after all that, honestly, standing alone on the ice, he wasn't sure if it made so much difference.

There he was in the middle of nowhere, if not quite the nowhere he'd gone looking for. And isn't that always the way?

ACKNOWLEDGMENTS

My deepest thanks (in the fairness of alphabetical order) to Michelle Bailat-Jones, Lacey Dunham, Roxane Gay, Lori Hettler, Tim Horvath, Michael Kindness, Ann Kingman, Ron Koltnow, Éireann Lorsung, Helen McClory, David Rose, Laura Ellen Scott, Laura van den Berg, and Will Wiles, who have served as first readers, supporters, generous blurbers, and most of all friends in so many ways. And to Lit Team Boston, aka Kevin Fanning, Robert and Karissa Kloss, Kate Racculia, and satellite members Amber Sparks and Chris Backley. Thanks also to Susan Tomaselli of 3:AM Magazine and Jason Cook of Fiddleblack for publishing early excerpts, to my students and colleagues at Emerson College, and to Robert Lasner and Elizabeth Clementson at Ig for taking a chance on a novel I worried nobody would.

A longstanding thank you to Professor Jackie Urla who generously guided the undergraduate research that eventually led (by way of many digressions) to this novel, and to John McCannon in whose book *Red Arctic: Polar Exploration and the Myth of the North in the Soviet Union, 1932-1939* a single unelaborated reference to the USSR's "Bureau of Ice Prognostication" kept my imagination going for the next fifteen years. And to photographer Richard Harrington, whose 1951 portrait of Theresie inspired a moment in these pages, as well as all the other authors, artists, and explorers whose own Arctic accounts I have read and returned to over the years.

Finally, thanks to Mom, Dad, Tim, Pete, and Theresa for years of support; and most of all to Sage and to Gretchen, my own true north.